HER FINAL WORDS

Emily Slate Mystery Thriller
Book 4

ALEX SIGMORE

Dark Woods Press

Prologue

"GOODNIGHT," I SAY, HESITATING IN THE DOORWAY A MOMENT longer than I should. He gives me a sweet smile before tucking his hands in his pockets and trundling down the stairs back out to the parking lot. The sound of fireworks pierces the night. They'll probably be going for a while longer, at least. But thankfully, no one in this neighborhood seems intent on setting off explosives for the country's birthday. I close the door, thinking back on the evening. Dinner, dancing, and a good conversation. It was practically the perfect date. That man definitely had a swagger about him, but it wasn't obnoxious. It was that endearing kind of confidence you only find in someone you truly connect with. I'm used to people pissing me off; he wasn't one of them.

I remove my light jacket and toss it on one of the chairs in the apartment as I head inside, slipping off my heels at the same time. I'm usually not so smitten, but that man's eyes could melt platinum if he stared at it long enough. And given my track record the past few months, it was nice to finally have some intelligent conversation for once, rather than just watch the guy stare at my rack all night.

But he never broke eye contact the entire night. I don't

know why I put this off for so long. He's been hinting at taking me out ever since we started working in the same office together. Maybe it's because of the kind of work we do; I'd heard inter-departmental relationships rarely worked, because of the stress of the job. With two people everything is compounded—squared, not doubled, and the pressure gets to be too much. Maybe that's still in our future, I don't know. But right now, I know things are good...good enough that I'm going to need a second date sooner rather than later.

I head into my kitchen, my thoughts swimming with the events of the evening. He was so charming. Part of it was his old-fashioned demeanor, but that wasn't all. He really listened, and was engaged, the entire evening. And he wasn't pushy, didn't try to cross my boundaries, and kept a respectable distance. And I think that's what made the entire thing even hotter. The brief moment when he placed his hand on the small of my back to guide me to the dance floor, I felt an honest-to-god jolt of electricity. We both stayed in perfect rhythm out there, anticipating one another's moves, keeping in time with the music while taking our cues off each other.

I haven't felt like that in a long time.

I grab a bottled water out of my fridge and down half of it in one gulp. I'm dehydrated not only from all the dancing, but the two glasses of wine at dinner. Most guys, when we go out, take the opportunity to try and order some manly drink —something they think makes them look cool and sophisti-cated. But he just had a tonic water, telling me he didn't want anything that might affect his memory or experience of me. He wanted to remember every second of it.

I set the bottle down. I think I might be in trouble here. Heading back over to my purse, I check my phone. It's already eleven-thirty. Damn. I need to talk to Sophie but I'm sure she's sound asleep by now. My sister isn't a night owl. She's one of those annoyingly-upbeat morning people who likes to be out of the bed at the crack of dawn. Which means this will have to wait until morning.

Part of me is wired while the other part is exhausted; it's like my body can't decide which. I need to wind down, though, or I'll never get to sleep. Those deep blue eyes keep invading my thoughts and I can't help but be a little disappointed that he didn't even try to come in for a nightcap. All I got was the tender brush of his lips against mine—brief, but full of so much potential—before he had pulled away, his lips quirked in a smile. It was as if the promise of that kiss had ignited something far fierier than anything else ever could, and he knew it.

Somehow, it was like he knew my weakness was for men like him; men who weren't afraid to communicate and be honest, who weren't so self-absorbed. And who were surprisingly rare these days. How many dates have I been on? And how many times has the guy ended up either talking about himself all night, or been distracted by whatever sports game happening at the moment, or couldn't quit talking about his ex who he misses more than life itself? I had grown so tired of it that tonight had been an unexpected breath of fresh air. Enough to even give me a glimmer of hope that maybe all of this wasn't for nothing after all.

I consider switching on the TV and just falling asleep on the couch, which was something I've taken to doing more and more these days. Sometimes it's just easier to distract myself with the sound of the TV rather than lie in the darkness of my bedroom, my mind swirling with the events of the previous day. Some days they're bad enough to give me nightmares for weeks, so the couch had been my go-to in times of crisis.

But tonight I wasn't thinking about the gruesome aspects of my job. In fact, I felt at peace for the first time in months—maybe even years. I guess all it takes is finding that one special person you know your heart needs to help everything fall into place.

Then again, I don't want to get ahead of myself. But if I was reading all of his signals correctly, then I see a lot more dates in our future.

I leave my water bottle on my small breakfast table and head into my bedroom, anxious to get out of these clothes and into something more comfortable. I can already tell I'm going to sleep great tonight, though I wonder if work on Monday will be awkward. I know there's no hard and fast rule, but we'll probably have to tell Warburton, just so he can make a record of it for the department. And I'll be sure to expect no lack of teasing from my other colleagues. But what can I say? It wasn't a bad decision at all and I'm not going to pretend like it's something to be ashamed of.

The real test will be to see how *he* acts.

I have to stop myself. If I allow my mind to run free, I'll make up a thousand hypotheticals before I even get halfway to sleep. I'd much rather ruminate on the memory of the night than make up what I think might happen in the next few days.

Maybe instead of texting Sophie I'll go visit her in the city. Sundays are usually pretty light for her and Zaid; I'm sure they wouldn't mind. At least for brunch if nothing else. Something this serious needs to be discussed face-to-face over brunch, a couple of poorly worded text fragments won't cut it.

I glance around for my phone, only to realize I've left it back in the living room, in my purse. I should probably grab that water too, just to have by the bed in case I need it.

When I step back into the living room, it takes me a moment to register what I'm seeing. The dark shape in front of me, however, doesn't hesitate, and instead swings something long and sharp in my direction. I barely have time to duck as it slices through the air over my head.

All I can think is I need to get to my service weapon that's in my bedside table. But before I can even turn, the shape has swung again, and this time the bar connects with my side, knocking me off my feet and sending me sprawling to the ground. My mind is awash with thoughts about how they got in here so silently, or how they could have gotten the jump on me. I can't see their face, it's shrouded under a hoodie and mask, but I feel their rage. Their frame is medium; if I can get some leverage, I might be able to take them one-on-one. But if I don't do something quick, this person is going to kill me.

I kick as hard as I can with one foot as they approach, which connects with a kneecap. They groan and stagger back, but I'm not sure I've done any real damage. All I've done is bought myself some time. I just need to get to my bedroom and—

Pain explodes across my head as my vision temporarily goes white. I lose all sense of what is going on around me as the room slowly comes back into view, though its spinning. At this point I can barely think straight, and my mind is awash with random bits of a thousand thoughts. I realize I'm looking up as I can see the blades of my ceiling fan. To my right is my television, mounted on the wall. To my left, the end table Sophie gave me as a house-warming gift. And above me stands the shape, only their eyes visible. I finally see what's in their hand: it's a fire poker, the kind you would use with an old-fashioned fireplace to stoke the logs.

But that doesn't make sense. I don't even have a fireplace. I never have because they are too much trouble. The soot gets everywhere. I remember helping my grandpa shovel it out every morning after he'd had a fire burning. The ashes went in a special bag...that much I recall.

I realize I can't move. Or if I can, I can't feel it, because I try to raise my hands and they don't appear in my vision. Part of me knows something is very wrong; that all of this shouldn't be happening. And some small part of me holds out for hope that I might still be able to get to my bedroom. But I've been a federal agent for almost five years now, and the practical part of my brain tells me this is already over. That this person has me and what feels like is taking forever in my brain is actually only taking milliseconds out in the real world. What's happening is I'm experiencing the final moments of my life, and my brain is firing on all cylinders as it's confronted with the certainty of its own mortality.

My mind rushes through the entire evening again, start to finish, and I'm able to experience the rush of endorphins for a fleeting moment, causing me to let out a gasp before I see the shape grasp the poker with both hands and drive it down, the spike aimed straight at my face.

Chapter One

"THAT'S IT," I SAY, CLOSING THE FILE FOLDER, YANKING IT OFF my desk and throwing it in one of the drawers, not caring that it's not alphabetized with all the other folders. I shoot up out of my chair and grab my blazer, pulling it on.

"Whoa there, bronco, what's the rush?" the woman with the platinum blonde hair sitting across from me, who also happens to be my best friend, asks.

"I'm tired and sick of being here," I say. "Bad enough we had to work fourth of July, but today too?"

Zara Foley sits back in her chair, a grin on her lips. "You're just not used to all this office work is all. You're like a wild horse, you need to be free." She bats her eyelashes at me. "Black Beauty, running off to the horizon."

"Shut up," I say, though I can't help but smile. "I just need a break. I'm going home for a few hours. See if I can't relax before coming back to try and sort through all this...stuff." Zara and I, and half of our department at the FBI have been sorting through a *massive* money laundering case that came through a few months ago. It's been all most of us have been focusing on for the past eight weeks. Given the number of

people implicated and their importance both in and out of the
federal government, it has been all hands on deck.

The only good news is it looks like things are finally
coming to a close…at least in theory. The sting operation is
due to go down next week if everything remains on schedule,
at which point we'll finally be able to start making arrests. But
the most infuriating thing about it is how much *paperwork* we've
had to sort through. Our unit usually deals with violent
crimes, but because of the size of this case, we were brought
on to assist until the Public Corruption Division no longer
needed us. Which means spending our nights and weekends
going over spreadsheet after spreadsheet of senseless data. It's
like reading hieroglyphics as far as I'm concerned, though
Zara seems to be having a blast with it. Given her affinity for
numbers and data, I'm not surprised.

"How about I just give you the rest of my stuff, since
you're so eager to keep going." I grab my keys and my badge,
making sure I have everything I need.

"No, thanks. I will take something from Taipei Palace if
you're coming back that way."

I check the time on my phone. Five-thirty. If I head home
and sleep for a couple of hours, I can be back by eight and be
ready to work through the night to try and finish all this up. "I
will if they're still open when I come back."

"Veggie Lo Mein, with a side of spring rolls," she says,
then goes back to her work.

"As you command, exalted one," I say then throw her a
wave as I head out.

Ten minutes later I'm halfway home and trying not to fall
asleep at the wheel. The past few weeks have been murder.
Plus, Zara is right. I don't do well when I'm stuck in the office
all day long. I work best when I can be out investigating a case,
but thanks to our recent workload, all of our current cases
have been put on hold. Not that we've had anything as

exciting as the serial murders in Charleston a few months back. It's been a quiet summer, which has been good for the local populace, and it's allowed me to catch up on some paperwork and older cases.

But simultaneously, it's given me a lot of time to think. Ever since we failed to find the woman who killed my husband in Savannah, I've been at something of a standstill. I still have some other addresses to search, but those are all on the west coast and I don't have the time or the money to get out there right now. Zara and I have continued the search, hoping to find something on the woman who seems to have half a dozen names but no true identity. I've searched them all: Kamilé, Siobhan, Caelan, and Antionette. I'm pretty sure that last one isn't real. In fact, I'm sure none of them are her real name at all, but I'm hoping one of them might lead me to a clue that would allow me to track her down.

It took me some time to get over what happened in Charleston. All those burned bodies…that isn't something I can easily move past. I still can't eat bar-b-que. But more than that it was what the man responsible for those deaths said to me: asking me how far I would go to find the woman who killed my husband. I have to admit, the longer this goes on, the more desperate I become. Not that I can let it show, but Matt has been gone more than six months now, and I'm no closer to finding his killer than I was the day he died. Given that I've been in the FBI over four years, I have to admit that's more than embarrassing. Not only that, but Zara has been helping. You would think with the two of us we'd be able to come up with *something*, but so far details have been sparse.

My only real lead was a landlord down in Savannah who owns an address matching the woman I'm looking for. When I finally persuaded her to release her rental records to me, all I found was the woman had faked all her application informa-tion, all the way down to what college she went to. It turned out to be nothing but another dead end. My only hope is one of the other addresses still has something I can trace, and that I can get out there before everything is gone. But given my limited resources and the fact my boss probably won't give me the time off to go on another wild goose chase, the chances of me actually investigating are pretty slim.

I pull into my building's lot, parking my car in my normal spot. I smell remnants of burgers and hot dogs on the air, no doubt people are cooking leftovers or still going strong from the celebration yesterday. Since fourth of July fell on a Saturday this year, everyone is off tomorrow. Which means another round of fireworks tonight. So I may as well be at the office, at least that way they can't keep me awake.

I open the door and am immediately greeted by Timber, my rescue pitty. He's up in my face, his tail wagging like crazy before I can even get all the way through the door.

"Hi, baby," I say to him, giving him a good face rub and hug as his whole body begins shaking with happiness. He always puts a smile on my face when I come home. "C'mon, let's get you a snack. About time for your dinner too, isn't it?" I ask as if I think he'll actually speak back to me.

After tossing him a cookie I take my blazer back off and lay it over the back of one of the stools up against the bar that looks into my kitchen. I hang my holster over it and grab Timber's leash so I can take him on a quick walk. He's been doing much better about being alone most of the day and is no longer tearing up the door when I'm gone. I think the times when he stays with my in-laws have really helped him cope with the loss of Matt, probably because Matt's brother has a familiar smell to my husband.

Fifteen minutes later we're both back in the house, Timber chowing down on his dinner while I pull on some sweats so I can at least get a few hours of sleep. I'm content to just leave him to finish his dinner while I lie down, and I make my way into the bedroom. But because I'm so bleary-eyed I don't see the squeaker toy until it's too late and I roll my ankle on it, causing me to crash into the bookcase, sending books scattering to the ground along with me.

Timber immediately leaves his food bowl, rushing over and sniffing my head. "I'm okay, bud," I say, embarrassed more than anything. "Momma just fell." He sniffs me a few more times while I check my ankle. It seems okay; had I not rolled with the fall I probably would have sprained it.

Timber looks at me again, and whines until I scratch behind his ears and snuggle his face a little. Then he seems fine and heads back to his bowl, but he stops only a few feet away just as I'm getting back up and putting pressure on my ankle again. He leans down, sniffing something among all the books that fell over.

"What'cha lookin' at?" I ask, taking a few ginger steps. The ankle is fine, not even a twinge of pain, thankfully. I'm almost content to leave all these books for later, but they'll only take a minute to replace. I bend down as Timber goes into full sniff mode, like he does when he's outside and has found another dog's markings. "What is it? You like the smell of books?" I can relate. Sometimes there's nothing better than the smell of an old novel.

But as I look closer, I realize he's not sniffing the books. Instead, there's something else among them, a small, black case that I don't recognize. "What the—?" I ask, peering at it. Timber's snot has already splattered the top, but as far as I can tell it's a featureless piece of black plastic that I've never seen before. I pick it up, realizing it's not as flat as it looked, and is instead more of the shape of a cube. But it's small enough to fit in my palm. And there are no markings on it anywhere. It just looks like a piece of junk.

Where did this come from? I remember placing all the books on the bookcase myself. Most of them I've already read once or twice, so I don't touch them that often, but still, I'll dig through them every few months. Whatever this is, it wasn't here a few months ago.

I'm about to shrug and toss it in the trash when I see the small red light illuminate on the longer side. And in that instant I know exactly what this is.

It's a remote camera.

Chapter Two

"ARE YOU ABSOLUTELY SURE, EM?" ZARA ASKS.

"I think I know a camera when I see one," I reply. "It's completely featureless, no port to plug it in, no lens, nothing. But, this little red light comes on behind one of the faces when I move it in a certain direction." I've never used anything like this before, which can only mean one thing: someone else put it here. Someone else has been in my apartment and I never even noticed.

"Motion sensor," she says.

"Yeah."

"Probably uses a remote upload too. And wireless charging. Designed not to be conspicuous."

"I want to know how it got in my apartment," I tell her. Timber is still trying to sniff my hand from where I held it. I set the camera on my countertop and covered it with a towel, though I'm sure that does absolutely no good. If someone is watching me on a live feed, they already know I've found it by now.

"Just hang on, I'm on my way," she says.

While I'm waiting on her I have half a mind to call in the FBI's forensic team. But I'm not doing that until I talk to

Janice. And I'm not talking to her until I know what I'm dealing with here. The fact that someone managed to break into my apartment, hide a camera, then get back out without me even knowing has set me on edge. Whereas I was exhausted before, now I'm completely wired, and my holster is back on over my shoulders. I don't even know if I can stay here any longer.

The entire time I'm waiting, I stare at the towel, wondering just who is watching me, and why.

Zara arrives fifteen minutes later, looking as frazzled as I feel. "Lemme see it," she says, pulling on a pair of nitrile gloves, which is something I should have done before handling it. But I had no reason to suspect it was anything nefarious. How often does someone find a hidden camera in their bookcase?

I remove the towel while she takes the small device and inspects it. She removes a small leather case from her back pocket and unrolls it along the counter.

"What are you doing?" I ask.

"Relax, I just want to get inside, see what this is. I'm not going to damage it."

"Good," I say, "because we need it intact for evidence."

Zara removes a sharp needle-looking device from the leather case and in less than five seconds, has popped off one of the sides of the plastic. Inside are a bunch of numbers, and some Japanese writing, all of which looks like manufacturer information.

"Definitely a camera. Capable of three-hundred and fifty hours of storage at a high resolution. Not a cheap piece of crap," she says, examining it. "Looks like it has a built-in microphone too."

"Great. Whoever is spying on me can listen to me talk to myself when I'm here alone."

She turns, her short hair flying out at the sudden movement. "You talk to yourself?"

"Doesn't everyone?"

She gives me the strangest look, like she thinks I'm crazy before replacing it with a huge grin. "I'm just messing with you. Of course we do. At least, those of us who are interesting."

"Can you tell where it's transmitting?" I ask, growing impatient.

"That's the thing, this unit doesn't have network capability. I assumed it did, but it's all internal storage. Which means someone has to come and retrieve it before they can see what's on it."

I rub my temples. "That's almost worse. That means someone could have been in here multiple times. You said three-hundred and fifty hours?"

She nods. "Yep, about two weeks, if it runs continuously. Which it looks like it does. The light you saw isn't a motion sensor, it's to indicate the unit is almost full."

"So then whoever put this here will probably come back for it soon." I glance down at Timber, who has laid down between us. Whoever they are, they managed to get past my dog without being noticed. Or, more likely, they came in when I have him at the doggy daycare. Or even worse, they come in while I'm on assignment somewhere. It's been roughly two months since I left for Savannah, they could have come in anytime then. But if that's true it also means they've been here at least three times since to retrieve the data.

"I gotta call this in to Janice." I take a deep breath.

"I was just about to suggest the same thing. Surveillance of a federal officer is no joke. And who knows how long this has been going on?"

I suppress a shudder. "I don't even want to think about it." My hand hovers over my phone before picking it up to dial.

"What?" Zara asks.

"I don't think I can," I say. "What is she going to say? I'm an FBI agent, for god's sake. I should have noticed when someone tapped my own apartment."

"Not if they did it really well," she says. "I guarantee you this isn't the only device here."

"You can't be serious," I say. My first thought is the bathroom. Then my bedroom. Has someone been watching me this entire time? I reflexively pull into myself.

"Em…" Zara says, a small frown on her lips. "It'll be okay. We'll catch this guy. Like you said, we're the FBI."

I shake my head. "No, I should have noticed something. I should have…I dunno, noticed a misplaced book or a footprint on the carpet."

"You mean you should have looked for something you didn't even know was there?" she asks. She turns to Timber. "I'm more surprised he didn't pick up on the intruder's scent, even if he wasn't here when it happened. That smell should have remained on the air for a while, for a dog, at least."

I don't know how to explain it either. Heat burns on my cheeks. Here I am, an FBI agent and someone has been spying on *me*. It's ludicrous. And I hate the idea of someone watching me, especially during what are supposed to be private moments.

"You think it's her?" Zara asks and it's like a jolt to my system. That should have been my first consideration.

"The assassin?" Zara nods. "Because we went down to Savannah?"

"She might be closer than we think." A chill runs up my spine. I've always assumed the woman I've been looking for has been half a world away, on some assignment. Given how she was able to disappear from Stillwater so effortlessly and the fact we haven't been able to find even a trace of her despite having the entire power of the FBI behind us, I assumed she had been in the wind for the past six months. But if she's still here in D.C., watching me…I might have the chance to catch her.

"What are you thinking?" I ask.

Zara shrugs. "She has to come back for this footage at some point. I say we make sure we're ready for her. You always said if you caught her, you wouldn't have anything to hold her on. I think this would qualify. Maybe then you could get the answers you need."

It's tempting. And this is probably my best opportunity to find her. But I have to consider her skill level. If this really is the woman who killed my husband, she's been able to sneak in and out of this apartment undetected for possibly months. There's no guarantee we could catch her in the act. It might not even be her; she could have hired someone to collect the camera for her. And if we capture that person, we'll never find her.

"It's a good idea," I say. "But I don't think we can do it on our own. I need to let Janice know."

Zara nods. "I understand." She puts her hand on my shoulder, giving it a supportive rub. "This is your show. You do whatever you need to feel comfortable. Still, I could set up a bunch of laser lines, they'd trip if someone even got close."

"Or she'd detect them and know we figured it out," I say. "She's a professional. I don't know much about her, but that is clear. This woman is clean in her work. If I hadn't tripped on Timber's toy, I probably never would have found this."

Zara holds up the unit again. "Well, you're going to have to do something. Because as soon as she looks at this footage she's going to know she's been discovered. Assuming it is her. And if that's the case, why is she still watching you six months after she killed Matt? I'm assuming if she wanted you dead, she would have done it already."

I get up and pace the room. "I have no idea. Maybe she knows I'm looking for her, and wants to see if I'm getting close. She's keeping an eye on me to see if I can really figure out who she is."

"Sounds plausible to me," Zara says. "Again, assuming this

is her and not some pervert looking to sell movies on the dark web."

"Don't even go there." I grab my phone and dial my boss's personal number.

"Simmons," she answers, her voice emotionless like always.

"Janice, I have a problem. I've just found a recording device in my apartment. Zara is over here with me now and has confirmed it's both audio and visual."

"Anyone other than management and maintenance have a key?" she asks.

"No."

"And I know better than to ask if there are any signs of forced entry." She waits a beat. "I'll get a forensics team over there right away. We could be looking at some form of espionage. Don't touch anything else, take as little as you can from the house and wait for me and the team to arrive." She hangs up.

Zara looks at me as I put my phone away. "Are you going to tell her your theory?"

Janice has always had my back, even when I've made questionable decisions. I don't think hiding this from her would be productive. If I'm ever going to find this assassin, I'm going to need some more help.

Half an hour later a white van pulls up to my apartment, followed by two other vehicles. One is Janice's Volvo, and the other is an SUV I recognize as belonging to Agent Wilson Dubois.

"Slate, Foley," Janice says, stepping out of the vehicle, followed by Agent Dubois. "You know Wilson."

I nod. "Thanks for—"

"Number fifteen, right there," she says, directing the forensics team to head into my apartment. The door is already ajar. Timber sits at my feet, panting in the evening heat.

"Hey there Emily. Zara," Wil says. He's been in the department a few years longer than either of us, though I haven't had much interaction with him.

"Dubois is going to be taking point on this one," Janice says. "I don't want either of you involved. You're both too close to the case and we all know what going down that road does." I inwardly grimace. No matter how many cases I solve, I'm not sure I'll ever be able to live down the stigma of the one that I royally screwed up. Even if she didn't mean anything by it, it's still in the unspoken words behind what she says. But, given the particulars of this case, I can't disagree with her decision. It would be a little odd to have me look into my own case. And Zara is much too close to me to remain objective.

"We'll start with the usual suspects," Janice says. "Then move out from there." She sucks her tongue behind her teeth while surveying the scene. "If you've got any theories, now is the time to voice them."

"My only guess is the woman I've been chasing," I say. "The one I went down to Savannah to find. She may not like me getting so close."

Janice puts her hands on her hips, staring at the ground. "Dammit. I was hoping that was nothing more than wishful thinking on your part." She looks up. "But we can't discount any possibility."

"The camera only holds about two weeks' worth," Zara says. "And the indicator means it's almost full. So whoever planted it will be back shortly to collect."

"When?" Janice asks.

Zara shrugs. "Depends on when they want to reset it. Could be anywhere from a day to a few weeks. We don't know how they're getting in and out of the apartment, so we don't know how often they've been in there."

"I can't spare anyone for more than a week, what with the sting set up to take place next Tuesday. Let's hope they retrieve it before then," Janice says. "In the meantime, Slate, I want you out of town."

"What? Why?" I ask, protesting more than I probably should. Even if I can't run the case, I still want to see how it progresses.

"Because if you're a target, any of our attempts to find the person responsible could backfire and they could suddenly figure out that you're too much trouble, especially now that you've found the device. Give us time to set up and catch this person. If they know you're out of town they're more likely to try and retrieve the data. Better chance for us to catch them." She looks down at Timber. "I assume you have somewhere for your dog to stay?"

"I was just going to take him with me," I say, defensive. "Since I'm apparently going on mandatory vacation."

"No, you're not," she replies. "There's a case up in New York that could use your attention. Just came across my desk this afternoon. I was going to pull you from the laundering case to investigate it anyway."

"What case?" I ask. We don't travel too far outside our given jurisdictions. But being the primary office here in D.C. gives Janice some latitude other SACs don't have. My last case outside of the D.C. area was the one down in Charleston, and that was only because we were headed back up from Savannah. But there are a number of offices up in New York full of competent agents. I feel like she really is just trying to get rid of me.

"It's a bad one," Janice finally says. "This time, it's one of our own."

Chapter Three

"Thanks for coming with me," I tell Zara. "This isn't the most pleasant of things."

"I get it. Family can be tough."

Timber sits in the backseat of my car, still panting, even though I have the a/c going full blast. The sun is almost down, but being July, it stays warm all through the evening. This is definitely not how I wanted tonight to go, but I've got enough adrenaline pumping through my veins to keep me awake for hours. I'll probably crash sometime around ten and sleep for a solid day when I finally hit the pillow.

We pull up to my in-laws' house. It's a nice craftsman-style home in the Van Ness area. Historic, but updated with a full yard and plenty of space for their dogs to run. It's not unlike the house Matt and I had together. The house I couldn't keep after he passed, as there were just too many memories, and it was too large for me alone. An apartment seemed like the better choice.

As soon as I open the back door, Timber is out like a shot, running up to the front door of the house, wagging his butt. It opens a moment later to reveal my raven-haired sister-in-law, Dani.

"Timmy!" she says in her best child-like voice and Timber's butt wags even harder.

"I'll be right back," I tell Zara through my open window. I've left the car running; I don't expect to be here long.

"Hey, Em," Dani says as I approach with Timber's small bag of treats and food from my apartment.

"Thanks for doing this on such short notice," I say. "I was just informed I'm headed to New York." I leave out the part about my apartment being bugged. Not only is it classified, but I don't need to get them involved in that. They already don't want to see much of me. At least, Chris doesn't. Dani's less...combative.

"Is that her?" I hear Chris yell. Timber zooms past Dani and almost runs into the man before skidding to a stop in the hallway. He leans down and gives Timber a quick scratch and couple of body taps before sending him on through the house to their dogs.

"Chris..." Dani begins.

"You can't keep doing this," he says, storming up to the door. "We're not your babysitting service. And we're not at your beck-and-call. At this point, we're little more than acquaintances."

"Chris!" Dani says.

"What? We're just supposed to be available twenty-four-seven for her? Not to mention the fact she doesn't even pay us."

I bite my tongue to keep something horrible from coming out. I already feel bad enough about losing my husband, but every time I come over here it's like I have to go through it all over again. And some deep part of me feels like that is appropriate, that I deserve the abuse for letting Matt die. Chris has never been shy about his disdain for me after what happened to Matt. Before he died, the four of us were close; we hung out, made plans. But after everything happened, it was like I not only lost Matt, but them too. If they didn't have such a love for Timber, I doubt I would see them at all.

"I know it's an imposition," I begin.

Chris shakes his head. "You can't just keep doing this, Emily. You need to let us take Timber...permanently. It's what's better for him."

We've had this conversation before. And I'm sure we'll have it again. I know my lifestyle isn't conducive to keeping a pet around all the time, given how many hours I work. But I've managed it so far. I just can't let him go. If I do, then I will truly be alone. Timber is the one thing in my life that I don't have to question. I know he'll always be there, waiting for me. And some part of me believes that with him close I'm still connected to Matt in a way. The two of them were insep-arable. "That's...that's not..." I begin but find it hard to get the words out. I can feel a wave of emotions threatening to overwhelm me and I can't even meet his gaze. I know he's glaring at me, daring me to challenge him, while my sister-in-law stands by and watches it all happen. Maybe if I just relent it will all be easier. I wouldn't have to have these conversations anymore. I wouldn't have to come over here anymore and face this abuse. But I would lose the most important thing in my life in the process.

"Hey, asshole!"

I turn to see Zara storming over, the passenger door of my car still open. "Where the hell do you get off?"

"Excuse me?" The heat in his voice is palpable.

"Don't you think she already feels bad enough for what happened? What are you going to do, beat her over the head with it until she collapses at your feet and begs forgiveness? She lost her *husband*, for Christ's sake."

"And I lost my *brother*," Chris says through gritted teeth.

"So maybe instead of looking to blame someone who loved your brother, maybe you should try to support her instead," Zara says. "Did it ever occur to you that she's hurting just as bad as you are? That you both feel the same pain?"

"I mean sure, obviously—" Chris begins.

"And yet, here you are, giving her shit for dropping her *dog* off when her high-pressure job requires her to go out of town. I don't know if you know this about the FBI, but a lot of times they don't give us much notice. We go when we're called."

I finally gather the strength to look at my brother-in-law, who still seems like he's fuming, though he's cooled a little. "I didn't mean—we enjoy taking care of Timber, it's just—"

"—just that you need to cut Emily some slack. I don't see her over here giving you the raw end because *you* weren't there to save him."

And there it is. The unspoken accusation that has hovered over my head for six months. "I didn't live with him!" Chris yells.

"And because she did, she should have been monitoring him twenty-four seven? What was he, a newborn?" she fires back.

"*Chris*," Dani says, taking her husband's arm and placing her other hand on his shoulder. He looks like he's going to say something else, but instead pulls away from her and storms back into the house. "We'll take good care of Timber until you get back," Dani says to me before following him inside.

"What a royal asshole," Zara says under her breath as we make our way back to the car. "I hope I didn't overstep a line there, but I couldn't just stand by and watch him blame you for something that's obviously not your fault."

Normally I don't let anyone talk to me the way Chris just did. If he wasn't Matt's older brother, I would have told him off the first time he came after me. I appreciate what Zara did, but in the end, I allow it because part of me thinks he's right. I should have been able to protect my husband, especially from the person who really killed him. I can't even imagine how Chris would react if he knew the truth. He still thinks that Matt's death was a fluke, a random heart attack that just happened to kill him out of nowhere. He thinks if I had been there, I could have called 911 sooner, could have saved him. But the truth is, had I been there when the assassin was, there's a good chance I'd be dead right now too.

"Em?" Zara pulls me from my thoughts.

"Yeah," I say, closing the car door and sitting behind the wheel, still feeling like I'm in something of a daze.

"Are you okay?"

"Fine," I say, turning and backing the car out of the driveway. I have to shove this all into a box in the back of my head. We have a job to do, which means I need to be focused. And I can't be focused if I'm distracted with all these thoughts. Maybe Janice is right. Getting out of town and working on this other case might be good—it might help me keep my mind off what's going on here.

As I pull out of the driveway, the last vestiges of light disappear from the horizon. The entire drive to the airport, it's as if the nighttime chases us, ready to swallow us up.

Chapter Four

DESPITE MY EXHAUSTION, I RUN THROUGH THE FEW KNOWN details about the case on the flight from D.C. to New York. There's not a lot in the case file yet, given the murder happened less than twenty-four hours ago. But from what little detail we have, an FBI agent, Melissa Green, was killed in her home by an unknown assailant. There's no sign of forced entry and the coroner's report hasn't come back yet. I'm hoping we can get some preliminary information tonight before starting properly tomorrow morning.

The flight is short, and we land in La Guardia around nine p.m. But because of all the holiday celebrations, half the roads are closed, and it takes us another hour and a half to get through the Bronx and into Yonkers. By then I'm nodding off from lack of sleep, so we decide to check into our hotel and start fresh in the morning instead.

I awake early, unable to stay asleep due to thoughts about what might be happening at my apartment swirling around my brain. Does the assassin know I've left D.C. yet? Will she try to retrieve the device herself or will she send someone else to do it? Or does she know that we're on to her and is already in the wind?

Finally, I realize I'm not going to get back to sleep and get up to take a shower. By the time I'm out, Zara is awake and trying to work the pitiful little coffee pot in the hotel room, to no avail.

"Let's just find some out," I tell her. "Better than to take a chance with the hotel brew."

"Or whatever the field office is offering these days," she mutters. Ten minutes later we're both polished and out the door and in a ride share. Ever since our case with Hannah Stewart's kidnapping, I can never look at ride share's the same way, but I doubt anyone is going to try and abduct two armed FBI officers. Our driver even gives us a heads up on some good coffee in this part of the city and makes a little detour so we can grab some real quick before dropping us off at the FBI office in Woodhurst. The building is nestled next to a residential neighborhood, sitting across a small pond from a row of nice-looking homes. When we step out of the car, all the hustle and bustle of New York is gone and it's like we've stepped into another world.

"Wow, this is…"

"I know," I say, taking a sip of my coffee, which turned out to be an excellent blend. "It's like suburbia up here. Weird that the city is so close."

"I at least expected you'd be able to still smell it," Zara says. As soon as we stepped outside of the terminal, we had caught the smell of the city on the air. The unmistakable mixture of people, garbage and pollution that permeates every big city. But it seems particularly noticeable in New York. Here, there's no trace of it. This is suburban America and could pass as any small town in just about any state.

"After you," I say, indicating the main entrance.

"Why, thank you, m'lady," Zara says and we both chuckle.

I'm feeling better after the confrontation last night. I think part of it is the serene nature of this place.

Inside we go through security. As we're picking up our

weapons and badges on the other side of the scanners, an agent in a smart navy suit comes trotting up. He's a little older than me, probably mid-thirties, but trim and with a mop of dark brown hair that he's tried to style in a way that it stays out of his face, though that's only been partially successful. To me, he looks more like a musician than an FBI agent, but that's kind of the point sometimes. We don't all want to look like the Men in Black, otherwise we wouldn't be very effective at our jobs.

"Agents," he says, slowing in front of us. "I'm Elias Detmer, your liaison here in Woodhurst. SAC Warburton assigned me to help you with whatever you need."

"Emily Slate," I say, shaking his hand with my free one.

"Zara Foley." Zara does the same.

"Flight and accommodations okay?" he asks. He's partially out of breath from his jog which makes me assume he ran down here as soon as he saw us coming through security.

"We would have been here last night," I say. "But the roads in the city were a mess."

"Always are for the fourth," he replies. "It takes them three days just to get everything back in working order. And you don't even want to know about the trash."

"Nothing like here, though," Zara says.

Detmer gives her a quick smile. "Nope. We've carved out a nice little section of the state here. And thankfully, we don't have to go into the city often. The office down there handles most things." He's got the nervous energy of someone who's had a few too many cups of caffeine.

He seems pleasant enough, which is a nice surprise. Sometimes you never know how a field office is going to react to agents coming in from headquarters. Usually it's not a big deal, but every now and again we'll get an office that seems to think they're an independent unit, and don't need any help. But as far as Detmer is concerned, he comes off as relieved that we're here.

"There haven't been many developments since last night," he says, leading us back to the entrance we just came through. "But now that you're here, we can head over to the medical examiner's office."

"Where's that?" Zara asks.

"Right beside New York Medical College," he says, "On the other side of Woodhurst. It's about a twenty-minute drive."

"We could have just met you there," I say.

He shoots me a quick glance before we pass back through security, heading out to the parking lot. "I just got the call five minutes ago. I'd planned on taking you through what we knew about the case so far—"

"—we've already done that," Zara says. "Unless there was something missing in your report."

"No, no," he says, almost tripping over the words. This guy is *wired*. "I just meant to make sure we're all on the same page and so you could meet everyone working on the case. As I'm sure you know, this is…I mean the Bureau can't afford to have someone kill an agent and just keep walking around freely." He directs us to his car, which is a newer black sedan. I motion for Zara to take the front seat. I want to watch him from the back. My initial assessment of this guy might have been off because I'm coming off some very long days working on that laundering case. I want to make sure I'm not missing anything.

"How well did you know Agent Green?" I ask as he opens the door to get in.

Detmer freezes for half a second like he's been hit with a taser before flashing me a quick smile. "Melissa and I…we'd known each other a long time." He's not wearing a ring. Coupled with his odd behavior, I already recognize some of the signs. Because they are things I've seen in myself. Not everyone processes grief the same way. And sometimes, when people that are close to us die, we have a hard time dealing with it, so we throw ourselves into our work. So much so that we become liabilities.

This man is doing everything he can to remain focused on the job at hand. He's so wired because he's trying to keep from thinking too hard about what happened. But this is also personal to him, because he had feelings for her.

"How long were you dating?" I ask.

Zara shoots me a quick glance from her seat before training her attention back on Detmer, whose face is contorting, trying to hold back the emotions that threaten to overwhelm him. Emotions I'm more than familiar with. "I guess I'm not doing a very good job of handling this, am I?"

"Don't be too hard on yourself," I say. "We've all been there in one form or another."

"Thanks," he says, and seems to finally relax a little. "We only had one date. It was that night, actually. It took me months to work up the courage to finally ask her." He shakes his head, starting the car.

"Do you mind if I ask about that night?" I say.

"I knew you probably would anyway," he replies, pulling out of the space. "The Bureau didn't know about us yet. We didn't want to disclose anything until we knew it was going somewhere."

"Was it?" Zara asks.

Detmer drives the car down the short road and gets on the interstate. "I always thought it would. And given how our first date went, I was pretty sure she felt the same way." He lets out a long breath, and a tear escapes his eye, which he wipes away quickly. "At least, that was my impression."

"What did you do on Saturday night?" I ask.

"Dinner. Dancing. Watched the fireworks. You know, normal people stuff."

I'm more than familiar. Sometimes it can be hard for agents to go do all the things the average person does. It's hard to go fishing without thinking about how many dead bodies are hidden under the water, or go to a baseball game without wondering who might be on the take and how many illegal bets are going on under the table. We see the potential for crime everywhere, which is why so many of us end up divorced. But when you can make a relationship with someone who already knows your world, it's much more likely to survive.

Matt wasn't like that though, strangely. It never bothered him when I would talk about the more gruesome aspects of my job. And he never complained that he thought I was being too cautious or over-protective in certain situations. He took it all in stride, which was one of the things I loved about him.

"I've been doing this job for almost ten years now," Detmer adds. "I know I'm going to be the first person you look at in your investigation. I think it's why my boss didn't want any of us working on this case. All of us were close with Melissa, though I was closer than anyone else. We all have our own biases and preconceived notions—"

"And your emotions," Zara says.

"You don't have emotions, Agent Foley?" Detmer asks.

"Me? I've got emotions out the ass. She's the impenetrable one." Zara hooks a thumb back to me and I catch Detmer's eyes in the rearview mirror. I recognize his pain all too well, and also the fire to find out who did this to her. They were smart to bring us on, rather than leave it up to her friends. While I have no doubt the agents here are more than capable, their connection to Agent Green might make them miss something crucial.

"If it makes you feel any better," I say. "You're not the only one who has been taken off their own case."

"Care to elaborate?" he asks.

I turn my mouth into a frown and give my head a quick shake. "Not really. I'm more interested in how your night ended. What time did you last see Agent Green?"

"I dropped her off at her place about eleven," Detmer

says. "She watched me pull away from her place. I didn't see anyone suspicious hiding in the bushes or walking around the parking lot. Plus, Melissa was a trained agent. She probably could have kicked my ass in hand-to-hand."

"So you had no reason to worry about her," Zara says.

"Right. I'm sure you guys have the same physical requirements we do. We have to maintain certain training regimens in order to stay active field agents."

"So what do *you* think happened?" I ask, taking another sip of my coffee.

He shakes his head. "I dunno. Maybe an old flame? Someone with a key to her apartment, for sure, because there was no forced entry."

Zara turns to look me in the eye. "Seems like a lot of that happening lately."

"What do you mean?" Detmer asks.

"Nothing," she says, "Forget it."

"Whoever they were, they had to be strong and fast to take down Melissa," Detmer adds. "And they must have caught her by surprise. It's the only way." He slows and takes an exit with the sign "New York Medical College". We sit in silence the rest of the way as I ponder the case. I'm sure Zara is already chomping at the bit to get a look into Detmer's background. We'll have to do it for all the agents Green worked with, just to eliminate them. But given they'd only been on one date, it doesn't make much sense for Detmer to be the person who killed her. Usually when it's a domestic partner, the couple has been together for some length of time, usually years. And often the dispute is about something that has built up over those years. There are cases where first dates have led to murder, but those have often been cases of stalking or situations involving mentally unstable individuals. Not trained FBI agents who have been through multiple psych evaluations.

Still, we'll need to run some background on Detmer just so we can eliminate him from the suspect pool.

"Here we are," he says as we pull up to a brick and concrete building with the words "Department of Laboratories and Research" emblazoned on them. I didn't miss the quiver in Detmer's voice as he made the announcement. This is going to be very difficult for him and might be enough to eliminate him outright. I'll have to keep an eye on him.

Chapter Five

THE WESTCHESTER COUNTY MEDICAL EXAMINER'S OFFICE IS like any other I've ever been in. Sterile, cold, and white. Most of that is practicality. It wouldn't make sense to have pictures of rainbows on the walls, or have the place decorated in bright, cheerful colors. This is a gruesome business, and it's better to keep things as clean and sterile as possible. So whenever we come into an ME office, they all generally look about the same. The only difference is the size.

Because the WCME is next to NY Medical, it's larger than most. And busier. The parking lot out front was almost full and there are a lot of people coming and going, many, I assume, who are students.

We head up to the main desk and show them our badges. They direct us back through doors on the right which lead to the examination rooms. Detmer gets about halfway down the corridor before slowing and putting his hand on the wall, as if he's being crushed by the reality of what he's about to see.

"You okay to do this?" I ask.

He shoots me a disingenuous smile. "Sure, of course." But his breathing has sped up and he's gone a few shades paler than normal.

I motion for Zara to head in while I try to calm Detmer. "You don't have to do this, you know. We've got the case covered. In fact, maybe it's better you don't see her. It's different when it's someone you know."

"I need to. I owe her that much," he says.

"I know it can feel like that, but this wasn't your fault," I say, feeling like a hypocrite. I know exactly why this man wants to go in that room. Maybe I shouldn't be trying to stop him.

"No, no, I can do it," he says again, taking a longer, deeper breath to steady himself. He stands on his own and draws in another breath through his nose. "I'm ready."

Maybe it's better he does see her; it will at least give me another chance to gauge his reaction. Though at this point I seriously doubt he had anything to do with Agent Green's demise.

As we head in, Zara is already speaking with the medical examiner, a somewhat rotund man with a full beard and moustache. "Hi there," he says, his voice more upbeat and jolly than I typically expect from someone in this profession. "Hadley Crawford." His grip is strong.

"Agent Emily Slate." I immediately like Crawford. He's got one of those magnetic personalities. Which makes it even stranger that this is the profession he's chosen. Most people in this job are heavy introverts, but Crawford seems like the complete opposite.

"Agent Detmer," the man behind me says, taking Crawford's hand.

"Ah, Agent, I'm very sorry. They told me you worked with her." I slide my gaze over to Zara but she gives me a subtle shake of the head. She hasn't said anything. Which means someone else has already been in contact with this office, possibly with Crawford himself. There are a lot of eyes on this one, something I'd do well to remember.

"Thanks," Detmer says. "I'd like to get this over with."

"Of course," he says. Behind him lays a body covered with

a thick sheet. I assume this is Agent Green. "Primary cause of death was massive hemorrhaging and brain damage. If it's any consolation, it was quick." He pulls back the sheet and I have to steel myself, even though I read the initial report. There's just something about seeing a body with its eyes gouged out that strikes you at your core. In some ways, it's worse than a body that's been ravaged, because it gives the face a very skeletal look, and it reminds me that we're all little more than meat and bones barely held together by nothing more than luck and time.

Other than the eyes, her face is mostly untouched, other than some damage around the sockets themselves. Her face is practically flawless, and I can see why Detmer was attracted to her. She strikes me as one of those tall, naturally beautiful women who don't need to put any effort into the way they look. But it seems someone was determined to kill her no matter how beautiful she was.

I turn to see Detmer staring at her, his face as pale as a ghost. He looks like he's about to faint again, but somehow manages to hold himself up as Crawford continues.

"She was stabbed through the eye with this," he says, holding up a steel fire poker that has been wrapped in a long, clear evidence bag. The sharp end is still covered in Green's blood. "Based on the blood loss, and internal damage, it looks like they shoved it through the left eye first, then the right."

Something tickles the back of my brain, though I can't put my finger on it. But something about this seems familiar. Perhaps an old case I studied at some point.

"The perpetrator used enough force to pierce the back of her skull," Crawford says. "But only on the second blow. The first blow killed her, the second was just for spite. As I said, it was virtually instant, so I doubt if she even felt it."

"Small comfort," Zara says, crossing her arms. I have to imagine she's as disturbed about this as I am.

"Anything else?" I ask.

"Yes," Crawford says, pulling on a glove. He lifts her hair on the right side of her head to show us an area that's been shaved away. The skin resembles a rotten banana it's so bruised. "She was struck on the side of the head here, more than likely with the same weapon. There are cracks all along the skull in roughly a straight line. It could have caused her to blackout, or at least temporarily incapacitated her. She also has some residual bruising around her ribs. It looks like she was able to put up a short fight, but flesh and bone doesn't usually hold up too well against steel." He pulls the sheet back over her and I let out the breath I've been holding. Detmer turns and walks back out of the room without a word.

"What was the time of death?" I ask.

"Between eleven and two a.m.," he replies. "She wasn't found until yesterday morning, but the apartment was well-cooled. Easy enough to extrapolate a time of death from the rate of decay."

"Any other defensive wounds?" Zara asks.

He shakes his head. "No skin under the fingernails or anything like that, I'm afraid."

"Caught off-guard," I say, even though I'm just theorizing. But I can't imagine it was a long, drawn-out fight. Not with a trained FBI agent. And so few other injuries indicates that the attack was swift and brutal. This person knew exactly how to take her out and fast. But I don't understand the significance of the fire poker. A knife would have made more sense if the perpetrator didn't want the sound of a gun to alert the neighbors. I need to get a look at the apartment.

"Okay, thank you," I say.

Crawford steps forward, as if to stop me. "There was one other thing, I don't know if Agent Detmer mentioned it or not. But we found some gray hairs on her clothes, short, curly ones."

"*Gray?*" I ask. "Like from an older person?"

"Our lab is taking a look at them now. We're not sure."

I hand him my card. "Make sure you keep us updated with what you find," I say.

"Of course," he replies. "Happy to do it. Good luck."

We return to the hallway to find Detmer, leaning against the wall. "Detmer?" I ask.

"Apartment?" he asks without turning around.

"Why don't Agent Foley and I drop you back at the office. We can investigate the apartment on our own."

He shakes his head. "Least I can do is drive you there. It isn't like I don't know where it is."

"No, you're done," I say, putting my foot down. "You can subject yourself to this personal torture on your own time. But we've got a job to do."

"What?" he asks, his tone almost pitiful.

"You don't need to be here," I say. "And right now, you're more of a hinderance than you are a help. We're dropping you off. I'd suggest taking a few days. We'll let you know if we come up with something."

He sighs. "Maybe you're right. The last thing I want to do is contaminate something by accident. But I needed to see her, at least one last time."

I swallow a lump forming in my throat. "I understand that. Probably more than you know."

We drop Detmer off back at the Woodhurst office and pick up one of the FBI general use vehicles there to drive out to Green's apartment in Adam's Hill. It's a small suburb just north of Woodhurst, nestled in the rolling hills of lower New York. No interstates go up there, but it's only about fifteen minutes from Woodhurst, and it's a beautiful drive.

"I could almost see myself living up here," I say as the wind blows our hair through the open windows as the car winds down along the sleepy streets.

"Nice place to visit, but I wouldn't want to settle here. Too...rural," Zara says.

"I know, you'd have a permanent high-rise apartment if you could, wouldn't you?"

Her platinum blonde hair whips around her head. "Great views, access to everything you could ever need, and someone else takes care of all the maintenance. What's not to love?"

"Green spaces?" I ask.

"Rooftop hanging gardens."

"I don't know," I say. "There's something to be said for nature. I bet they have some great hiking up here." For some reason I'm feeling sentimental about a place I've never visited before and I don't know why. I just find it calming, which is strange. I figured New York was urban sprawl for a hundred miles in every direction of the city. I had no clue it could be this desolate so close to the biggest city in the country.

"Since when did you get so outdoorsy?" she asks.

I shrug. "Maybe I need a vacation."

"You *definitely* need a vacation. Preferably somewhere tropical. And somewhere that has drinks that come with little umbrellas."

I laugh as I pull off the main road onto a side street which leads to a cluster of apartments nestled into a wooded area. The first thing I do is check the sightlines from the road. The complex isn't hidden, but it's not easily visible either. Somewhere in between. Which would have made it easy for someone to lie in wait.

"There it is," Zara says. The yellow tape gives it away. Looks like Green had an end unit, which could have given the intruder additional access from the side instead of just the front and back.

We park next to the tape but before we're out, we're stopped by an older gentleman in a tweed suit. "If you can't tell, this is a crime scene," he says brusquely. "You'll have to clear off."

"Agents Slate and Foley, from D.C.," I say, showing him my badge. "We've been assigned the case."

"Where's Agent Detmer?" he asks, his gaze flipping between me and Zara.

"Back at your office, Agent..."

"Williamson," he says. "They didn't tell us you'd be a couple of trainees."

I do my best not to show any emotion on my face. "Guess you didn't need to know," I reply, letting him wonder if we actually are trainees or not. Sometimes I'm more than happy to correct people when they mistake us for people five or six years younger. And sometimes I can feel the energy coming off someone and decide I'd rather not waste my time. If Williamson wants to bring it up with his boss, that's none of my concern.

I push past him and duck under the tape. The apartment is set up more like a condo, with an entrance up a half flight of brick steps that lead to a small porch with an overhang. The door is already open, and I make sure to pull on a pair of gloves before entering. I can't help but think about what's happening at my own apartment as we enter. Janice or DuBois would have called if anything interesting had happened, but the urge to check anyway lingers in the back of my mind.

As far as I can tell, nothing seems disturbed, at least in this part of the apartment. It's more spacious than the average apartment, and it's furnished with clean, modern fixtures and furniture. There's a lot of light in here, but my eyes are immediately drawn to the dark bloodstain in the middle of the floor, halfway between the kitchen and the hallway that leads to the bedrooms. The blood has seeped into the wood itself, but it's unmistakable that something very bad went down here. I crouch down, peering at what used to be the puddle. Near the far side is a deep gash in the wood.

"Where the fire poker stuck," I say, pointing it out to Zara.

"Through her eye, then the back of her skull and embedded into the wood," she says. "Why leave it?"

"Maybe they couldn't get it back out on their own?" Though that's unlikely. Someone with the strength to do this could have dislodged it as easily as they drove it. "Or they were afraid of getting caught. Didn't want to take the time."

"Yeah…" she trails off, lost in thought.

I look around the rest of the apartment and something strikes me as odd. "Do you happen to see a fireplace anywhere?"

Zara glances around at the walls, noticing what I have. "Bedroom maybe? Some have that."

"Maybe." Though I doubt an apartment of this size would have a fireplace exclusively in a bedroom, even if it's faux.

She turns back to the puddle. "The perp brought the fire poker with them?"

I give the rest of the apartment a cursory glance and don't find any other fireplace tools, no brushes, clamps, or shovels that would be used with hot ash. In fact, the fire poker we saw was older, and almost all of Green's furniture and accessories are new items. I see very little vintage or sentimental in here. "Looks that way," I say. "Which means they might have left it for another reason."

"Which is?"

"They wanted to send a message," I say.

Chapter Six

WE TAKE OUR TIME GOING THROUGH THE REST OF THE apartment, checking all the entry points for any signs of disturbance. It turns out there is no fireplace anywhere in the unit, and I'm willing to bet none of these units have them; they all looked identical from the outside. Which means the killer was determined to kill her with the fire poker. If I can figure out why, I'm betting we can track them down.

Other than the main disturbance in the middle of the apartment, nothing else seems out of place, removing any potential that this was a robbery. And given Agent Green wasn't sexually assaulted, it makes finding a motive other than murder difficult. If the killer came in here just to kill her, it means her death benefited them in some way. Unfortunately, I think that means we're going to need to take a look at her case files and see who had grudges against her. It's very likely this could be a revenge killing for someone she arrested or incarcerated on one of her past jobs. And if that's the case, they may not stop with just one FBI agent.

Zara and I take another few rounds through the place, just to rule out anything we might have missed. But given all the windows are secured and the patio entry is locked tight with no signs of anyone forcing their way in, I have to conclude the intruder came through the front door. The question is how they were able to gain access and how quickly. The evidence suggests Agent Green was taken by surprise, and since there is no damage around the door from being forced open in any way, I'm going to assume the killer had a key.

"Feel familiar at all?" Zara asks once we finish and head back outside.

"You don't think this is related to what's happening at my place, do you?" I ask.

"Probably not, but it does seem strangely familiar," she replies. "Someone finds their way into the home of an FBI agent, no forced entry, no sign of them being there. You can't ignore the similarities."

"It's something to keep in mind," I say, though I really don't think this has anything to do with my apartment back in D.C. I've never met Agent Green before; and I knew nothing about her until this case. Why would someone target the two of us? The only thing that connects us is that we both work for the FBI. "Williamson," I say, walking up to the sour-faced man leaning against his car.

"You two finished? Can I leave now?" he asks, his body radiating impatience. He's drawn himself up like he's trying really hard to show us just how much larger he is than us.

"Has your forensics team done an electronic sweep of the apartment?" I ask, ignoring his bravado.

"Electronics sweep? For what?"

"Hidden cameras, bugs. Anything that indicated Agent Green might have been under surveillance."

He bristles. "We didn't have any reason to. Who would want to surveil her?"

"Who would want to kill her?" Zara asks.

"I need you to call in your team, get them back out here and have them go over the apartment inch by inch. I want to make sure there isn't anything in there that could have been used to tell the killer when she was at her most vulnerable."

He huffs, pulling out his cell phone. "I didn't sign up for this."

"Excuse me?" The words come out razor sharp and he looks taken aback for a moment. "Is there a problem?"

He seems stunned at my reaction, and it takes him a moment to process. "No. I'll get the team back out here to check."

"Thank you," I say. "Where's the office for the apartment block?" He points further on down the row to a large white building clad all in siding. It features a pitched roof that follows the curve of the building and on top, a rooster weathervane.

Zara and I head down the row of apartments, the light filtering through the thick trees that line the parking lot on the other side, creating pinpricks on the ground.

She leans over to me. "I love it when you get forceful with them."

"Sometimes I just get so sick of it, you know? It wears on you. I guarantee if Detmer had given the order he wouldn't have even questioned it."

"No, he wouldn't. But that's part of why we're here, right? The dynamic duo, out for action," she says, her palm flat as she wipes an imaginary arc in front of us. "We're gonna change all of this. At least, I am. You'll get partial credit."

"Uh-huh," I say. "Let's just see what management has to say first. We need to figure out how many people have a key to that apartment."

Inside we're greeted by a large rotunda that's two stories tall. The back of the office curves around, matching the roofline we saw from outside, and everything inside seems new and fresh. It's almost more like the lobby of a hotel than the management office for an apartment complex. A young fresh-faced woman with honey blonde hair sits at a desk off to the right, beside some tasteful cabinets that run the length of the wall.

"Hi," she says, getting up before we can take more than a few steps inside. "Welcome. How can we help you today? Are you looking for available rentals?"

I show her my badge. "Agent Slate. This is Agent Foley. We'd like to ask you a few questions about what happened."

The woman's face falls. "Oh, you're here about what happened to Ms. Green."

"*Agent* Green," Zara corrects.

"Yes, I'm so sorry, were you friends of hers?" the woman asks, motioning for us to come take a seat in the chairs that face her desk.

"No, we're from the D.C. branch," I say, coming up to the desk but waiting until she sits down before I take my seat. "We didn't know Agent Green personally."

The little plate on her desk says her name is Angie. "I spoke to another agent yesterday. He seemed very upset."

Angie doesn't come across as particularly disturbed about a murder in her apartment complex. Her posture is balanced and she has great eye contact. I guess I shouldn't expect anything else from someone who has to sell rentals for a living. Though I do find it curious.

"Can you tell me who found her?" I ask.

"That would be Adrijus, our maintenance man. Ms.—Agent Green had been having some cooling issues in her apartment but because of the fourth, we couldn't get to it until Sunday. He knocked, but when there was no answer he figured she wasn't there, so he let himself in."

"What happened next?" I ask.

She straightens a little. "He phoned us first, which, I told him he's supposed to call the police, but...well, you know. Anyway, as soon as he called the office to let us know, we called the police who showed up less than ten minutes later."

I lean forward. "What's *you know?*"

She sighs. "Adrijus is from Lithuania and doesn't speak great English. I think he's afraid to call the authorities himself."

"Were you aware Agent Green worked for the FBI?" Zara asks.

"I was, yes. As were most of the residents. That's not something that stays secret very long. As soon as one person finds out the news tends to spread. People like knowing an FBI agent lives—lived here, it made them feel secure." Angie crosses her long legs, leaning back in her chair.

"How many keys exist for her apartment?" I ask.

Angie turns to her laptop, opening it and typing a few characters. "Four. Two to the resident. One to our maintenance team and one for the main office, here." She stands and heads over to one of the cabinets, unlocking it with a key on a ring that she's pulled from her desk. The front door swings to the side and she rolls a drawer out of the top, in which are set three dozen keys, all marked with their respective numbers. "Here's hers, number seventy-two." She holds up the key to show us.

"How many people have access to that drawer?" I ask.

"Just me and the other manager, Tom. Our parent company doesn't keep master copies; they leave all of that up to us."

"Which one of you was working on Saturday night?"

She shakes her head. "Neither. We both had the day off. The office was closed for the holiday."

I turn and look up at the camera positioned right above the door we came through. "I'm going to need the footage for that camera," I say.

"It's motion-based," Angie replies. "So it only records if something trips it." She returns to her laptop and taps a few more times, before turning the computer around to face us. "Since the office was closed and locked, there's no footage from Saturday." The computer shows a log of each day, along with timestamps of when motion was detected in a long spreadsheet. The field beside Saturday, July 4th is empty. The first entry after that isn't until eight-oh-two on Sunday morning.

I sit back. It's possible someone could have gone in and erased the footage, but there's a more likely explanation at the moment. "The maintenance keys, where are those kept?"

"In our maintenance building," she says. "But you don't think anyone on our maintenance team would have done this, do you?"

"I don't know what happened," I say. "I just want to know how easy it is to access the maintenance keys. Looks like you have these locked down pretty well. But if someone can get to those easier, then all your precautions here are worthless."

Angie pinches her face together, like I've just insulted her dog. Apparently, she takes her job very seriously. "We have the highest hiring standards, and we perform full background checks," she says. "There is no doubt in my mind everyone on our team is of the highest integrity."

"How many is that, exactly?" I ask.

"Right now we only have three. We're a small complex and usually don't need more than one at a time. Adrijus and Mikhail trade shifts for most of the week. Tasmin is our emergency person who normally covers the third shift if there are any calls."

"Then Tasmin would have been on call Saturday night?" I ask.

She nods. "We always make sure at least one of them is available twenty-four-seven for emergencies. Though we didn't log any calls into maintenance on Saturday night."

"We're going to need to interview all three of them," I say.

"Is that really necessary?" Angie asks. "I'm sure—"

"Until we can be sure they weren't in that apartment on Saturday night, they're suspects," Zara says. "Like it or not, they all have access to the murder scene. As do you." Angie looks taken aback. "Where were you on Saturday night?"

"At home, with my family," she says, her voice hardening. "We were having a bar-b-que with my parents. There were at least ten people there, including Tom and his wife, if you're curious."

That should be easy enough to verify and takes the office managers out of the running, which is fine with me. Angie doesn't strike me as the kind of person to kill one of her residents in cold blood. And given that the keys in the office are locked down tight, we have to turn our attention to the maintenance workers.

"We'll need the addresses and phone numbers of each of your maintenance personnel," I tell her. "As well as names and numbers of the people who were at the get-together on Saturday night."

Angie sighs, pulling out a small notepad. "If you insist."

Chapter Seven

"THIS IS OUR MAINTENANCE ROOM," ANGIE SAYS, OPENING THE door to an industrial-looking room on the backside of the office. Exposed HVAC ducts run the length of the ceiling, then funnel down into a large metal box at the far end of the room. A wooden workbench sits off to one side, covered in parts and outlet boxes, as well as a few tools. The rest of the tools are either up on the wall behind it or in the rolling toolbox right beside the table. There are also stacks of old microwaves off in one corner, as well as a couple of other, larger appliances.

"Keys are right here." Angie leads us over to a metal box secured by a heavy padlock. She searches on her keyring before finding the right one, then opening the box to show us. Much like the rows in the office, the keys are lined up in order, with each one corresponding to another. Agent Green's key is right where it should be, though two others are missing. I point to the empty spots. "Numbers thirty-one and nineteen both had maintenance requests today."

"What about older residents?" Zara asks. "When someone moves out of your apartments, do their keys still work?"

"They're required to turn them back in at the end of their

lease," Angie says. "But we're aware some people may copy them for their own purposes while they live here. We re-key each lock at the end of the lease for a new tenant, so they don't have to worry about security."

"Who is on maintenance duty right now?" I ask.

"Adrijus," she says. "Mikhail doesn't usually start until two, but he's off today."

I check my phone for the time. "Which unit is Adrijus working in right now?"

Angie shakes her head. "No clue. He runs his own schedule depending on what he thinks is best." She's grown colder since our meeting in her office, probably due to us practically accusing her of being a suspect. The friendly smile is gone, replaced instead by impatience and pinched features. The list of names and numbers she gave us is in my pocket.

"Very well, thank you for your help," I say. "If we need anything else, we'll be in touch."

Angie locks the key safe back again and escorts us out of the maintenance room, locking it back as well. I have to admit, anyone who wanted to get into Green's apartment had to really want it. This was no crime of convenience.

Once we're back outside, without so much as a *hope you find the person who murdered someone on our property* from Angie, Zara and I make our way to the closest apartment on the maintenance schedule: number nineteen.

"Anything seem off about that to you?" I ask.

"You mean the fact she doesn't seem to care if we catch this person or not? Yeah," Zara replies.

"What did you notice?" I've come to rely on Zara observing from the background while I engage with our potential suspects. It allows her to observe things I might miss and keeps whoever we're talking to focused on me. That way they tend to forget she's even there and might make a slip.

"Image-conscious, but that's obvious," she says. "She seems more concerned with maintaining a façade rather than finding out the truth behind all this. She probably just wants it all over with as soon as possible so they can re-rent the apartment."

"That was my assessment as well," I say as we trudge up a small hill to another row of homes. It's a callous world, that's not news to anyone. But if a federal agent was murdered on my property, I think I'd be as cooperative as possible to get to the bottom of it. But then again, I have to look at this from the company's perspective. The last thing they want is a fleet of news crews here, splashing the story all over the place, telling the public how unsafe this area is that even an FBI agent can meet their end inside a locked apartment. Considering Green's neighbors have already been interviewed, I'm sure it won't take much longer for word to spread anyway.

Number nineteen is three units down out of eight total. We scale the steps and I rap on the door a few times. A moment later a woman in a bathrobe opens the door, her hair up in curlers.

"Yes?"

"Excuse us, is the maintenance man here right now?" I ask.

"Oh," the woman says. "Yes, he's right in here."

"Adrijus?" I call out.

I hear some rustling in the apartment's kitchen, before a face appears from around the corner. He's got light skin, with tawny hair and stubble that looks a few days old. That combined with his blue eyes make Adrijus more handsome than I would have suspected. He narrows his eyes when he sees us. "Yes?"

"Could we have a word with you?" I ask.

"What's this about?" the woman asks, pulling her robe tighter. I realize now she's got on a full face of makeup, even though she's just wearing the robe. Her hair is shiny as well, something I missed when she first opened the door.

"We just have a few questions," I say, showing the woman my badge. Her eyes go wide and she backs out of the way.

Adrijus approaches slowly, like an animal who suspects a trap. He's wearing a full toolbelt, and a button-up shirt that outlines his physique. A gold band encircles his left ring finger, though I'm not sure that matters much to the tenant, who is watching us carefully.

"Let's speak out here," I say, and I see his eyes flash down to my badge.

"You're...you're FBI?" he has a particular accent that hangs over his words, making them rough, but clear. "About... the lady?"

I nod and step out of his way so he can join us on the porch. "This will only take a moment," I tell the tenant, and close the door again.

"We'd just like to ask you a few questions," I say, introducing us. Zara stands on the other side of the porch, leaning up against the railing while I face Adrijus. I can tell from his stiff posture and shifting eyes he's very uncomfortable. Then again, I would be too had I just found a dead body. The fact that he isn't in the wind is a point in his favor, but not all killers are looking to get away. Many like to stick around and see the havoc they've caused.

"Can you tell us what happened yesterday morning?" I ask.

"S-sure. I was on maintenance schedule for morning. First on list is seventy-two. Green. Her air conditioner needs coolant. But company couldn't send until late Friday, too late before holiday. So I set up to fix on Sunday morning. I knock, no answer, so I think no one home. But when I open..." he trails off.

"That's when you found her."

He nods. "Yes. On ground."

"And her door was locked?" I ask.

"Yes. Needed key."

That matches up with the initial report. So far, so good. At least he's not changing his story. "What did you see, exactly?"

He winces, like it's difficult for him to remember. "Ms. Green. On ground, with pole…" he makes a motion toward his face. "Like flag."

"It was still standing up, is that what you're saying? The weapon?" He nods emphatically. "Did you touch anything?" He shakes his head. "What happened next?"

"Called boss. Police." He holds out his hands.

"Adrijus, where were you on Saturday night?" I'm still trying to gauge him. The language barrier makes his involuntary cues even more important. I'm almost not listening to what he says, and instead watch *how* he's saying it.

"Family," he says. "For celebration. Holiday." I'm not picking up anything deceptive from him, though he does seem nervous. Depending on his history, he may have an ingrained distrust of law enforcement, which may be why he called the office before calling the police. But we'll need to run background checks on all three of the maintenance personnel regardless.

I shoot a glance over his shoulder at Zara, who gives me a subtle shake of her head. "Okay, Adrijus, thanks for your help. We'll let you know if we need anything else."

He nods, then pulls out the key again to unlock number nineteen's door. The woman inside stands quickly from her couch and in that brief moment I catch the edge of a negligée under the robe. I'm not sure if Adrijus knows what's in store for him or if this is business as usual, but it opens another possibility I hadn't considered until now. I carefully watch Adrijus until the door closes. As far as I can tell, I don't see any lust or even recognition in his eyes about what the tenant is planning.

As Zara and I make our way back down the hill, I voice my concern. "Did you catch that back there?"

She gives me a sly grin. "Oh, you mean the hanky panky stanky? Yeah, I saw it."

"How common do you think that is here?"

"You don't think Green could have been involved with him, do you?" she asks.

I shrug. "Who knows? He's a handsome man, and she was downright gorgeous. Who's to say they didn't have a little fling on the side. But then she starts dating Detmer, and sees it could be something serious. Adrijus doesn't like that idea, instead decides if he can't have her, no one can."

Zara shoots me a glare. "That's a lot of *ifs*, Em."

"I know, just thinking out loud. We'll see if his alibi checks out first. Plus, I want to get a look at the other two. Someone else used a key to get into her apartment."

We reach the parking lot, making our way back to Williamson. Zara perks up before we reach him. "Something you said back in the office made me think about that. What if Green herself made a few extra copies? She could have given them to friends or family in case of emergencies."

Shit. She's right. There's no telling how many copies of the keys could be out there, floating around. And chasing them down is going to take a lot of time. We already have to investigate two more maintenance people. And then there's the whole ritualistic nature of the killing. Why the eyes and why the fire poker? I would have understood if it had been a shower curtain rod or something that Agent Green already had in her apartment, but the killer specifically brought the poker with them...why? There must be some significance. Again, something familiar tickles the back of my brain every time I think about the weapon, but I can't recall what. It's like smoke that passes right through my hands as I try to grab it.

"Williamson," I say as we approach.

"Agents," he says. "Forensics is on the way. Should be here in another half hour."

"Good," I say. "We need to go run some background

checks. Can you handle things here?" He nods, seemingly more cooperative now. I hand over my card, so he'll have my cell number. "Please let me know if they find anything."

"Sure," he says.

We thank him, then head back to the car. We've got a long afternoon ahead of us and I'm not looking forward to it with Detmer hovering over my shoulder. But we need the resources of the Woodhurst office if we want to get this done in a reasonable amount of time.

"Okay," Zara says, looking over the top of the car at me as we open our doors. "Taking bets. I say the twenty-four-hour maintenance guy has no alibi."

I let out a long breath. "What's the punishment?"

She sticks out her tongue. "You're no fun. It's not punishment!"

"With you, that's debatable," I say.

"If I win, we go to Six Flags, you eat two funnel cakes, then get on Firebird."

I shake my head. "Z, teenagers do that crap."

"Aw, c'mon, when's the last time you were even on a roller coaster? They're a lot more fun now that you're tall enough to fit." She laughs hysterically.

"Okay, just for that, if I win, we're going to the Natural History Museum. All day."

"Good," she says, sticking out her bottom lip. "I *love* history."

"*Good*," I emphasize, knowing full well she hates walking through museums as she finds them boring as hell. "You're on."

We both get in and slam our doors in unison.

Chapter Eight

"DAMMIT," ZARA SHOUTS AS SHE SLAMS DOWN THE PHONE. The entire desk shakes.

I look up, a sly smile on my face as I drink this in. "Problem?"

"Turns out the twenty-four-hour guy is really a twenty-four-hour girl, and she was in the hospital with her mother Saturday night because someone had mixed nuts into the snack mix they were all eating, and her mother had an allergic reaction. Nurses confirm she was there with her all night." She crosses her arms, huffing.

"Does this mean I win?" I ask.

She eyes me for a minute. "Fine, I'll go. But I'm wearing headphones so I can drown out anything boring you might have to say."

I cock my head. "I don't think that's fitting with the spirit of the contest. I mean, I had to risk eating and throwing up. All you have to do is walk around and look at some exhibits."

"That's so much worse!" she says. "I'd rather puke my guts up all day."

"I thought you *loved* it," I tease, mimicking her voice from earlier.

"It's not over yet," she says. "What about the third guy, Mikhail?"

I check my notes from all the phone calls I've had to field. "At least now I know why he was on call and Tasmin wasn't. But he was at his church from four until eleven-thirty. They do some kind of Fourth of July celebration there for the kids; I didn't really understand it."

"Eleven-thirty?" Zara asks. "Where is the church in relation to his house? Could he have swung back by the apartments on his way home?"

I hold up a finger. "The party turned into a sleepover for the kids. He was one of the five chaperones there all night with them, keeping watch. He didn't get back home until nine a.m. the next morning."

She cranes her head back toward the ceiling. "Ugh."

"I also spoke with Adrijus's wife. She confirmed he was home all night as well. But given our choices, his is the weakest alibi."

Zara runs her hand through her hair, leaving part of it sticking up from the static. "Maybe you're right. Maybe Agent Green did have—"

"Afternoon." I look over to see Agent Detmer entering the room. When we got back to the office, Detmer showed us where we could set up, which is a small room off the main bullpen where there are a few extra desks, phones and computers. Enough that we could do all the research we need. "Find anything?"

"Still working on it," I say, trying to maintain my façade of patience. He's been all over us all afternoon, just like I thought he'd be. Even though he's technically not on this case, he can't help but want to be a part of it. I know how he feels, every hour or so I have a reflexive need to call Janice, but I know better than to put my own life in my hands like that. Maybe I should take a page out of her book and insinuate if he keeps interrupting us, he might lose a few fingers.

"Looks like the alibis on the maintenance workers check out."

"I just can't believe there are no solid leads," he says.

I catch Zara glaring at me. Her eyes shift to Detmer, then back to me. I know what she's doing, and I mouth the word *no*. She mouths *yes* back. I shake my head, now is not the time.

"Hey, Detmer," Zara says. "Did Melissa ever mention any of the maintenance workers to you?"

Creases run up his forehead. I'd be willing to bet Detmer hasn't gotten much sleep in the past few days. "Not particularly, why?"

She gives me a mischievous smirk. "Did she need to get a lot of maintenance work done? Those looked like nice apartments. They were probably pretty prompt with maintenance requests."

"If she did, she never talked about it with me. Why do you ask? I thought you'd cleared the maintenance crew."

"We have, for the most part," I tell him. "I just need to pull some more background information on one of them." I need to change the subject. "You don't happen to know if they got any prints on the murder weapon, do you?"

He shakes his head. "It was clean. No prints, no oils, nothing. Not even evidence someone wiped it down. The murderer probably wore gloves."

The more I think about this, the more I can't help but imagine some kind of forbidden tryst between Adrijus and Agent Green. He looks to be a strong, capable man. Definitely someone who could drive a fire poker down through another person's face. But I didn't sense any malice from him when he mentioned Agent Green. He seemed contrite, which is a lot harder to fake when English isn't your first language.

"Which one of the maintenance people are you still looking at?" Detmer asks.

"Andrijus Vilmantas," I say. "His wife confirmed his alibi,

but wives lie for their husbands all the time." Not to mention her English wasn't the best either. She seemed to understand what I was asking, but could it all just be a ruse? Are we getting played here, or am I thinking too hard about this?

I rub my face a few times before checking the time. "I'm going to call it for the day. I need sleep."

Detmer checks his watch. "It's barely past six."

"Our boss had us working long hours on this nationwide laundering thing," Zara says, getting up with me. "Everyone was putting in a ton of overtime."

"Trust me," I say, "I'm better when I've had some rest. We'll start again first thing in the morning."

Detmer looks like he wants to argue, but there's not much he can do. Zara and I are the leads on this case, so what we say goes. The rest of the team has to follow along. In the past, Janice has accused me of spending too much time on a case— to my own detriment. Sure, I could probably stay here and rack my brain but I would just end up spinning my wheels all night and getting nowhere. Better to get some sleep and start over tomorrow.

"I can't believe you asked him that," I say once we're alone outside.

"What? I needed to assess him, see if he knew about it. If Green was involved with Adrijus, odds are, either he or Detmer killed her."

"Look," I say. "What we saw today could have been nothing more than a one-off. A tenant hoping to get lucky with her hot maintenance man. There's absolutely nothing connecting Adrijus to her death other than a weak alibi—"

"—and the fact that he found her body. He could have been feigning to cover up any guilt."

It's possible, but I'm not convinced. "Let's just take a fresh look at it tomorrow. Oh, and get ready for a field trip, because as soon as we get back, we're going to the museum."

Zara gives me the evil eye halfway back to the hotel. But by the time we reach it, it seems she's forgotten all about it; instead she's buried in her phone, looking at whatever it is she does on there all the time.

When we got in last night, I didn't really take the time to appreciate our hotel. It's not one of those chain places, or at least, if it is, they've done a good job disguising it. The sign out front says *Elk Lodge Inn*, and the inside reflects that promise to the extreme. It looks more like a log cabin inside, with carved wood bannisters and railings, as well as huge wooden pillars holding up the two-floor lobby. A giant stone fireplace sits in the middle of the room, surrounded by large leather chairs, as well as tables and ottomans. On the far wall are shelves of books, games, anything anyone could want to pass the time, with one exception: there's no television anywhere.

"Did I miss something, or did you book us in the kitschiest place in New York?"

"Are you just now noticing it?" Zara asks.

"Give me a break, I was exhausted last night. I barely remember the flight."

"I think you slept the entire ride here," she says before changing the timbre of her voice so she's mocking me. "Do you recall which floor we're on?"

"Yes," I hiss and head for the elevators. But the bookshelf draws my eye. I didn't bring anything to read on this trip and while I'm tired, reading might be a good way to wind my mind down so I can look at this case fresh tomorrow. "You go on up, I'll be there in a minute. I want to find a good book."

"It's room four-twenty-five if you forget." She chuckles as she gets on the elevator. I have half a mind to toss something at her but the only thing is a random coaster on the table that sits in between the elevator shafts. She shoots me a wink as the doors close and I let out a huff as I head over to the bookcase. I love that woman, but she can tire me out sometimes. I don't know where she gets all her energy.

I scan the books on the upper shelves, looking for something interesting. There's a small placard beside the shelf with a sign: *Woodhurst: home to National Bestselling Author Ruby Blackthorne!* I look over and see there are a few books with Blackthorne's name on them, and I recognize some of the titles. I believe I've read some of her stuff before; though I didn't know she was local here. I pull the first book off the shelves: *"X" Marks the Spot*, and flip through it. After a few minutes I recall the story: it's about a deranged priest who carves crosses into his victims. A little gruesome, but I think I enjoyed it.

I go through the next few, but one catches my eye. *Flame's Ember*. The worn cover is bright red, and in the center, the unique tip of a steel fire poker.

Suddenly my heart is hammering in my chest as I flip through the pages of the book, searching for what is slowly beginning to coalesce in my memory: the familiarity I was feeling when examining the facts of the case. I scan through the climax of the book, familiar passages jumping back out at me now, jarring my memory into remembering.

I slam the book shut, tuck it under my arm and run for the stairwell. I can't wait for the elevator. I take the stairs two at a time, scaling them like I'm being chased by a rabid wolverine before I finally hit the fourth floor. Scampering down the hallway, I fumble with my keycard before finally getting it out just as I reach our door. I burst through, causing Zara, who is sitting on one of the beds with a grin as wide as her face, to jump.

"Jesus, woman!" she yells, hiding her phone under a pillow. "What the hell?"

I hold up the book, pointing at the cover. "It's in here," I say, almost manic.

"What is?"

"The whole thing! The fire pokers, the eyes, all of it," I say.

Zara gets off the bed. "Emily, calm down. What are you talking about?"

"Agent Green," I say. "This book describes exactly how she died."

Chapter Nine

"I THINK I'VE FOUND HER," ZARA SAYS, SITTING ON THE BED, cross-legged, her face in her phone. "Stephanie Murphy, 9 Winding Road, Richney, New York."

I glance up from my own phone. "How did you do that?"

She grins at me, then tosses her phone so it does a helicopter spin before landing on the bed. "I didn't spend two years as an Intelligence Analyst for nothing."

"Yeah, but still, figuring out her real name and her address in under an hour? That deserves some accolades."

"And a trip to a certain roller coaster, I believe." Zara winks.

"You've lost that bet, give it up," I say. After I managed to calm down and catch my breath, I showed Zara the passages in the book that describe Agent Green's death. Except in the book it's obviously not Agent Green. It's a corrupt police officer named Wilma Fallows, who arrests innocent people on trumped-up charges and then kills them, making their deaths look like suicides. The protagonist finally gets the upper hand on her by stabbing her through the eyes when Wilma breaks in her house to silence her investigation. The story itself was good; it kept my attention, but that's what had been nagging at my mind ever since we got to New York. I'd recalled some of the details about the case from the book, but I'd thought it had been an old case instead.

The facts of the case match up, but not exactly. In the book, Wilma manages to steal a master key from the protagonist earlier without her knowledge, giving herself access to the house late at night. But it turns out the protagonist set a trap for her, and is already waiting. While Wilma makes her way through the house, looking for her prey, the protagonist sneaks up on her from behind, blindsiding her with the fire poker before shoving it down through her eye. In the book, Wilma still twitches after the first impalement, so the protagonist removes the poker and shoves it through the other eye, hard enough so that it goes all the way through and sticks into the wood floor. It's very dramatic. The police arrive moments later, and the books wraps up shortly after that.

In our case, Agent Green isn't a police officer, and she's not a serial killer, at least not to my knowledge. But everything else matches up. The way someone gets into the house, sneaks up on her and kills her. It's just the roles are reversed. The person breaking in is the killer in our case, instead of the victim. But the way the poker was shoved through both eye sockets, then left sticking up in the ground is what really intrigues me. Someone went to a lot of trouble to copy the scene from this book. We now have an explanation for the ritual itself, but we still need a why.

Zara hops off the bed. "So? We headed there now?"

I shake my head. "I want to go back to the Bureau tomorrow. See if Detmer or anyone there knows anything about this first." After we both read the end of the book again, Zara immediately got to work on finding out the real name of *Ruby Blackthorne*, the author who is apparently local to Woodhurst. I'm not sure if that's coincidence or not, but it's looking less and less likely Adrijus had anything to do with this. The language barrier would have made it more difficult for him to

read the details of the book and get them exactly right. I
checked and *Flame's Ember* hasn't been translated into his
native Lithuanian. It also doesn't make much sense. I'm just
using generalizations, but the demographic for this kind of
book isn't middle-aged men. There are always outliers, of
course, but my gut tells me we're looking for a woman, as she
would have been much more likely to have read these details
which inspired Agent Green's death.

"How many female agents in Detmer's department?" I ask
Zara.

"Five, I think," she replies. "You think this was an inside
job?"

I shake my head. "Just mulling things over." I'm very interested to talk to the author herself, to see if she's received any
kind of communication from a fanatic or someone who seems
like they're disturbed in some way. Usually a killer doesn't start
by murdering, they work up to it. Either through physical or
psychological means. Someone may have started out as a fan
of her work, only to eventually incorporate it into their ritual,
almost like a calling card. With any luck, the author will have
something for us.

"Let me see her house," I say, getting off my bed and
sitting beside Zara. She picks up her phone again and pulls up
a satellite image of the house. It's nothing short of palatial.
Given the success of *Ruby Blackthorne's* books, I can't say I'm
surprised. I always get announcements when her next book is
coming out, though I haven't read anything of hers for a year
or so now. I just haven't had as much time, especially since
Matt.

"Looks like a modern-day castle," Zara says. "Fountains
out front. Two pools out back. Are we sure she isn't an
athlete?"

I chuckle. "Getting to her isn't going to be easy. I'm
hoping we meet up without arranging some kind of appointment with her people. Rich people protect their privacy."

Zara raises an eyebrow. "Even from us?"

I stretch my arms above my head, feeling the effects of the adrenaline wearing off. If we want to get a jump on this tomorrow, I need to hit the sack. "I guess we'll find out."

After a surprisingly good continental breakfast surrounded by mounted heads of half a dozen animals in the restaurant that's attached to the hotel, Zara and I head back to the office to get there before Detmer and the others.

Once there we dive into Stephanie Murphy's background, to see if she's ever made any kind of complaints of stalking or surveillance. But her record comes up clean. No domestic reports and nothing to the police indicating she feared for her safety.

I'm not discouraged though. It doesn't mean she hasn't received something in the past, she may have just disregarded it.

Because we're already here, I keep doing my due diligence on Adrijus, though my searches don't pull up anything I didn't already see last night. On a whim, I gather all the names of the female agents who work in this office—anyone who would have had constant contact with Green. One FBI agent killing another is virtually unheard of, but at this point I can't discount any possibilities. The details from the book have set the idea in my mind that we might be dealing with someone in law enforcement. Someone who would have had easier access to Agent Green. But I still need a motive.

"Agents," Detmer says, poking his head into our office, coffee in hand. "You're here early."

"I told you," I say. "Early night's sleep makes for a productive morning."

"Found any new leads?"

"What do you know about a woman named Stephanie

Murphy?" I ask.

Detmer furrows his brow, taking a slow sip from his cup. "Murphy? Sounds familiar..."

"She's the real person behind the author Ruby Blackthorne," Zara says.

Detmer snaps his fingers. "That's it. She's something of a local celebrity around here. We have a fair share of famous people who commute up here from the city, but she's lived in Woodhurst most of her life, I believe."

"Know anything else about her?" I ask.

"Not much. She does a few book signings around town sometimes at the local shops. But other than that she and her family keep to themselves. I know she lives in one of those big houses out on Marnmouth Island. Why? What does she have to do with this?"

I give Detmer a brief explanation of the end of *Flame's Ember*, only for him to arch a skeptical eyebrow when I'm done. "So you think a fan of hers is responsible?"

"Maybe not a fan, but at least someone who is familiar with her work," I say. "It can't hurt to check with her to see if she's received anything out of the ordinary lately. Our person might be looking to impress her." Considering we don't have many other solid leads at the moment, I feel it's worth a look.

He gives me a small shake of his head. "I suppose. Though it seems like a waste of time to me. I think you should concentrate on this Adrijus person."

"Don't worry," I say, grabbing my jacket and slipping my arms through. "We're not done with him yet." I want to take a stab at Murphy first, while this is still relatively fresh. Adrijus isn't going anywhere.

"Hey," Detmer says, his gaze dropping to the ground. "I wanted to let you know there's going to be a service on Thursday...for Melissa. The Bureau is handling her funeral costs, thankfully, since her parents and sister don't have much money."

"Oh." I pause. I hadn't even thought about a service for her. Seems sudden, especially since we don't know who killed her yet. But if the forensics team has already gathered all the evidence from her body, there's no need to keep her in storage, I suppose. I just hope they haven't missed anything. "Is she being buried?"

He shakes his head, and I can tell he's trying to keep a lump from forming in his throat. "Cremated. That's what they wanted. I don't think she had a will. You're both welcome to come, if you want to."

"We'll leave that to her family and friends," I say. "But thank you. I'd rather find out who did this. With any luck, we'll know who was responsible *by* Thursday." Though a service might be a good time to spot the killer. As odd as it sounds, some killers actually attend the funerals of their victims. Some out of a sense of guilt, others to witness the results of their actions in person. The narcissists are the ones who can't seem to help themselves. "Will it be open to the public?"

Detmer finally meets my eye. "I think so. Why? You thinking the killer might show up?"

"Exactly," I say. I turn to Zara and she nods. "We might attend after all. Let me know what time. If we don't find who we need by then, it will be a good opportunity."

The man makes a face. "Do you really think they'd be stupid enough to come to a funeral full of FBI agents?"

"Maybe that's part of this. There's obviously a performative aspect to the murder. Whoever this person is, they want attention, and they want to show off their power. Being at the funeral might be the ultimate expression of that."

A small smile quirks at the edge of Detmer's mouth. "They told me you were good."

"Nah," Zara says, winking at me. "She's just lucky."

"Maybe this Murphy thing will pan out after all," Detmer says. "However it goes, good luck."

Chapter Ten

THE SUN WARMS MY ARM AND THE WIND WHIPS OUR HAIR AS we head to Stephanie Murphy's house on Marnmouth Island. Large fluffy clouds dot the sky, momentarily blocking out the sun as we drive, alternating us between sunlight and shade. The air coming off the ocean is salty, but without the brine that I normally associate with the sea.

As we drive the roads get smaller and smaller, until we're finally confronted with a small gatehouse as we try to turn on Murphy's street. It's barely more than a shack with a long pole extending across the street behind it. An older man in a security uniform pops his head out of the gatehouse when our car doesn't automatically raise the gate, though he's on Zara's side.

"Help you folks?"

I show him my badge. "We're here to see one of the residents."

"Oh, o'course, o'course," he says, heading back into the gatehouse. A moment later the gate opens. "Always happy to help out officers of the law. Drive safe, speed limit is twenty."

I give him a small finger salute and continue down the small road which is barely a lane and a half wide. Off to our left is a small sound where houses dot the other side; homes we passed on the road in. While those were at least twice as large as the biggest house I've ever lived in, the ones that pass by on our right are downright *massive*. Huge, circular drives cut in from the road, winding back into the beautiful landscaping and winding back out again. The homes are no more than two or three stories tall, but they're sprawling. A few we pass have tennis courts or additional buildings on this side, I'm sure so they have unobstructed views of the ocean on the other.

"Can you imagine this?" I ask. "Living in something this large?"

"Just give me a loft and a foldaway bed," Zara says. "As long as I'm up high, that's what counts."

A few moments pass and I can feel her staring at me out of the corner of my eye. "What?"

She casts her gaze down. "You seem really gung-ho on this author theory."

Am I being too obsessive about this? I feel like there's a connection here, and I don't want to miss it. But what if I'm letting my personal feelings get in the way? Being the first one to recognize a link no one else does gives an investigator a certain…ownership over proving their theories right. Maybe I'm being too biased. "Don't you find it weird?"

"Weird, yeah. But how do we know it's not just some nut who happened to pick up this book looking for some inspiration? They might not even know who Ruby Blackthorne is."

I shake my head. "People don't need inspiration to murder. It's not a contest to see who can be the most creative. This was done for a reason, I'm sure of it."

Zara tips an imaginary hat at me. "Okay. But if you're wrong I'm gonna tell Janice and then *I* get to be in charge."

"Thanks for the support." I don't try to hide my sarcasm.

"Hey, I'm just here for the glory," she says, grinning.

I roll my eyes before we come up to number nine. Like

most of the others, the house is massive. But there's no individual gate on the property. That's something I've noticed about this neighborhood. I guess that guard gate down at the entrance is enough to ward off any solicitors.

The house is a two-story colonial, with a large attached building off to the left and a large row of thick trees on the right, separating the property from the neighbor. A black Audi R8 sits out front, pulled slightly to the side so a vehicle can pass all the way around it. A BMW SUV sits beside it, but I don't recognize the model. The house looks like it could pass in Williamsburg, it's that traditional.

"Guess this is it."

Zara leans forward. "I can't wait to see their faces when they find out who we are. That's my favorite part."

"You're awful," I say, pulling our vehicle into the semi-circle driveway, past the other two cars already sitting out. I park off to the side, careful not to drive on the perfectly manicured lawn. As we step out of the car, I notice the left side of the house doesn't have nearly as many trees to mark the property line. But when I walk a little closer I realize why: someone has taken the time to create a French-style garden, complete with hedges and pathways.

I let out a low whistle. We definitely aren't in D.C. anymore.

"Excuse me." A woman in her mid-forties stands at the top of the stairs that lead into the house. She has shoulder-length blonde hair, which frames a graceful face. She's wearing a baggy shirt which falls off one shoulder, revealing the strap of a sports bra. I suspect her leggings are lululemon or some other name brand. But even from where we are, I can tell this is the woman we're looking for. She matches her author photo almost perfectly. As if it were only taken a few days ago. "We don't allow solicitors on our property," she says, dismissive.

"Mrs. Murphy?" I ask. Before she can respond I hold up my badge. "Agent Emily Slate, FBI. This is Agent Foley."

Concern crosses her face as she takes a few steps down toward us. "FBI? What is this about? Is it Dylan? Or Harper?"

Right, the kids. If my memory of the files we pulled is correct, he's eleven and she's eight. "No ma'am, nothing like that. We're investigating a case and we were hoping you might help us."

"I don't understand," she says, cautious. "Does this involve me?"

"In a way, yes," I say. "May we come in?"

"Oh," she says, as if she's just now realizing we're still outside. "Yes, of course. Please come with me."

As I take the steps up to the house, I can't help but wonder what happens when the Murphy's have someone who needs accessibility over to their home. Maybe it's easier to get in through one of their garages.

"I'm sorry about earlier," Stephanie Murphy says, pointing to a small keypad inside the front double doors, which she holds open until we're inside. "I saw you pull up on the security cameras. We didn't have any maintenance scheduled for today so I figured you must have swindled your way past Gus."

She's direct, I'll give her that much. Maybe that's a talent benefiting an author, I don't know. But as far as I can tell, Stephanie, or *Ruby Blackthorne*, is doing pretty well for herself. Unlike the outside of the house, the interior is modern and updated. The foyer is all marble, and open to the second-floor, allowing the light from the upper windows to filter through and hit the crystal chandelier in the middle of the room, scattering shards of light everywhere. It's not overly opulent, but it's not modest either. "Would you like some iced tea?" she asks. I detect the hint of an accent under there somewhere. Southern. I heard it all the time down in Charleston, but this is a little different.

"That would be great," I say, trying not to gawk at the home.

As we're walking through the hall, two small Pomeranians appear, fluffy like clouds. I expect them to bark, but instead they fall into step behind us, their little legs doing the best they can to keep up as we wind through the house behind Murphy to the kitchen.

"Don't mind Elena and Nadia," she says. "They just want to smell you, then they'll leave you alone."

We walk into the kitchen and I'm dumbstruck. The room is larger than my entire apartment, clad in a mixture of stones and metals. Blue cabinets with gold handles run along the bottom halves of the walls, while open wooden shelving holds perfectly stacked rows of plates and glasses along the top. In the center of the back wall is a massive stove with six burners, and looks like something out of a steampunk movie.

Our host grabs two tall glasses off one of the open shelves and takes them over to what looks like the most expensive coffee maker I've ever seen, which is odd. True to her word, the Pomeranians take a few sniffs of our legs once we stop before turning and disappearing into another one of the home's rooms. The back of the kitchen features windows that run almost all the way across the wall above the lower cabinets, featuring beautiful views of the ocean beyond.

"Nice kitchen," I say.

"Oh, thanks," she replies, pulling a part of the machine away which looks like a built-in pitcher. She then pours the tea into the glasses, complete with ice, before setting them before us. "I cook a lot. It's kind of my hobby."

"Should we refer to you as Stephanie or Ruby?" Zara asks, taking a sip of tea. Her eyes perk up when it touches her lips.

A smile plays across the author's face, and she glances down a moment before looking back up. "I guess I should have figured you knew who I was. It's not something I advertise, but I suppose the FBI has ways of finding these kinds of things out." She pauses. "Steph is fine."

"It's actually your work that brings us here," I say, pausing a moment to take a sip of the tea. As soon as it touches my lips, an explosion of sugar coats my tongue. I glance over at Zara, my eyes wide. *See?* she says with a look. *Told you.* "This is…potent."

"Oh, sorry," Steph says. "I should have warned you. I forget ya'll don't like it sweet up here; it's a force of habit." She reaches for the glasses to take back. "How about some coffee instead? We have it imported from Colombia every few months. My husband has a friend who invests in a farm down there."

"That's not necessary," I say, setting the glass down. I'm going to be tasting sugar for hours. "Is your husband here?"

Steph shoots a look over her shoulder. "I'm sure he is. Probably in the garage tinkering with something."

It boggles my mind just the two of them live here with their kids. This house is big enough to hold at least two large families, maybe more. While part of me feels the injustice, I have to remind myself that Mrs. Murphy built her fortune from scratch. She wasn't one of those generational wealth people. And if a woman can make all this happen for herself, then I'm not about to disparage her for it.

"Mrs. Murphy—Steph—have you received any threats lately?" I lean forward. "Any suspicious communication from any of your readers? Could be emails, messages, even letters."

"I don't get many letters these days," she says, smiling. "And there is always the oddball or two who like to ask everything about your life from what kind of socks you wear to who grooms your dog, but I wouldn't call any of them threats."

"Are any of your fans what you would call…obsessed?" Zara asks.

Steph laughs. "Well, I do have some that will buy almost anything I release, if that's what you mean. But no one's ever showed up at my doorstep like you two have. Then again, most people don't know my real name." She has an easygoing manner about her and for a moment I'm a little bit starstruck. It isn't often you think you'll meet the person who writes the books you enjoy reading; she's kind of like a famous actor that way. Except in her case, she's managed to stay out of the limelight.

"Is there a particular reason you use a pen name?" I ask. "Just out of curiosity."

"Privacy, mostly," she replies, leaning up against her back counter. "I never wanted to be famous. Plus, my publisher thought it would be a good idea. Ruby Blackthorne is a lot more intriguing than Steph Murphy. They said it had something to do with marketing." She seems very at ease with us. Most people either have one of two reactions when they see the FBI at their doorstep: they either become defensive and combative, or they try to over-cooperate, falling over themselves to prove they had nothing to do with whatever we're investigating. Murphy is neither. Instead, it's like we're a couple of old friends visiting over some cold glasses of tea that's much too sweet.

"I know I'm probably not supposed to know, but can I ask what this is about?" she finally says. "I have to admit, you've piqued my curiosity."

I exchange glances with Zara. Typically, we don't reveal details about a case unless we're sure the person we're speaking with can give us something in return. So far it doesn't look like Murphy has anything and this has just been a bad call on my part. "I'm sorry, but we can't speak about the details of the case."

"Can you at least tell me what's happened?" she asks. "I mean, you're basically asking me if I have a stalker. Am I in danger here?"

I suppose she does have some right to know. We're not sure if the person who committed the murder is looking to show it off to Murphy in any way, whether that be by a letter or some other communication to Blackthorne. "We don't think so, no," I say. "As I said before, the case is only tangentially related. We're investigating the murder of an FBI agent. The manner in which she died was…peculiar."

"Peculiar how?" Murphy asks.

"As in someone took a page from one of your books," Zara says. "*Flame's Ember.*"

Murphy's hand goes to her mouth. "What?" She looks shaken.

"The murder recreated a scene from the book," I add. "Where the protagonist kills Wilma at the end. It's hard not to look for some kind of connection."

She turns around for a moment, looking out to the ocean through her large windows before turning back. "And you think one of my fans did this?"

"We don't have any evidence to support that yet," I say. "All we can really infer is that the killer read your book at some point before the murder. We were hoping if you'd had communication with someone that seemed 'off', it would provide us with a lead."

"God," she says, shaking her head. "I just can't believe it. I never thought…" Her eyes begin to well up with tears. "It's my fault."

"That's not true," I say, trying to nip this in the bud. I can already see the spiral she's headed down. "You can't control who does and who doesn't read your work. You're not at fault for this."

Her eyes shimmer for a moment before she swallows and nods, though I can see this is going to affect her for some time. "Do you need to sit down?"

She shakes her head. "No, I'm fine." She looks around like she's in a daze. "Let me, uh…let me get in touch with my publisher. See if they've seen anything. My agent usually lets me know if anything weird comes across, but it happens so rarely, she may not even think about it. Is there somewhere I can get back in touch with you?"

"Of course," I say, fishing a card out of my pocket and handing it to her. "Feel free to call anytime."

"I wish I had more for you, I really do," she says again, still in a state of shock. "I think I'll contact our security company as well and make sure they're aware of the situation."

"That's not a bad idea," I say. "Though at this time we still don't have any reason to believe the killer even knows who you really are."

"Let's hope it stays that way," she says.

Zara and I ask a couple of follow-up questions, mostly to help Mrs. Murphy calm down. Finally, she escorts us out. On the way I get a glimpse of her office which I missed when we came in. It's sparse, mostly a desk with a bookcase behind it, looking out onto the ocean. I think if that was my view, I'd sit around and write all day too.

As soon as Zara and I are back in the car she flashes me a Cheshire cat grin. "Well, any other ideas?"

I hate to say it, but it looks like this might be a dead end. I was really hoping she might have something for us, especially given her proximity to the murder. What I didn't tell Mrs. Murphy was that the killer might have fixated on her *because* she's local. But at the moment that's pure supposition, and I don't need to go around scaring our potential informants. But it does linger in the back of my mind.

"I guess it's back to the office," I say, dropping my shoulders in defeat.

Chapter Eleven

WITH NO REAL PROGRESS ON THE MURPHY FRONT, WE'RE forced to return to our original investigation. Since Adrijus is our best lead, I decide to pay his home a visit on the way back to the office, just to get a feel for the place.

Zara directs us through downtown Woodhurst until we turn north, heading back in the direction of Green's apartment. But before we're out of the city completely, we turn off to a small adjoining apartment complex that straddles its parking lot on both sides. It looks relatively nice, though the units don't seem very large. Being the middle of the day, most of the spaces are empty.

"Which unit is it?" I ask.

"Fourteen, there," Zara says, pointing to the second-floor.

I glance around, looking for security cameras. I catch sight of a couple positioned on the parking lot itself. "Bingo," I say. "We can verify if he was here or not ourselves."

I pull into one of the spaces and we step out, headed for the small office near the back of the units. It's on the ground floor, and decidedly less impressive than Agent Green's apartment office, seeing as it is really only one room. A young man in a polo shirt and glasses looks up as we enter.

"Can I help you?" His tone has an edge of superiority to it, like he thinks it's beneath him to deal with us.

"We need to see your parking lot footage from two nights ago," I say.

"And who are you? We don't just—" My badge in his face stops him from saying another word.

"Don't just what?" I say, taking a small bit of pleasure from being able to shut him up. He strikes me as one of these overprivileged college kids who's been forced to get a summer job as the first bit of real work they've ever done.

"Nothing," he says, and I can still see a bit of fire in him. But he can't be more than twenty and he's not about to antagonize two FBI agents. "It's around here."

We walk around the counter to a computer monitor near the back of the room. The image on the monitor is split into six segments, each on a different angle of the property. Zara sits down and picks the one that's closest to Adrijus' apartment without an invitation from the kid.

"You just—"

"I know how to use it," she says without taking her eyes off the screen. A second later the images are rewinding so fast everything becomes a blur.

"Thank you," I tell the kid and he takes the hint to return to his post and leave us alone. "Adrijus drives a Silverado, right?"

"Yep," Zara says, "Dark green." Though that won't help much, given the images are in black and white. She scrolls all the way back to Saturday morning, where Adrijus's truck is clearly visible in the parking lot, parked right under unit fourteen. We see him head out to the truck, get in, and drive off. Zara fast forwards until around noon when the truck returns. "Looks like he's getting ready for his family gathering." Both his arms are full of groceries.

"Keep going," I say. "All the way past midnight."

She fast forwards again, the light fading and eventually

disappearing from the parking lot. But there's enough ambient light from the surrounding area to still give a good view of everything. "Wait a second," she says, peering closer to the monitor. "He's going back out."

I check the time on the security tapes. It reads ten-fifty-six p.m. "Green was killed between eleven and two, right?"

Zara nods.

I pull out my phone and do a quick maps search, plotting the time it takes to get from here to Green's apartment in Adams Hill. "He could have made it. It's only a twenty-two-minute drive."

"Probably less that late at night," Zara says.

"Keep going, let's see when he comes back." She forwards it again, and Adrijus doesn't return in his truck until well after three a.m.

"Not looking too good for our boy," Zara says.

"It's still circumstantial," I say. "It just proves he and his wife lied to us, that's all."

"But it's enough to bring him in." She turns and looks up at me.

"Sure is."

When I call the apartment complex, Angie is the one who answers. I had been hoping it would be the other manager, as I wanted to get a feel for him, despite the fact he already has an alibi.

"Avalon Hills," she says, her voice chipper.

"Hello, this is Agent Slate with the FBI. We spoke yesterday?"

"Oh, yes," she says, her voice clipped. The cheerfulness disappears immediately. "How can I help you?"

"Is Adrijus still there for his shift?" I recall her telling me he worked the morning shifts, but it's a little past noon already and I'm not sure how early he gets started.

"He's still here, yes. Do you need to speak with him?"

"No," I reply. "I was just curious." I realize as I'm speaking, Angie might warn Adrijus off if she suspects something is up. "What time does Mikhail come in?" I ask, attempting to deflect the attention of Adrijus.

"Not until two-thirty."

"Okay, thank you," I say and hang up. "C'mon, we gotta go," I tell Zara. "He's still at the apartments and I don't want to lose him." I get the kid's attention. "We need a copy of this file."

He sighs and digs around in one of the drawers under his desk for a thumb drive. As soon as he finds one he trudges over and hands it to me without a word. Zara copies the file quickly and we thank him on our way out. I swear I hear him say something under his breath but at this point I'm too concerned with our main quarry to care.

"How about you drive and I stick my head out the window and make the siren noise," Zara says as we hop in the car.

"Only if you want to cause more accidents than you prevent," I say, backing the car out quickly and heading back for the main street.

"Do you really think he did it?" Zara asks.

"I don't know what to think," I say. My gut tells me no, but I've been wrong before. Adrijus could be playing us, thinking we're stupid enough to overlook him because he stuck around. Perhaps he didn't think we'd check his alibi once we spoke to his wife, who obviously knows something as well. But again, they could both play the language card and say they didn't fully understand what we were asking. I've seen it done before to avoid a perjury charge.

We speed down the roads, and I'm pushing the speed limit at every turn. The roads up here aren't very large, which means the speed limit usually stays between thirty-five and forty-five if I'm lucky. No longer do I feel like this is a relaxing drive. I just hope Angie didn't show our hand prematurely.

When we finally pull up to Avalon Hills, I scan the parking lot close to the office for Adrijus's pickup, but don't see it. I curse myself for being too unsure and calling ahead. If we'd just come up here, we would have caught him in time.

I park right beside the main doors in the handicapped spot and jump out, running into the office. Angie sits behind her desk, just like yesterday, though there's another man here as well, at the desk on the other side of the room. Tom, I assume.

"Where's Adrijus?" I ask.

Her face blanches. "I—uh…" She checks a schedule on her computer. "He should be over at the pool."

"Where's his truck?" I ask. "It's not parked outside."

"He was just in here a few minutes ago," she says. "I told him you called asking about him."

Shit. I turn back to Zara. "He's in the wind."

"I'm sure he's just—" Angie begins, but I don't stick around to listen. Zara is already headed back outside and I'm hot on her trail. We hop back in the car and circle the parking lot, scanning for his truck, but it's nowhere to be seen.

"Call Detmer," I tell Zara as I continue to search the parking lot. "Tell him to notify the local police to be on the lookout for a dark green Silverado. And see if he can't get someone back over to Adrijus's apartment; it's more than likely the first place he'll go."

She's on the phone, making the calls as we keep searching the parking lots of Avalon Hills. But it's clear to me he's already gone. I let my anxiousness to find him override my better judgement. But the strange thing is I didn't get the sense that Adrijus was a threat when we spoke to him earlier. Then again, he did lie to our faces and neither Zara nor I saw it. I need to get him in an interrogation room, really put the pressure on. I pull out of the lot and head back in the direction of Woodhurst.

"Detmer says one of his guys is ten minutes out from the apartment," Zara says, cupping her hand over the phone speaker.

"Tell them we'll meet them there. If he's running, he might stop off to get some supplies first. And check to see if he has any other family in the area. Anyone he might go to for help." I press the accelerator hard, frustrated that I've missed this. Zara relays the information and hangs up.

"He's going to call me back in a few." I can feel her eyes boring into me from the passenger seat. "Don't do this to yourself, Em."

"Do what?" I ask, pressing down even harder.

"Blame yourself for missing this. Neither of us saw it. You're not a mind reader."

"I should be," I say. "I should have seen it. What good am I if I can't even tell when someone is lying straight to my face?" It's the same feeling I felt when I was back in that elevator in the Stillwater hospital, and I came face-to-face with the woman who killed my husband. I should have been able to see something wasn't right immediately, but I was too focused on getting to Wright to pay enough attention. I rub my leg absently, a dull ache growing from the spot where I was stabbed.

"Do you blame *me* for not seeing it?" she asks.

"No, of course—"

"Then give yourself the same courtesy," she replies. "We're not going to catch him if you're sitting there beating yourself up."

I ease off the accelerator a bit, which is a good thing as I'm doing almost twenty over. "You know, a supportive friend would help me when I need to beat someone up."

"In every other case, yes. But not when you're doing it to yourself," she says. I'm very lucky to have Zara in my life. I can't imagine where I would be without both her and Matt. I'm not even sure I'd still be in the Bureau at this point—probably would have been discharged after my incident six months ago. But she's kept me tethered so I don't go too far over the edge. I want to tell her how much it means to me that she's been there for me, but I can't seem to get the words out. I'm not great at expressing my emotions, at least when they are these kinds of emotions. It's so much easier to focus on the case at hand and catching the people that need to be caught.

Fifteen minutes later we're three blocks from Adrijus's apartment complex when Zara's phone rings. "Foley," she says, putting it on speaker.

"My guy at the apartment just watched him pull in. He ran into his unit, somewhat frantic."

"We're right around the corner," Zara says. "We'll go cover the back, just in case he tries to leave without anyone seeing."

I make the next turn, taking us down a side street which runs parallel to the apartment complex. There's a small opening where our car fits through, that leads to the back alley behind the building itself. Sure enough, we see Adrijus climbing down what looks like one of those emergency fire ladders from his second-floor window to the ground. He's wearing a large backpack.

I gun it and he looks up, fear in his eyes. As he jumps down the last few rungs, he lands wrong and crumples on the ground, crying out. I bring the car to a stop and we both get out, training our weapons on him.

"Adrijus Vilmantas," I say. "Don't move. You're under arrest for lying and obstruction."

"I do nothing," he pleads, as he rocks back and forth, holding his ankle. Looks like he might have sprained it on that last jump.

"Do you have any weapons on you?" I ask. He shakes his head emphatically. "Don't move." Zara keeps her weapon trained on him while I walk over and carefully remove his backpack, frisk him, then help him stand up, keeping the pressure off his bad ankle. I take a moment to cuff his arms behind him. "We need you to come with us. We have some questions for you."

"I do nothing," he says again.

"Adrijus!"

We look up to see a woman looking out the window, her face blanched with tears. The wife, I presume.

Zara stows her weapon. "Call Detmer," I tell her. "We've got a mess on our hands."

Chapter Twelve

I'M SITTING ON THE OTHER SIDE OF A LARGE PIECE OF GLASS, my arms crossed, and my legs stretched out in front of me, frustrated to no end. On the other side of the glass sits Adrijus, an ice pack on his ankle, and a bottle of water on the table in front of him. He keeps shooting the glass itself looks, even though he can't see beyond it. I've just spent the past two hours interrogating him and getting nowhere.

We decided not to bring in his wife, since they had two small children at home, but an agent is keeping an eye on the apartment to make sure they don't flee. Though, given what I've learned from Adrijus, I'm not sure that's likely anyway.

The tech who is running all the recording equipment looks back at me. "Are you going back in or..."

I shake my head. "Let him sit in there a while." Maybe he'll be more cooperative after a couple more hours alone. But I don't like it. His excuse for running was because he thought we were affiliated with ICE, and that we were there to deport him. It seems Adrijus and his wife didn't come here via the most legal of ways. But their children were born here, which means if ICE gets a hold of them, they'll ship the parents off and leave the kids to fend for themselves. I'm not about to report either of them but at the same time he won't tell me where he was on Saturday night. He just keeps shaking his head, refusing to talk about it.

The problem is I don't have anything tying him to the scene. The report on those hairs the medical examiner found isn't back yet, and his fingerprints aren't on the murder weapon. They are, however in the apartment, but that can be explained seeing as he had been doing maintenance in there earlier in the week. I'm sure if I talked to the District Attorney he would tell me it's not nearly enough for a murder conviction, though I can feel the pressure from everyone else in this office, especially Detmer. They're out for blood for their fallen colleague, and Adrijus just happens to be in the crosshairs.

The door to the observation room opens and Zara walks in, a grim look on her face. "Just spoke to Williamson," she says. "No surveillance equipment at the apartment. Nothing to indicate someone was watching Agent Green."

"There goes that theory," I say, craning my neck back, trying to get it to crack. I shake my head as she takes the seat next to me. "I'm just not sure about this. He's hiding something, but it doesn't feel like the murder of a federal agent. Not to mention we still don't have a motive."

"There's the sexual angle," Zara suggests.

"Maybe," I say, but he just doesn't strike me as the type. We're missing something big here, I just don't know what. My stomach grumbles in response to having nothing but coffee and sweet tea all day. "Let's grab a bite while he stews. Maybe things will be clearer once I actually have some food on my stomach."

"Yo," Zara says, and the tech turns to her. "What's a good place to eat around here?"

"Head over to Purdy and Purchase," he says. "Ton of places over there. Anything you could want."

"Let's kick it." Zara is up and I'm right behind her, though I throw one glance back at Adrijus, feeling the bitter sting of disappointment rising again. I need to do better. Food first, then I'll take another shot at him.

———

Downtown Richney is an eclectic mix of fancy restaurants and bars for the late-night crowd. It's an easily walkable area, so we just park and stroll along until we find something good: a seafood joint. I typically don't do seafood, but given our proximity to the ocean, I'm thinking they might have some fresh options. Fortunately, we've come before the dinner rush and snag a table quick.

Zara waits until a pink cosmopolitan is sitting in front of her and a scotch on the rocks is in front of me before she begins an interrogation of her own.

"On a scale of one to ten, how likely is it he did it?"

"If one is no chance in hell and ten is he held the bloody poker himself, I'm at about a three," I say. I've interviewed a lot of killers. They're all a little bit different, but they usually have something in common: they're classic narcissists. It may not be plainly obvious on the surface, but you can tell in how they react to certain questions, how they view the world: everything always leads back to *them*. Adrijus isn't like that. He's much more concerned with other people than himself, a trait rare in someone who kills for a reason other than self-protection. It's obvious from the evidence the intruder didn't fear for their lives. Agent Green didn't even have her service weapon on her; it was still in the drawer in her bedroom. So self-defense is out. Which brings me back to my original hypothesis: whoever killed Agent Green had to benefit from it in some way. It had to help them.

It has only seemed to make Adrijus's life worse. While it's not unheard of that someone like him is capable of cold-blooded murder, the statistics don't support it. Unless we're just *that* unlucky.

"You look like you're going a million miles a minute," Zara says, taking a sip from her drink. "Take a breath already."

I smile, knowing she's caught me. I sip from my own drink, it's smooth and peaty, just what I need. "Okay then, I have a question. *Not* about the case."

"Shoot."

"Last night, when I ran in the room. What were you doing?"

Zara's cheeks blush. I've never seen that happen before. "What do you mean?"

I lean forward. "I mean, you were deep in your phone, and made a point to hide it when I came in with the book. What exactly were you doing?"

"You're too observant for your own good," she says, before taking another long sip of the drink, making a point to keep eye contact with me as she does. "Fine, I was talking to someone."

"Someone who?"

"Someone I plan on meeting soon, nosy." I narrow my eyes, staring straight into her soul. She puckers her lips for a minute, trying to look away before she finally gives in. "Gawd, it's a guy, okay? I met a guy."

I reset my face with a pleasant expression, though there's a small knot forming in my stomach. "Oh yeah? Where?"

"In a sketchy internet chatroom, where else?" she asks before giving me her own death glare. "On a dating website, obviously."

I drop the pretense. "I didn't even know you were looking."

"I wasn't, not really. I just happened to have my profile up there and was checking…we got to talking and…I don't know. He seems nice. We're supposed to meet in person when we get back to D.C."

"What's his name?" I ask.

"Ian. He works for one of the international banks based out of Switzerland, but his office is here." The blush has returned. She really seems sweet on this guy.

"I assume you've already done a full workup on him." I take another sip of my drink, willing myself not to down it all in one go.

"Pssh. I had that finished five minutes in," she says. "He's recently divorced. Married too young, I guess."

"Kids?" I ask.

She shakes her head. "Not as far as I can tell. He travels back and forth to Switzerland about once a month. And he's already invited me on a trip with him."

"You haven't even met him yet," I say. "How can you think about going across the world together?"

She shrugs. "Eh. Meeting in person is overrated. I already know a ton about the guy, enough to know I'll like him. We've been talking for the past couple of weeks."

"And when were you going to tell me?" It comes out as more of an accusation than I mean. I'm happy for her, I really am. But selfishly, I know that a boyfriend means I'll lose the one tether I have left in my life.

"I was hoping to see how the first date went," she shoots back. "I didn't expect the third degree so soon."

I'm being too harsh, and I know it. "Sorry, it's just...this is sudden."

Zara leans forward and extends her hand. I take it and give it a quick squeeze before withdrawing again. "Em, I didn't want to say anything because I know with everything you've been through, romantic relationships aren't really on the top of your list right now. I didn't want you to feel like I was rubbing it in."

I shake my head, embarrassed at my own reaction. "No, of course not. It wasn't that. I'm just...today has been frustrating for a lot of reasons. I didn't mean for it to seem like I was taking it out on you."

She's about to reply when the waiter stops by our table with our meals. Cod with fries for me and a grilled chicken salad for Zara. I'm thankful I ordered something on the heavier side; Zara's news is the cap on a crappy day. I wish I could let go of my personal feelings and just be happy for her, which part of me truly is. I don't want her to be alone forever either, and I know she wants someone to come home to, just like anyone else would. But it reinforces the fact that my home is empty, and as far as I'm concerned, will always be empty. I can't even imagine trying to date after losing Matt.

"Let's talk about something else," she says after a few moments of silence. I feel like this news has erected some kind of invisible wall, even though that wasn't my intention. "Are you going to give Janice an update?"

I take a few bites of the fish, which turns out is excellent. I was right, it's a fresh catch. "Not until we have something concrete on Adrijus or someone else. Otherwise she'll probably think I'm just calling to check on the sting."

"What are you going to do when we get back?" she asks.

I haven't given it much thought. Someone who can get past me *and* Timber is not someone I want to be messing with. But it's not like I can just move on a whim. I have a lease, not to mention moving is time-consuming and expensive. "I could probably stay in one of those extended-stay places for a while, assuming they accept dogs."

"You could stay with me," she says.

"But you just said—"

"I said I was going to meet him, not ask him to move in." She digs into her salad, her next words muffled by the crunching of her greens. "It would be a bit tight with the two of us and Timber, but we could make it work, short term. At least until you get this situation figured out."

"Thank you," I finally say. I'm honestly touched. "But only as a last resort. Best case scenario is Janice manages to catch her in the act, then I don't have to worry about it anymore."

She points her fork at me. "Yes."

As soon as I move to take another bite, my phone vibrates in my pocket. I pull it out, seeing it's Detmer. "Slate," I say.

"Just got a call from local PD," he says. "We've got another one."

Chapter Thirteen

WE PULL UP TO A MID-SIZED HOUSE ON A SMALL LOT. LIKE most of the homes in this neighborhood, it doesn't have a garage, only a couple of concrete pavers leading from the house down to the street. Most of these homes were built around the second world war, and thus are smaller. A few are renovated so they take up much more space of their lots, but not this one. It looks like the only changes it's had over the past eighty years has been a few new coats of paint.

Two police cruisers and an ambulance sit outside, along with Detmer's car. He and Williamson are already out, waiting for us when we arrive.

"What's the situation?" I ask as soon as we're out of the car.

"Come with me," Detmer says, "I'll show you." Williamson hangs back at the car while Zara and I follow Detmer up the concrete steps and along the walkway. A local officer lifts the tape for us to step under. "I got a call from a friend in the violent crimes division, we've known each other for years. Ever since you told me this was related to that author I've been putting my feelers out to see if anyone else has seen something similar. He called me about an hour ago, guy's wife came home to find him."

"Where's the wife now?" I ask.

"She was understandably upset, so I had one of my guys take her back to the Bureau to try and help her calm down. We didn't get a full statement yet." Detmer leads us through the front door and into the house proper. It's small, with a long hallway leading to segmented rooms. The opposite of "open concept".

"Anyway, after you left this morning, I got to thinking about what you said regarding Blackthorne. It got me curious, so I started researching some of her other books." He stops short, and moves out of the way, showing us the body.

It looks to be a middle-aged male, roughly two-hundred pounds or so. Light brown hair, thinning along the top. And he's completely naked, lying spread eagle on the ground. In the middle of his chest, is a jagged cross, carved deep into the skin. Blood is pooled all around the body, and his eyes are open, staring up at the ceiling.

"Jonathan Nicks, accountant," Detmer says. "Wife came home from grocery shopping to find him like this."

I snap into investigator mode, careful of where I step. I grab a couple of gloves out of my pocket and snap them on, bending down to get a better look at Mr. Nicks. "Recognize the mark?" Detmer asks.

"A cross," I say. "Looks like it was carved while he was still alive." I think back, trying to recall these details.

"He matches the description of the victim in '*X Marks the Spot*' by one Ruby Blackthorne," Detmer says. "I pulled a copy off the internet to make sure. Same M.O. Naked body, open eyes. Cross carved into the chest, left for everyone to see."

"Damn," Zara says, putting her hands on her hips.

Damn is right. If the same person who killed Agent Green killed Mr. Nicks, then it couldn't have been Adrijus. We've had him in custody ever since early this afternoon. "Do we know how long he's been here?"

Detmer shakes his head. "Can't have been long. The wife did manage to tell us he wasn't home when she left for the grocery store, which was around five."

I look a little closer at the body, a small gray hair catches my eye. "Evidence bag?"

"Hang on," he says and heads back out the door.

"What do you see?" Zara asks.

"Looks like the same hair the medical examiner found on Agent Green," I say. "Which means it's very likely this was the same person."

"And not the guy we currently have in an interrogation room," she says.

Detmer returns with the bag, and I carefully slip the hair into it, sealing the bag and returning it to him. "I assume Crawford is on his way?"

He nods. "I'll make sure he gets it."

"If it comes back a match to the one on Green's body, we'll have to cut Andrijus loose."

"But what about that time he was gone on Saturday night?" Zara asks. "Maybe he had an accomplice or something."

I shake my head. "It's not enough to hold him. We'll keep an eye on him for now, but I don't want to spin my wheels on someone who can't have possibly been here. Adrijus is a stretch anyway. The guy is more worried about getting deported than anything else. He's not out for some kind of ritual killing." I look over at Detmer. "Let me guess, no forced entry."

"I haven't done a full check yet," he says. "But the front door doesn't show any signs of damage."

I make a circle motion with one finger to Zara. She nods and we both go about checking the place, seeing if there are any unlocked windows or other access points where the killer could have come in. After about fifteen minutes, I'm satisfied that there was no break-in. Either Mr. Nicks knew his assailant, or, like in Agent Green's case, they had a key.

"Thoughts?" I ask Zara as we return to the body. Crawford and his team have arrived, and begun their inspection.

"We're in trouble here," she says. "Someone seems to really like their Ruby Blackthorne books."

"We need to figure out what the connection is between these two," I say. "Someone obviously wants us to know. Otherwise, why be so performative?"

I glance over to Detmer, whose face is pinched in worry. "I don't like it," he says. "As soon as the media gets ahold of this, we're going to lose any lead we could possibly get."

"Then it's your job to keep it off the media's radar," I say. I glance down at Crawford who has begun his investigation. "Crawford? Can your people keep this quiet? At least until we have a suspect in custody?"

"You don't have to worry about us," he replies, his voice still upbeat, despite the circumstances. "We wouldn't be in this job if we didn't respect the dead."

Detmer motions for us to follow him back out to the front of the house. "The wild card will be the wife. As soon as we let her go, there's no telling how quick it will spread. You two need to work fast."

"How long can you hold her?" I ask, checking my phone for the time. A little past eight-thirty. It'll be hard to talk to anyone tonight. But we can at least begin looking into the links between Green and Nicks.

"Maybe until morning. We still have to get her statement and she obviously won't be coming home. I'll see if we can't coax some of her family to come to the Bureau and sit with her, give you a little more time."

"Thanks," I say, nodding. With Agent Green we had the luxury of Adrijus being the only person who saw the body before Detmer and his team showed up. He may have mentioned the state of her body to his wife but I'm betting he kept it to himself, not wanting to get wrapped up in this any more than he already is. But with a second body being a civilian, this whole thing is about to get a lot messier.

Zara and I head back to the car. "Good thing we got some sleep last night," I say. "Because tonight is going to be a long one."

A bleary glance at the clock on the wall reminds me it's past two a.m. We've been back at the Bureau nearly six hours now, going over Green's case histories, trying to find a link to our newest victim. So far there's been little to find. Most of her work involved public corruption, particularly environmental violations. I can't imagine that made her many friends in the private sector, especially with some of the big energy companies. But there's nothing in her files to indicate anyone was mad enough to retaliate, especially like this. It feels almost like a non-issue. Still, that doesn't mean we can stop. We need to poke into every corner of her work life, see if we can't dig up *something*.

"Hey," I say, and Zara looks up, her eyes drooping. "Could the fact that Green's profession was an FBI agent have been a coincidence?" I ask. "Maybe she wasn't targeted because of her job."

She folds her hands in front of her like she's about to scold a child. "We've already ruled out personal relationships, for the most part. Now you want to cut out professional ones too? Where does that leave us? That it was random?"

I quirk my mouth. "Seems unlikely, doesn't it."

"FBI agents don't get randomly killed in their own homes. At least none that I know. Unless the killer was *extremely* lucky, they had to be prepared to fight someone who was also trained to kill."

I put my elbows on the desk and rub my face up and down. "You're right. I'm just exhausted. And running out of brainpower."

"Okay, I'm calling it," she says, getting up. "We can finish this tomorrow. Or, in a couple hours. We need the sleep."

"What about Jonathan Nicks' wife?" I ask. "Detmer will have to release her soon."

She shakes her head. "As you've told me plenty of times, we can't control everything. If she's going to talk, she's going to talk. We'll deal with the media when we get there."

I know she's right. But my stupid brain just doesn't want to quit. I know there's something big here I'm missing, but I've been firing on all cylinders for twenty hours straight. Not to mention I only had one good meal today. I need to do better about that.

"C'mon," she says. "We need to head back to the wilderness lodge. Get at least a few hours in." I stand, begrudgingly. "The saga of Ruby Blackthorne will have to wait until tomorrow."

The saga of Ruby Blackthorne. It sort of feels like that, like things keep pointing back to her. "Wait a second," I say. "What if we're looking at this from the wrong angle."

"What do you mean?"

"We've got two murders. Both imitate deaths in books Ruby—Stephanie wrote. Someone is looking to gather our attention, and not trying to hide their actions. What if they are building up to something? What if Stephanie is the ultimate victim?"

Lines form in Zara's forehead. "You're saying someone is telegraphing what they're planning on doing?"

"How many books does she have out?" I ask.

"Um…six. The most recent was just released a few weeks ago."

"*Flame's Ember* was her breakout book, I remember. Was *X Marks the Spot* her second?"

"It was," Zara says.

I can't believe I didn't see it before. Someone is going down the line of Stephanie's releases, killing in the order she wrote the books. "We need to speak with her again," I say. "Her initial fears about being a target might be more accurate than I'd been willing to admit."

"But why?" Zara asks. "Why go to all this trouble? To scare her?"

"I can't answer that," I say, shaking my head again. "All I know is we need to talk to her as soon as we can. First thing tomorrow. Or…today."

Chapter Fourteen

CONTRARY TO THE LAST TIME WE WERE HERE, THE SKY IS overcast when we arrive at Stephanie Murphy's house the following morning. A strong wind blows off the sea, ushering in a storm somewhere on the horizon. Whether it will reach us here or not I don't know, but it looks like a powerful one. The cool breeze makes me glad for once I'm wearing a suit in the middle of summer.

Gus the guard recognized us from last time and waved us through without hesitation, which makes me wonder just how secure this neighborhood really is. Do they check the credentials of everyone coming and going? What's to stop someone from infiltrating one of the lawn care or maintenance crews that come through, keeping everything beautiful and in working order? I don't want to frighten the woman, but I think some caution is prudent.

We make our way up to the house, and this time there's no one to greet us at the door. I know if they're home, someone has seen us on their security system. And judging by the car parked in front, I'm assuming at least one of the two adults is here.

I give the door my signature "police" knock, as Zara likes

to call it, and step back, watching her wipe a smile from her face. We wait outside longer than I would think necessary for someone inside to reach the door, so I knock again, this time ringing the bell beside the door as well.

A few moments later, I hear the deadbolt slide in the door and one of the two opens to reveal Steph Murphy again. "Agents," she says, her voice colder than last time. "To what do I owe the pleasure?" There it is again, the accent. Just barely hidden under a couple of decades of New England living. Some people don't care how they sound, but I can tell Mrs. Murphy has worked hard to try and conceal the natural twang of a Texas drawl.

"We're sorry for the intrusion," I say. "But there have been some developments in the case. May we come in?"

"If you must," she says, stepping out of the way and swinging the door wide. She waits until both of us are in before closing the large door behind us. Half a second later the two Pomeranians appear again, trotting after us as Steph leads us into a sitting room right off the main foyer. No tea today, it seems. "You know, I would appreciate some heads up before you show up at my door. I do most of my writing in the morning, and was in the middle of an important scene."

"I apologize," I say, "But this couldn't wait. Have you had any luck with your publisher or agent?"

She shakes her head. "It's barely been a day. I don't expect to hear back from them until at least Friday. I'm not the only client they have."

"I would think this deserves some urgency," Zara says.

"You said I wasn't in danger," she replies, her gaze widening. "That it was unlikely to come back to me."

No sense in beating around the bush. She already knows about the first. Might as well get it out there. "There's been a second murder."

"What?" she asks, seeming to shrink back into her chair. "Not another FBI agent?"

I shake my head. "No. But he was…he was positioned exactly like one of the victims in your second book: '*X Marks the Spot*'."

She bites her lower lip. "The cross? On the chest?" I nod. "Oh, God," she says, standing and going to one of the windows. "What is going on?"

"That's what we're trying to find out, Mrs. Murphy," I say. "I think it's more urgent now you get in contact with your agent and publisher. We need to know if they have received anything odd in the past six months related to you in any way. I don't care if it was nothing more than a blank postcard."

"I can't believe this is happening," she says. "I thought maybe it was some kind of fluke, like someone had read my book a long time ago then happened to remember it or…I don't know. Not this. Do you have any idea of who is doing it?"

I shake my head. "We thought we had a suspect, but they were in custody during the second murder. We're still looking into it."

She takes a few deep breaths. "I'll—I'll call them back this morning. My agent lives in the city, she'll…she can come up here if necessary."

"Is your husband home?" I ask.

She turns back to me. "No, he's out playing tennis. Why?"

I exchange a glance with Zara. Two trips here and no sign of the husband. A husband that doesn't work, from what I understand. "We think it would be prudent he know all the details of the case as well."

"You think he has something to do with this, don't you?" she asks, a hint of fire in her voice.

"We just need to speak with everyone that—"

"Trust me, it's not him," she replies.

Might as well get this out of the way now. "Can you tell us where he was between eleven and two on the night of the fourth? And between five and seven yesterday evening?"

"On the fourth he was home. We have a security system that's armed every night and that's monitored by a central station. Check with them, you'll see the system was on all night. No one could have come in or out of the house." She crosses her arms.

"And yesterday?"

"Here. He was working on a project with the kids for one of their camps while I finished up for the evening. But again. We have cameras outside the house. If he'd left, they would have picked it up." She pulls out her phone to show me the app. "Nothing from that time."

"We have to ask, you understand," I say. "It just makes our job easier."

"No, I get it," she says. "I write enough of this stuff. I'll tell him, obviously, but—" she's interrupted by the front door opening. I'm immediately on my feet, my hand going straight for my weapon. A woman shuffles through the door in a long sundress and wide-brimmed hat, looking like she might be spending a day on the beach, were it not for the weather. She's got soft features, and strawberry blonde hair. There's a moment where she doesn't even realize we're there as she drags in a large bag full of what look like gardening tools. But she must sense us, because she begins talking before she even turns to look at anyone.

"Wow, I picked the wrong day for this, didn't I?" she turns, a wide smile on her face, which disappears immediately. "Oh."

Stephanie sputters out introductions. "This is my friend, Erin. We went to college together." She goes over and embraces Erin in a hug, which seems to surprise the other woman. She gives us a half smile as she closes in around Stephanie.

"What's going on?" the other woman asks.

"They're with the FBI," Steph says, letting go and turning back to us.

"I'm Agent Slate," I say. "And this is Agent Foley."

She gives us a friendly nod. "Erin Barnett. I still don't understand. Has something happened? Is everyone okay?"

"I'm sorry, we can't really discuss—"

"No," Steph says, interrupting me. "Erin is like a sister to me. You can tell her. I trust her with my life."

Zara gives me a palms out gesture, as if to say "what are you gonna do?" I'm not in the habit of revealing sensitive information to someone I had no idea existed five minutes ago, but Murphy seems to trust her, and I need Murphy's cooperation. Plus, this woman may be able to provide emotional support that could encourage Murphy to help.

"Steph, you're scaring me," Erin says. "Will someone please tell me what's happening?"

"There have been a series of murders," I begin, "both where the victim's death and body placement mimic what is described in Mrs. Murphy's books. We're trying to determine why someone is doing this, and if there is any threat to Mrs. Murphy."

"Oh my God, Steph," Barnett says, and leans into Murphy again, giving her a tight hug. "I'm so sorry. Are you okay?"

Murphy shakes her head. "No. I don't know what to make of any of this." She turns back to us. "Why would someone do this?"

"It's hard to say without knowing who it is," I say. "I'd rather not make suppositions until we have more facts."

"Here," Barnett says, leading Murphy back to one of the loveseats. "You need to sit. Can I make you something? Some chamomile tea? Or the lavender?" Barnett's accent isn't quite as subdued as Murphy's, though I can tell it's been softened from years of being in the northeast.

"If you don't mind me asking, what were you doing here?" I ask before Barnett can leave.

"Oh, I'd planned to do some gardening before I had to

head into work. Steph lets me keep a garden on the front side of the property and I'd just dropped Joey off at camp. But this storm came in quicker than I thought."

"Joey?" Zara asks.

"My son. He's seven. He's doing this week-long soccer camp where he's there most of the day. Kid can't get enough of soccer."

I nod, wondering how often Barnett is over here given she just walked in like she lived here. Now that we have a second victim and the only thing that connects them, for the moment, is Stephanie Murphy, we need to start looking into her life, figuring out if she is a target or just the unwitting accomplice to someone's sick game.

"I'd really like a chance to speak with your husband," I say.

Murphy looks up for the first time in a few minutes. "Brad? Why?"

I can't tell her the real reason I want to speak with him— that I now have to consider him a possible suspect, though I think that's premature. "In addition to informing him about what is going on, I'd like to see if he's noticed anything out of the ordinary over the past few months. Anything that you might have missed."

She shakes her head. Barnett has wrapped one of her arms around Steph's shoulder. "I guess. He's over at Westing Country Club, it's on the other side of the island. But Brad doesn't have anything to do with my books. He doesn't even read them."

"Really?" Zara asks, sending me a glance.

"He's just not a reader," she says. "Never has been. Ironic then that his wife turns out to be a writer."

"I love her books," Barnett says. "She's so creative, and the stories are so engaging. Have you read any of them?"

"I have," I say, "It's how I knew about the connection." While her books are good, I wouldn't necessarily be gushing over them the way Erin Barnett is. It's almost like she's trying to ingratiate herself to her friend. There's more to that, but I'm not sure what. "Are you here every morning?"

Erin lets out a small chuckle. "Not *every* morning, but I do come over some days just to check on Steph, see how the writing is going. And to work on the garden, of course." As if on cue, rain begins to pepper the windows, coming down in sheets. "But clearly that's not going to be happening today." She pats Steph on the knee. "Let me go get you that tea."

After she leaves, the two Pomeranians trot closely behind her all the way to the kitchen, while Murphy leans closer to us. "What kind of security do I need? Don't bullshit me; if someone is coming after me or my family, I need to know."

"I wouldn't take any extreme cautions," I say, "Not until we know more about what's happening here. Keep your doors locked, your security system armed, and keep an eye on your kids. Other than that, wait to hear from us. We're doing everything we can to find this person."

She sits back in the chair, like I've just given her the most disappointing news she could receive. I'm anxious to meet the husband; see how he fits into all this. But before we go, I have one further thing I need to ask. "Do you know a Jonathan Nicks?"

She rubs the back of her neck, kneading hard. "I don't think so. Who is he?"

"The second victim," I say. "He was an accountant."

"Not mine. I use Lloyd O'Brien with Sharp, O'Brien and Hayes. They've always handled my affairs."

I shoot a glance out the window, not looking forward to getting soaked trying to get back to the car, but it's showing no signs of abating. "Thank you for your time. We'll be in touch soon with further developments." Zara and I stand.

"What should I do in the meantime?" she asks. "I can't work under these kinds of conditions."

"I understand it's stressful. We're doing everything we

can," I say, hoping to placate her. I don't know much about the profession, but I imagine it takes a lot of concentration. And unless we can find whoever is doing this, I'm not sure Mrs. Murphy will ever be able to fully relax again. "Just hold tight."

She shoots me a glare, but I ignore it, and instead Zara and I excuse ourselves from the sitting room.

"Leaving already?" Erin is approaching with a small tray of teacups.

"Yes, but thank you anyway," I say. "Pleasure meeting you."

"You too," she calls after us as we head out into the pouring rain. "Be safe out there!"

Chapter Fifteen

"THOUGHTS?" I ASK ONCE WE'RE BACK IN THE CAR AND I'M halfway soaked through. The seats are already slick with the rain and there's a small puddle in the floorboard at my feet.

"Next time, pack an umbrella," Zara says, shaking water off her blazer. It splatters everywhere, but by now, both of us are so wet it barely matters. "She's not telling us everything."

"What makes you say that?" I ask.

"She didn't ask any details about the crimes. Don't most people want to know as much as they can?"

I shrug. "Some people have an aversion to it. They don't like morbidity. Her reaction seemed genuine to me. She's scared."

"Yeah," Zara says. "But doesn't she write this stuff? She should be used to it by now. Plus, I think she might go over-board on the security. She doesn't seem like the kind of person to take chances."

"Are you thinking we'll need to get past a personal security guard next time we come see her?" I turn the heat on if for no other reason than to try and dry us out a little. Not to mention the rain is freezing.

"I'll be surprised if she lets us in again," Zara says. "She was a lot more reserved this time. Yesterday it was almost like she was—I hesitate to say giddy—but I think part of her was intrigued someone had turned her words into an actual murder. That has to stroke the ego on some level, right?"

"Maybe for a moment, until you realize what it really means," I say, backing the car up and pulling out of the circular drive. "If she was intrigued before, she's terrified now. And we need to figure out what all of this means. Are we looking at four more possible victims? Four more bodies before the killer decides to do whatever they're going to do? What's the third book she wrote?"

Zara opens her phone. "*Deadly Stacks.* Something about a long-haul trucker?"

"Oh right," I say, recalling it. "I remember that one. Someone had all their fingers cut off by a crazy truck driver, right? From what I remember it was gruesome, even for a book."

"We can't very well stop every tractor trailer between here and Connecticut," Zara says. We pass the guard station again, which has been shuttered. Inside we see the elderly guard who gives us a friendly wave as we drive by. I turn left to head to the island's country club.

"Let's see what the husband has to say about all of this."

"You think he's involved?" Zara asks.

"If Stephanie is the eventual target, then yes. He could even be an unwitting accomplice; someone could be working him to get to her. Especially if they're trying to circumnavigate their security. Who better to befriend than the husband of your target?"

"*If* Stephanie is the target," Zara says. "We still don't know the killer's endgame."

"Right. But as of now, she's the only thing that connects these two murders. So that's where we need to focus our efforts." I check the time on the dash. It's about nine-thirty. Which means Jonathan Nicks' wife has probably left the

Bureau and is out in the wild. I don't expect it will be very long before the media vultures begin to swarm.

As we pull up to the country club, I realize we've come in on a side road, and not the main entrance, which is a long, grand entryway with one-lane roads on each side, bordering a beautiful array of trees and flowers down the middle. Even in the pouring rain, I can see how it is meant to frame the main building of the country club so that's where all your focus is when you're driving up. It's what I'd call a classic New England style building, all white with a dark roof and a center rotunda that ends in a spire. In a way, it reminds me of Agent Green's apartments in its ostentatiousness. The lawns are perfectly manicured as expected and there is a fountain out in the middle of the green, still going strong even in this weather. I pull the vehicle up as close to the front doors as I can get, but there's no overhang. A porter appears in the doorway, and I see the frustration on his face for a split second before he comes running out in the rain with an umbrella and opens my door.

"Ma'am," he says, trying to cover himself and me, but the wind is pushing the rain sideways, and the umbrella isn't doing anyone much good.

"We won't be long," I tell him, leaving the keys in the car. He nods and offers me the umbrella which I reluctantly take as he gets in. By the time I reach the steps, Zara is already inside the front door, being held open by another porter. As soon as I reach a dry patch I close the umbrella and hand it to him and follow Zara in.

"I think it actually soaked me more," I tell her once we're both inside. The interior of the club is understated, which surprises me. It feels more like a large living room than a country club. A few leather couches surround small tables and a plush carpet covers most of the floor. Before we can reach it, we're approached by a man wearing a suit that probably costs half my annual salary.

"Good morning, ladies," he says. "How may we assist you?"

I show him my badge. "We're looking for Brad Murphy," I say. "His wife said he was here playing tennis." The rain rails against the windows overlooking the beach and ocean beyond. Unless they have indoor courts, Brad Murphy isn't playing anything.

"Mr. Murphy is enjoying our lounge until the weather turns," the man says. A skeptical look from me does nothing to unseat the false pleasance of his demeanor. We stare at each other a moment before he finally pinches his features together. "This way."

We follow the man as he does an about-face, and I roll my eyes at Zara, who grins. I expect people who join places like this expect they'll be insulated from the outside world, regardless of the consequences. After all, that's what this place is, right? An oversized fence to keep the underprivileged out.

We enter the lounge via a diagonal hallway that splits off from the main room and follows the back wall of windows, so the view of the tumultuous ocean is never obstructed. White caps stretch out as far as I can see as the storm rages. There is a door to the lounge, but it's propped open, revealing the lush, wood-grain interior of the large room. Several pool tables sit inside, as well as high-backed leather chairs which are paired up, but don't seem to be in any particular configuration. To the left, on the far side of the windows, is a U-shaped bar, stocked to the brim with every kind of alcohol you could imagine. For not yet ten in the morning, it's surprising how many people are in here. Half a dozen men are gathered around the bar itself, all sipping something different while they watch sports on large screens suspended in the upper corners of the room. A few others are playing pool with a couple of women, while others sit in the chairs, deep in discussion.

The porter directs us to a man in one of the chairs, leaning suspiciously close to a brunette-haired woman in a white polo shirt and tennis skirt. He's also in his tennis outfit, down to the visor that's still on his head. Brad Murphy is a handsome man, and it looks like he's using that to his advantage. Chiseled jaw, thick, wavy hair, and from what I can tell, penetrating green eyes. The woman he's speaking with is practically swooning over him.

"You want to take this one?" I ask Zara.

She gives me a smirk. "I'd love to." That gives me a chance to step back and watch Murphy's body language. Even as we approach, he still hasn't taken his gaze off the woman, who isn't wearing a wedding ring I see.

"Mr. Murphy," the man in the suit says, finally drawing his attention. "These ladies are with the FBI and have some questions for you."

"FBI?" He looks up, frowning.

The woman, on the other hand, looks as though she's been caught with her hand in the cookie jar. Eyes wide, she's out of the chair. "We'll talk later, okay?"

"Jessica," Brad says, but it's too late. She's already gone.

"Would you like another chair?" the porter asks.

Zara takes the one next to Brad, smiling at him. "We're good," I say and cross my arms, standing off to the side.

Murphy eyes us, one at a time, before picking up his glass and downing half the brown liquid inside. "What's this about?"

"You don't know?" Zara asks, the hint of accusation in her voice. I know she's just toying with him, but considering he was about five inches from sticking his tongue down that young woman's throat, I can't really blame her.

"Oh," he says, recognition on his face. "You're the ones who harassed Steph yesterday."

"I'm Agent Foley," Zara says. "And this is Agent Slate. We'd like to ask you a few questions."

Brad Murphy drains the rest of his drink, then holds up the glass. A waiter comes of a moment later and takes it from him without a word. "Look, I don't know anything about my wife's business. She handles all of that."

"Have you noticed anything strange over the past few weeks or months?" Zara asks. "Anything that might have given you pause?"

"No," he says, as if that's the final word on the matter. Clearly, he doesn't know how these things go. He's very withdrawn, not open at all. I don't know if that's because he's hiding something, or because he was just caught in a possibly compromising position.

"Your friend is cute, what's her name again? Jessica?" Zara asks, giving Brad a mischievous grin.

"What, do you think I care that you saw that?" he asks, growing more combative. "It's no secret Steph and I haven't been getting along very well lately." I'm surprised at the admission this early. We've barely even begun and he's already trying to justify his behavior. Brad Murphy comes across to me as the kind of man who is used to getting his way. Rigid, inflexible. Zara just needs to apply the right kind of pressure.

"Fair enough," she says. "I assume your wife at least told you why we came by to visit yesterday."

"She said someone got killed and the killer used something from one of her books," he says. "I wasn't really paying attention."

Wow, Stephanie really picked a winner when she married this guy. I want to jump in, but I'll let Zara handle it. I know she can take care of this.

"That's right. And last night, we found a second victim." *This* causes him to finally make good eye contact.

"Wait…what does that mean? Was she right? Is someone stalking us?"

"We don't know yet," Zara says, then leans forward. "Which is why we're here talking to you."

"You don't think I had anything to do with this, do you?" he asks, going on the defensive. "You can't possibly—"

"Did you?" Zara pins him with a heavy stare.

"No, of course not." He's gone from defensive to indignant quickly and by the way he's pressing himself deeper and deeper into that chair, I can tell this is not a man who likes being under the microscope. I can't help but wonder what he's hiding under all his wife's money. Probably nothing more than a few affairs and possibly some recreational drug use, but if there is one thing I've learned about people, it's that you never really know a person, no matter how much you think you do. We all hide deep, dark secrets we don't let anyone ever see.

"Where were you between five and seven last night, if you don't mind me asking," she says.

"I do mind," he replies, trying to regain the upper hand and failing.

"See, when you get all defensive, my little suspicion siren in my head goes off," Zara chides. "I don't like that siren. Gives me headaches."

"I was at home, all night, okay?" he asks. "We have a security system. It's always on, so you can see who comes and who goes. I stayed in the garage most of the day, then went inside to watch some baseball in our movie room."

"I have to ask," Zara says, relaxed. "You understand. But given this second murder, we need to investigate all avenues. It is possible someone is targeting your wife, in a very strange and roundabout way. You're sure you haven't seen or noticed anything odd lately? Anything that would have stood out to you?"

He shakes his head. "Steph has been under a lot of pressure lately. Her last book didn't do as well as the publisher hoped, and she's worried about this next one. She's been working twelve hours a day on it, if not more. She'll get up at five and start typing and not finish until dinner is ready."

"You cook?" Zara arches an eyebrow.

He barks out a laugh. "Maybe when we're having a party.

But for just us? It's not worth the time. We have an in-house chef who comes by once a week and prepares meals for us."

"How many people have access to your house?" Zara asks.

"The cleaners come twice a week," he says. "We have a maintenance company on call for any emergencies, but they're usually there at least every other week doing preventative work on either the appliances, air conditioner or some other bull-shit. I'm sure they're taking us for a ride, but Steph doesn't want anything breaking down and it's her money, so whatever. The landscapers are there twice a week, but they don't come into the house."

"Anyone else?" Zara asks, a hint of sarcasm in her voice. I admit, it's a lot of people. I wonder how Stephanie is able to concentrate on her work with all those people coming and going from her house all the time.

"Just the kids and their friends," Brad replies. "The occasional parent who will drop one of them off or pick them up."

"It sounds like a lot of activity," I say.

Brad looks at me for the first time, like he's forgotten I'm there. "It's why I'm normally here."

"What about Erin Barnett?" Zara asks.

It's subtle, but there's a shift in his posture. He closes in on himself a bit more at the mention of her name. "How do you know about Erin?"

"We met her, this morning when we went to see your wife again," I say.

"Oh," he replies. I thought he might react to us going back over to his house again, but he seems more distracted now. "I forget about Erin, she's there so much."

"How often is she around?" Zara asks.

"If it's not every day, it's almost every day," he replies.

Zara picks up on his cues. "So then you're close."

"*I'm* not. But she and Steph are. They went to school together. They've been friends ever since. Sometimes she will stay in the guest house, on the nights when she doesn't have her son. Of course, he's over almost as often as she is, with our kids."

"I see," Zara says. "Well, if I were you, I'd limit who has access to your home until we catch whoever is doing this."

"*Are* we in danger?"

"That's unclear right now." Zara stands and joins me. "But right now it won't hurt to be cautious. Your neighborhood security isn't the best. If someone wants to get to you, we need to make it as difficult as possible."

The waiter who picked up Brad's drink before returns with a full glass, setting it on the table between the two chairs before leaving again. "You're asking us to barricade ourselves in our own home."

"We're just telling you to be cautious," Zara reiterates. Brad Murphy picks up his drink and takes a sip, watching us over the lip of the glass. Zara smiles. "Enjoy your tennis match."

Chapter Sixteen

"Bleh," Zara says, shaking herself off once we're back in the car again. "That guy has slime written all over him."

"You have to give him a little credit; it's not like he's trying to hide it," I say. "Interesting that he mentioned marital troubles though. Mrs. Murphy never said a word about that."

"There was a lot he wasn't saying," Zara adds. "Like whatever happened between him and Erin Burnett."

"I saw that too." His body language was unmistakable. The way he was caught off-guard when she mentioned Erin's name. "You think it's an affair?"

"Not sure what else it would be," she replies. "Especially given how he was all over that other girl when we arrived."

I sigh. At least I never had to worry about that with Matt. But it's part of the reason I don't think I can ever get back out into the dating pool. After four years in this job, it's hard to trust people anymore. "Well, whatever is going on with their relationship, I'm not sure it's related to the murders. Last time I checked, it wasn't illegal to cheat on your spouse."

"He didn't strike me as the kind to set up an elaborate series of murders designed to mimic his wife's books. Especially since she said he doesn't even read them."

"There are certainly easier ways to begin divorce proceed-ings," I say, chuckling. "Though we should find out if they had a prenup. If they get divorced and he gets nothing, it would give him much more of a motive to do something like this. As crazy as that sounds."

"You're right, it does sound crazy," she says, running her hands through her hair some more, trying to dry it out.

I pull out my phone and call Detmer, turning the volume up so I can hear over the rain pounding on the windshield. "Slate," he says, picking up. "Any good news?"

"Nothing on this front," I say. "No one seems to know anything. What's the story with Adrijus?"

"We're cutting him loose. The D.A. doesn't think we have a case with him and I'm inclined to agree. But I just got a call from Crawford. He wants you over at the medical examiner's as soon as you can get there. I'm pretty sure he's spent all night with the body."

"Alright," I say. "We're about twenty minutes away."

Thanks to a traffic accident, it takes us nearly an hour to get back over to the medical examiner's. Apparently this happens a lot up here, because even though we tried a few alternate routes, we found all of them blocked as well. It doesn't take much to muck up the whole system. Along the way, Zara manages to verify both Brad and Steph Murphy were in their home during Agent Green and Jon Nicks' murders.

Crawford is already waiting for us when we arrive, the body of Jonathan Nicks on the same slab where Agent Green was not too long ago.

"Agents," he says. "Pleasure, given the circumstances. How are you this fine morning?"

"It's raining buckets," I say, my shoes still soaked from the country club. "Is this your idea of a fine morning?"

"Sure," he says, drawing out the word. "Days like this are my favorite. I can hear the rain pounding on the building, there's a nice, gray overcast feel to everything and the streets are empty of people. It's a great time to be out."

"Yeah, well your beautiful weather is about to land you another patient," Zara says. "We passed a wreck on the way here. I wouldn't be surprised if you get them by the end of the day."

"Don't misunderstand me," he says. "I don't wish for death on anyone. I just happen to like the dreary days better than the sunny ones."

"Fair enough, what do you have for us?"

"I figured this was rather time sensitive," he says, scratching his long, scruffy beard. "So when we transported the body over this morning I just stayed to do the examination." He leans over to the table next to the body and picks up a small, plastic bag. "As you so deftly observed, the same hairs that were found on Agent Green's body were found on Mr. Nicks. We've determined they're canine hairs, but not sure what breed yet."

"*Canine* hairs," I say. The hairs inside the baggie are light gray and curly. I don't recognize what breed they could belong to, but I'm sure it isn't Pomeranian, considering those dogs are as white as snow. Which pretty much eliminates Brad Murphy from our suspect pool.

"We've tried to fast track the DNA identification," Crawford says. "But it can still take a few days. As soon as I know, I'll be sure you do too."

"What else can you tell us about him?" I ask, handing the baggie back.

"Death was from rapid blood loss, due to his heart being punctured," Crawford says. "The murder weapon was a knife with a blade of at least nine inches, given the depth of the injury." He indicates the vertical section of the "cross" on Mr. Nicks' body. "Then a smaller incision was made here, drawing horizontally. This was more than likely done with a much smaller, sharper instrument, such as a scalpel."

"So we're looking for someone with access to medical equipment," I say.

He shakes his head. "You can buy scalpels off Amazon these days. But it is interesting they used two different knives for the carving. The long blade actually ended up breaking two of his ribs, it was driven down with such force. The smaller cut is much cleaner and deliberate, made after the subject was already dead."

We got lucky with the first murder, given the murderer left the weapon there for us to find. "I don't guess there's been any sign of either the knife or scalpel."

"When we left with the body, no," Crawford says. "But they could have found something by now."

"Anything else?" Zara asks.

"Yes, the victim has bruising along his upper neck and the back of his skull, here." Crawford points to the affected areas. They're purple with damage. "More than likely, he was struck from behind, with a heavy, metal object, though I can't tell you much more than that."

"The killer snuck up on him, just like with Agent Green," I say.

"Not exactly," Crawford says. "Agent Green's injuries suggested she was facing her attacker when he hit her. Mr. Nicks would suggest he was facing away. A slight difference."

"But an important one," I say, cursing myself for not remembering the detail. That isn't something that should have passed by my notice. "What was the time of death?"

"Lines up with the wife's story," he replies. "Between five and seven last night, given his body temperature."

"*Anything* else?" I ask. "Trace evidence, sweat, spit, hair dander, anything?"

Crawford shakes his head. "Whoever they are, they know how to keep a scene clean. I haven't even seen any evidence of anything being cleaned. Which means they have to be wearing close to full-body suits not to leave anything other than a few dog hairs."

"Thanks," I say. "I just hope we can stop this before we see you again."

"As do I," he replies, his voice taking on more of a regal tone. I can't tell if he's trying to be funny or not. "As much as I enjoy your company, I do not wish it at the expense of others."

Zara and I bid him farewell and make our way back out to the car. The rain has begun to let up, but only barely. "We get caught in the rain one more time and I'm going back to the hotel to change," she says.

I can't say I blame her. The inside of the car smells like a combination of body odor and stale water. It doesn't make for a very enjoyable ride.

"We need to figure out if there's any other connection with Green and Nicks," I tell her.

"You think it's something other than Murphy?" She's giving me that skeptical look. The one that makes me feel like maybe I'm going down the wrong path.

"I don't know what to think. But so far, we've run into dead ends out there."

"Maybe we need to speak to someone else."

I turn to her. "You're thinking about Burnett, aren't you?"

She gives me a small shrug. "Maybe. She's in there, entrenched with them. She might see things they don't. Plus, there's something else going on there."

"I felt that too," I say. "It's a good idea. Brad was obviously worthless. But Erin seems much more supportive of Stephanie. If there's anything going on, she'd know more than the woman's husband."

"Don't forget about the affair angle," she says.

I shake my head. "I don't think we'll need it. She seemed very personable back at the house. Can you figure out where she works? Didn't she say something about heading to a job later?"

"One second," Zara says, diving into her phone. She chuckles at something on the screen quick before pounding away on the keypad. "Got her. Instagram account. The woman posts all the time." She turns the screen to me. "Look."

I take the phone, scrolling through the pictures. Most of them are of her at Steph's house. Some in the same rooms we were in before, others in the garden she mentioned. Most seem to be flaunting a lifestyle that doesn't exactly belong to her. "Only misrepresenting real life by a little," I say, handing the phone back.

"That's what Instagram is all about, baby. Making other people feel bad because they don't have the fake life you do." She laughs and scrolls through some more, until she comes to a stop. "Plug this in. Long Gone Cat Café, downtown Richney."

"Didn't we pass that place last night when we went to eat?" I ask.

She looks up. "Oh, yeah, I guess we did."

"We could have walked right by her and not even known." I check the time. It's close to lunch, but I have no idea what time Burnett is working today. "Want to go grab a bite to eat and wait for her?"

Zara shoves her phone back in her pocket. "I'd love nothing more."

Chapter Seventeen

THE LONG GONE CAT CAFÉ IS A CUTE LITTLE HOLE-IN-THE-wall place that looks like it's been here a hundred years or more. Not the business itself, but the building and the space it occupies. It's small and narrow, shoved between two larger buildings, though it advertises a healthy meat-free lunch.

"Looks like your kind of place," I tell Zara as we head in.

"Oh, quit your whining," she says. "Get a salad or something."

The sign inside the door offers for us to seat ourselves, so we choose a small table close to the window where we can keep an eye on everyone who comes and goes from the café. Zara chooses some kind of tofu plate while I opt for a rice and bean bowl as we wait for Erin Burnett to appear. It doesn't take long. Before either of us is finished, she makes her way in from the back, wrapping an apron around herself and tying her long hair back. She's changed out of the sundress she had on earlier and is instead in a short-sleeve shirt and black pants.

She doesn't leave the area behind the bar-slash-counter, instead takes over for one of the other waitstaff and starts making all the coffees and drinks. I have to admit, I'm perplexed. Any friend of Steph's I assumed would have been from the same tax bracket, but Erin looks right at home working here, like she's done this for a long time. Is that why she stays over with Steph so much, because she doesn't have a lot of money?

We manage to finish our meals without her noticing us, seeing as we're tucked in a small corner. Finally I get up and walk to the counter.

"Hi, do you need—" She looks up and her eyes go wide before an easy smile spreads across her face. "Oh. Wait, from this morning, right? That's a weird coincidence," she says. I can't tell if she really believes we're here just out of cosmic randomness or if she's trying to hide her true surprise. But I'm not seeing any of the classic signs of deception.

"Mrs. Burnett, we're not here by accident." Zara joins me at the counter.

"It's Ms.," she says, her voice a little smaller now that there are two of us. "Haven't used Mrs. since my divorce."

"Would you mind if we took a few minutes to ask you some questions?" I ask.

Erin looks around, scanning the café. It's still relatively busy given it's the end of the rush hour. "Can it wait about forty-five minutes? There's no one here to cover my shift."

I nod. "Sure. We'll be right over there when you're ready," I say, indicating the table. We head back over, leaving her to her work.

"Way to scare the crap out of her," Zara says as we retake our seats.

I shrug. "Sometimes intimidation is a good tactic. We'll be able to judge how well she responds after having some time to think about it. She obviously didn't think she'd see us again."

"Obviously not."

The entire time we're waiting, I catch Erin shooting us furtive glances in between making drinks. Every time we catch her looking, she offers us a pleasant smile. She doesn't seem overly nervous, but she doesn't seem eager either. She's acting like someone who has nothing to hide, but is still hesitant about talking to the FBI. I just hope she can give us some insight into Stephanie's world that we haven't uncovered yet. Steph may have told Erin something she later forgot about, or that she was deliberately trying to hide. I can't say why yet; I just know something about all this feels…off, and this author is at the center of it. If Erin yields nothing, we might want to consider speaking with the rest of Stephanie's family.

Someone has to know something.

"Thanks for waiting," Erin says after almost an hour has passed. "Usually, the crowd dies off a little earlier. I guess more people were eager to get out of the rain."

"Are you here every day?" I ask.

"Oh, no. Just Wednesdays, Fridays, Saturdays, and Sundays. The café is closed on Monday and the other days I'm off." Again, she works more hours than I would have expected.

"How long have you been working here?" Zara asks.

"About three years. I like it, the people are nice and the work isn't too hard." She's trying hard to remain chipper, but by the way her hands fidget, it's obvious she's nervous about speaking with us.

I try to put her at ease. My earlier tactics might have been a bit too aggressive. "Listen, we understand this can be frightening; we're just looking for information related to Stephanie. Can you tell us if you've noticed anything strange over the past few months?"

"Strange how?" She seems genuinely curious.

"Steph acting different, calls, odd mail. Anyone hanging around when you're out with her, or any communication she might have received and brushed off," Zara says.

Erin pinches her features together in concentration. "I don't…think so. Nothing that I've noticed, at least. But then again, Steph doesn't tell me everything that happens with her business. It's not like I see all the fan mail she gets either."

"Does she get a lot?" I ask, trying to follow where Erin wants to lead us.

"Oh, sure. Mostly emails and messages through her website and stuff like that. I've seen the number that come through—has to be at least hundreds a day. Not to mention all the people she interacts with on social media."

"Social media?" I wasn't aware authors ran social media campaigns. I figured the publishers did all that for them.

"Yeah, she's got a couple groups on Facebook, and a Twitter feed. You know, all the big ones. People sign up and then can meet other people who like her books, talk about them, or even ask her questions."

"And Stephanie actively participates in these groups?" I ask.

"Not *all* the time, obviously. But sometimes she'll pop in. You know, as a thank-you to all her fans." Erin has gone a bit starry-eyed, though I'm not sure if it's because she admires Steph's work, or she just likes the thought of lots of people fawning over her.

"Are you in those groups?" Zara asks.

"I wouldn't be much of a friend if I wasn't," she replies. "I was one of the first members, you know, back when Steph was just starting out. I've always tried to be supportive of her work."

I lean back to give her some room. "She said you went to college together."

"Yep, that's where we met. Both graduated the same year, both of us majoring in English." Her nervousness has fallen away now, replaced by the confidence of reminiscing in the past. "Of course, she reached our dream a lot quicker than I did."

My eyebrows shoot up. "You wanted to be an author as well?"

"Yeah," she says, looking away, as if she's embarrassed. "Ever since I was little. I've been writing a long time. But

Steph…she picked it up so quickly. She didn't start until college, when the professor began to assign us fiction projects. She has a natural talent for it, I guess, considering she signed with McCallan and Press less than a year out of school."

I detect a hint of jealousy, though I'm not even sure Erin realizes she's projecting it. It's subtle, which is opposite of how I see Erin, being more animated and exuberant. "Don't get me wrong," she continues. "I'm so happy for her, and I admit I live vicariously through her sometimes. Signing that contract was the best thing that ever happened to her."

"Hasn't she tried to help you get your work published?" I ask. "I would think with the number of resources she has—"

"Oh," Erin says, brushing it off. "Yeah, she's tried. She sent my work to her agent a few years ago, tried to get me a jump-start." She gives a small shake of her head. "Just…didn't work out."

While not exactly damning, this does provide us with another angle I hadn't considered. We'll need to take a closer look at Erin's past, see if her jealousy has ever manifested itself before.

"Steph says you stay over sometimes," I say, leading her off the topic before she becomes suspicious.

Erin chuckles. "We've named the guest house 'Erin's Room' unofficially. She's been really good to me. Ever since my divorce, things have been tough with my son. But every time I need something, Steph is right there. I can always count on her."

"And Brad?" I ask. "What about him?"

There's a noticeable shift in her body posture. It's very similar to what we saw with Brad back at the country club. "What about him?" she asks, trying to mask innocence.

"How does he feel about you being around all the time?"

She gives us a small shrug. "Fine. We don't talk much. He's usually out in the garage or in the adjacent wing in the man cave. I really don't see him that often."

"How is the relationship between Steph and Brad?" Zara asks, picking up from my cues.

"Okay, I guess. I think things have been a little rough lately, ever since Steph's last book didn't perform like the publisher had hoped. She provides everything for that family, so if something happens to her income…"

"It puts a lot more pressure on their marriage," I say, finishing the thought.

"Yeah. It's tough, for her. It's a lot of pressure. She's worried this next book won't do as well, but she's said that about every book she's ever released. Constant pessimist, I guess."

"What about your son?" I ask. "Does he get along with the kids? Does he like staying over?"

"He usually doesn't stay over when I do," she replies. "He's with his dad those days. But when I bring him over to play, they always get along really well, even though he's a little younger. They've all grown up together. Steph had Dylan early, but then she and I were pregnant at the same time when she was carrying Harper. How funny is that? But things got harder and Justin and I…" She leaves us to fill in the blanks. It's not hard to tell which of the two women has gotten the better deal in life, but despite all the drawbacks, Erin maintains a positive attitude. But every time she mentions Steph, it's almost as if she reveres the woman; like Steph represents the best version of what she could become. I see a longing in her that I don't often see with people.

"Erin," I say, lowering my voice. "I have to ask. Can you tell us where you were last night between five and seven p.m.?"

"Um…" she checks her phone, absently though, just to see the time. "That was after my shift was over, so I was at home with Joey, probably feeding him dinner and getting ready for bed."

"Anyone else with you?" I ask. She shakes her head.

"What about the night of July fourth? Do you remember what you were doing that night, around eleven p.m.?"

"Am I in trouble here or something?" she asks, all hint of the former smile gone. "You don't think I had anything to do with those people, do you?"

"It's just routine," Zara says. "We ask everyone we speak with, as a precaution."

"Oh," she says, like she only halfway believes us. "I was home with Joey that night too. He's afraid of fireworks, so I got him these noise-cancelling headphones so he could sleep while they were being set off."

"Just you and Joey that night," I say.

She nods. "That's right. Unless you count our dog. But she's deaf as a doornail, doesn't hear a thing."

"Oh, I love dogs, what kind do you have? I've got a pit bull my...husband and I rescued."

"That's so sweet," Erin replies, her former self returning now that the hard questions are over. "Ours is a poodle mix, I think. We rescued her too, but my husband didn't want her in the divorce, so she stays with me."

"What about the nights you spend at Steph's?" Zara asks.

"Oh, Puddin comes along. She's got a nice little dog bed right beside the regular bed."

I shoot Zara a look. This is the first possible lead we've had. Crawford said the hairs found on the body were canine hairs, though I can't exactly see Erin killing someone in cold blood. Still, I have to ask. We still don't know what kind of dog hairs they are, but if we could get ahead of this thing...

"What color dog is she?" I ask, trying to keep the upbeat tone in my voice, as if I'm genuinely interested.

"She's white," Erin says, "And is a bear to keep clean. Especially when I'm not a professional groomer. But she doesn't shed very much which is a big plus."

I sit back, deflated. Our hairs are gray, not white. And poodles are notorious for not shedding, so the likelihood of the hairs matching Erin's dog are slim. I don't really have her pegged as a killer anyway, but I had to ask, if for no other reason than to eliminate her.

"I think we've taken enough of your time," I say, standing. Zara follows suit. "Thanks for sitting down with us."

"If I think of anything, can I give you a call?" she asks, and I gladly hand her a card. It's nice for someone to ask, for once.

"Take care, Ms. Barnett," I say as Zara and I head back out into the rain.

"Well," Zara says. "At least we got lunch."

Chapter Eighteen

WITH NOTHING BUT DEAD ENDS ON THE STEPHANIE MURPHY front, Zara and I head back to the office to do some more research on Agent Green's cases. Since my theory about Murphy being the link between the two victims didn't pan out —at least not yet—we have no choice but to keep going through her case files to see if we can find anyone who looks even the least bit suspicious.

It turns out Agent Green worked mostly white-collar crime, specifically fraud cases, which makes this even more difficult. Typically, people involved in fraud don't go out and start murdering people, even if the FBI closes in. It's a long shot, but at this point, I'm willing to try anything.

As we work, my mind drifts back to home and what is awaiting me there. Every time I think about someone breaking into Agent Green's apartment, my mind finds its way back to D.C. I'm desperate to call Janice for an update but stay my hand because I know that will lead nowhere good. I just can't get over the fact someone broke into my apartment without my knowledge and set up those cameras. She must be damn good if she can get in and out of there without Timber detecting her scent, because that dog can smell a snausage from across the whole apartment.

It upsets me even more that I was so blind to it. Had I never tripped on Timber's toy, who knows how long she could have kept an eye on me? What does she want with me? Is she spying because she's afraid I'll uncover something about her? Or is there another reason that I can't even fathom? The only plus side to this is it gives Janice a reason to finally listen to me about her. I know Janice has been humoring me up to this point about the specifics of my husband's death, and for good reason. It isn't like I have any hard evidence. Just a coincidence and a hunch. If we can catch her, we can make her talk. And then maybe I can finally find out *why* she decided to destroy my life from the inside out. I trust no one else better than Janice to find this person and bring them into the light so I can finally get some answers.

"I swear, there isn't one violent criminal in here," Zara says, pushing herself back into her chair so hard it rolls away from her desk. "They're all just pencil pushers and wannabe money launderers. Nothing that would indicate any of them were willing to kill to keep their operations going."

"Maybe we need to look at associates of the people she was investigating," I say. "Instead of the people themselves. Perhaps someone had a vested interest in one of her targets, and they got wind of what she was doing. Decided to take her out before she could disrupt their operation."

"And don't forget, they're big Ruby Blackthorne fans," Zara says with a wink. She pulls herself closer to the desk again. "I guess it's worth a look. It just means we're going to be here until midnight."

"I know," I say, keeping my head down as I do the research.

"Funeral is tomorrow," she says after a few quiet moments.

"Yeah."

"Think we should go?"

I look around my computer so I can catch her eye. "It's worth taking the time. We can keep an eye on things while everyone else takes time to grieve. It's what we're here for."

"You still think they'll show up. With fifty FBI agents there?" Zara asks, shaking her head. "I keep telling you, you're crazy."

"Maybe not completely crazy yet," I say. "But getting there." If I have to go through any more files, I think my eyes will fall out. "Let's call it, we can start up again early in the morning. Knock a bunch of these out before we're due to leave for the funeral."

"Yeah, okay," Zara says, extricating herself from the chair.

On our way out, we pass Agent Detmer, who looks like he hasn't slept in five days. "Headed out?" he asks.

"We'll be back early in the morning to keep going over her cases. Do you have anyone keeping an eye on Adrijus, just in case he's working with an accomplice?"

He nods. "I got one of my guys stationed at the apartments, keeping an eye on him if he decides to move."

I give him a reassuring nod before we head for the door. "Hey," he calls after us. "It was a good idea to look at Murphy. Sorry it didn't pan out."

"Me too," I say.

After an actual night's rest and a filling breakfast made up of more than just liquid caffeine, Zara and I are back in the office again. With fresh eyes I find the work a lot easier, and I'm able to zero in on a couple of them that I think I skimmed the afternoon before. I pull the very last case Green was working on before she was killed—a case she was about to submit to the D.A.'s office for approval on an arrest. It involves someone named Eve Nelson, who seemed to be perpetrating an advance fee fraud; catfishing unsuspecting people into giving her fees for the promise of a bigger payout later.

It isn't particularly interesting, or unique in any way that I can tell, except for the fact it was her last case before she was killed. Had she lived through the weekend, her paperwork says she was due to submit it to the D.A.'s office so she could go get an arrest.

Again, white collar crime is not violent—most of the time. What Eve Nelson was doing was akin to a ten-year-old stealing a pack of gum in how important it is in the big scheme of things. People run these kinds of scams all the time, and lots of them go unnoticed by the FBI. But for some reason, Green managed to find this one and begin exploring it. It didn't take her long as it was an open and shut case, which was why she was probably submitting it so soon.

"Did you see this one?" I ask, sending over Eve Nelson's case file to Zara's email.

"Yeah, so?" she asks.

"So? She was working on this case when she died," I reply.

"She was working on *all* these cases when she died, that's kind of the point of us doing this," Zara replies.

"No, I mean, she was ready to submit this one. Whoever this Eve Nelson person is, they are extremely lucky she died when she did." Maybe it's not completely rational, but I am grasping at anything I can get here. Anyone who happened to benefit from Agent Green's death, as I've always said. Eve Nelson happens to fit, more urgently than any of the rest of Agent Green's cases.

"So what, you want to go after this Nelson person?" Zara asks.

"I think it's worth a shot," I say. "At least look into her. We can still file for the arrest warrant if she looks like she might be good for this."

Zara gives up, holding up both hands. "If you insist."

I check the time. "Hey, we better get going. It starts in less than half an hour." By the time we head out of the office, a lot of the other agents have already left for the funeral. I've never been much of a funeral person myself, opting to have a short service for Matt before he was cremated. I went through a few long funerals as a kid, which only ever seemed to be an excuse for people to get up and preach instead of actually remember the people who had died. I didn't want that for Matt; and I couldn't bear sitting there, listening to someone go on about what a great person he'd been. I knew all that already. I wanted someone to get up in front of that crowd and tell me *why*.

The service is held outside, in a private rose garden belonging to some wealthy socialite or another; a friend of Green's parents, I'm told when I ask. As Zara and I approach, many of the white seats are already filled, as people from all ages and walks of life have come to remember Agent Green. In addition to the FBI agents, I see her family, huddled near the front, sitting closest to a small urn that has been placed upon a pedestal under a rose canopy, like the kind people often get married under. The backdrop is a field of verdant green, peppered with flowers that stretches out to a large, tall hedge at the edge of the property. If I didn't know better, I'd say this *was* a spot for marriages; though it seems Green's family has decided this is where they'd like to last remember their daughter.

Zara and I settle in the back, standing behind the glut of FBI agents who have gathered. Detmer sits closer to the front, his head hanging down and his face pale. "He must have had a crush for a long time," Zara says when she sees me staring at him.

"I don't think it was a crush," I say. "I think it was love."

"They only went out on one date," she reminds me.

I shake my head. "I knew after one date with Matt." I wouldn't have admitted it to anyone if they had a gun to my head, but I knew right then that he was the one. Of course, I didn't know if he felt the same way or not. But still.

"I have to count myself lucky I got as much time with Matt as I did. They only had one date. Sometimes it isn't the quantity of time we spend with people. Sometimes you just click."

"That doesn't bode too well for me then," she says. "Because I don't know if he's the one or not."

"You haven't even met Ian yet," I say. "You have to at least give it a once-over in person first."

"Why must you have so many rules?" Zara says, possibly a bit too loud. A couple of people turn in our direction, and we mouth *sorry*. "See what you made me do?"

"I didn't make you do anything," I say. "It was all you."

A man stands up in front of the gathering and a hush falls over everyone. He positions himself beside the urn and gives it a long, loving look before opening his mouth. "Ladies and Gentlemen, thank you for being here today to celebrate the life of Melissa LaRue Green. We're so glad you could join us. If you don't mind, I'd like to begin with a story…"

I assume this man is her dad, given his gray hair and fair complexion that matches what I've seen of Melissa in pictures. As he speaks, I scan the crowd, looking for anyone who might be out of place. The FBI agents are all easily visible in their near-matching suits and emotionless facades. I guess sometimes that training we undergo to help us deal with stressful situations can be applicable when we're not in mortal danger.

The rest of the crowd is made up of people dressed in nice clothing, appropriate funeral attire. But given the way Mr. Green is going on, he's using this opportunity not to mourn their loss, but instead to celebrate her life. It's so refreshing to hear someone tell all the funny and sometimes embarrassing stories that I'm sure someone with a good sense of humor would have laughed at right alongside everyone else. I can't imagine with a father like him, Melissa didn't grow up without at least a small amount of humor. When I look at Detmer again, I can see even he is smiling, though there are tears in his eyes. Some of the other agents have begun to break ranks and tear up as well.

I smile, glad that her memory can still provide comfort and joy to people. But as I'm finally beginning to relax, I catch sight of someone I did not expect to show up at this funeral. I nudge Zara and nod in the direction.

"What is she doing here?" Zara whispers.

"I don't know, but we better go find out," I reply. She's got on a shawl that covers most of her hair and dark sunglasses, but it's definitely her.

Stephanie Murphy has decided to put in an appearance.

Chapter Nineteen

As the funeral progresses, Zara and I make subtle moves along the back of the crowd, inching closer and closer to Murphy. She hasn't spotted us yet, but if she does, I don't want to spook her and cause her to run. I can't imagine why she is here at all and think back to if I even told her about Agent Green. I mentioned the death of an FBI agent, but I don't think I ever said her name. So how would Murphy know to come here? Does she have more to do with this than I originally thought?

I look over at Zara, hoping to get a second opinion, but she's zeroed in on Murphy like a bloodhound, determined not to let her get away. The other woman happens to look over her shoulder, straight at us, but then turns back to the service. I'm partially flabbergasted; I suppose I suspected she would try to run when she saw us approaching, but that's only because I was thinking of her as a possible suspect. Why else would she come to Green's funeral? But she obviously wanted us to see her or doesn't care. Either way, as soon as this service is over, I'm finding out exactly what she's doing here.

A couple more people get up to speak, each with their own humorous anecdotes about Agent Green. Even some of her colleagues from the FBI. I expect Detmer to get up and say something, but when there is a call for anyone else, he remains seated. Though he's no longer staring at the ground. Instead, his eyes are locked on the urn.

Through all of this Murphy keeps a respectful silence, occasionally dabbing a tissue under her sunglasses, one eye at a time. A million different scenarios run through my head as I try to determine her purpose here, but nothing is coalescing. The problem is I don't know Stephanie Murphy very well, and so it's difficult to get a good read on her. Plus, I have heard that writers tend to be difficult subjects to profile because they're like chameleons, they can have the traits of anyone. They have to, in order to inhabit all those different characters they create.

The service ends and everyone who was seated stands and begin to break off into smaller groups. Some heading for the family, while others head back out of the opulent settings for the parking area just off the other side of the road.

We don't even have to go to Stephanie Murphy, she comes to us instead, still dabbing her eyes. "Agents," she says. "How are you?"

"How did you know who the victim was? I never told you her name," I say, perhaps coming on too strong.

Murphy doesn't seem to notice. "After you left I checked the local obits. There was only one woman mentioned under the age of thirty who worked for the federal government. Wasn't that hard to figure out."

"I suppose not," I say. "But why come? You said you didn't know Agent Green."

"I didn't," she replies, removing the sunglasses. Her eyes are puffy from tears. "But like you said, this is all centered around me. I had…" She trails off, looking back at Green's urn. "I had to be here for it to be real. To see it for myself. I think if I hadn't, I would have been able to convince myself you were wrong, or this had all been a bad dream."

"Did you manage to speak with your publisher and agent yet?" I ask.

She nods. "I did. Nothing from either of them. They assured me if they'd seen something concerning or out of the ordinary, they would have informed me immediately."

I'm almost surprised Murphy doesn't receive semi-concerning letters on a regular basis as it is. Most famous people, or at least, people with a following, will always attract those who are looking to stand out in some way. The ones who will do anything for a little attention, even make toothless threats or send cryptic messages intended to scare the person they admire. People can be really strange sometimes.

Agent Detmer comes up, his hands in his pockets. "It was a nice service." Before we can agree he puts his hand out to Stephanie. "Elias Detmer."

"Stephanie Murphy," she replies, taking his hand. Detmer's gaze widens, then shifts to me and Zara before he releases her grip.

"Mrs. Murphy came to pay her respects," I say.

"I feel like it's partially my fault," she adds before I can say anything else. "If I hadn't ever written that damn book—"

"The killer would have just used another one," he finishes. "We appreciate you being here."

"Did you work with Agent Green?" she asks.

Detmer shoots us a quick look. "I did. She was a fantastic agent. The Bureau is really going to miss her." Smart of him not to mention their personal relationship to a civilian. He turns to me. "I just got a call from Williamson. The local news just got wind of it."

"I'm surprised it took this long, honestly," I say. Mrs. Nicks must have finally broken down and told someone, or her family did. I don't blame her for wanting to get the story out there, if anything I understand exactly where she's coming from. If I had learned Matt had been murdered immediately, rather than thinking it was an accident, I would have wanted every news station from WJLA to CNN to run it.

"Well," Murphy says, slipping her sunglasses back on. "Guess I'll be informing Gus. He'll need to add extra security. I'm sure they'll be wanting an exclusive." She turns to me. "Brad told me you came to see him. He said you threatened him?"

I have to keep from laughing out loud. "No, that's not what happened. If we'd threatened him, there would have been no question."

"We're not in the business of threatening people," Zara says.

"I didn't think so, but he seems to have some kind of axe to grind with you. I don't know why, but he was very put-off by the visit."

"Tell him not to worry," I say. "I doubt we'll be questioning him again anytime soon."

She nods. "If you need to talk to me again, please call first. With all this media frenzy it's going to be a madhouse over on the island. I'll have to make my apologies to all my neighbors before things get bad."

I can't imagine the old gatekeeper doing much to barricade the gate. It isn't like he has a lot of resources to stop people who really want to get in. Plus, how late can he work? "That's probably for the best, anyway," I say. "Like I told you before, until we determine who could be doing this, keep all your doors and windows locked."

"Don't have to tell me twice," she says, then returns her attention to Detmer. "Agent, sorry to meet under such poor circumstances." She heads off toward the vehicles. "Oh," she says, returning and removing the sunglasses again. This time her attention is completely focused on me. "I wanted to apologize about Erin yesterday. She didn't tell me she'd be dropping by or I would have warned you. I saw you both go for your guns when she barged in."

"She just startled us, is all," I say. "You're very observant."

"It's my job to watch people," she replies. "I've been doing it most of my life. It's how I find new ways to bring characters to life. But again, she shouldn't have frightened you like that. I've told her she needs to let me know when she's going to be stopping by, Gus seems to think she can come and go as she pleases."

"I'm sure that must be disruptive," I say.

"You have no idea," she says. "Especially now that I'm under this deadline. I can't have her tromping and stomping all over the house while I try to work."

"Have you spoken to her about it?" I ask.

She harrumphs, then gives me a look that says "are you kidding?" before slipping her sunglasses back on and heading back to her car without another word.

"That was…odd. Does anyone else think it's weird she was here?" I ask once she's out of earshot.

"I imagine she does feel some level of responsibility," Detmer says. "Even though something like this is completely unpredictable."

I turn to Zara, looking for her opinion. "I dunno," she finally answers. "I think you could make a case either way."

"I guess," I say. I just find it strange that as soon as I feel we've moved past Stephanie Murphy, she inserts herself right back into our midst.

Chapter Twenty

AFTER THE SERVICE, THE FAMILY MAKES IS CLEAR THEY HAVE A
private service that will be for family only. Zara and I leave
with the other agents, heading back to the office. Just because
there has been a tragedy, doesn't mean we stop working.

We loop Detmer in on what we've discovered so far
regarding Agent Green, even though it isn't much. As I
continue working on pouring through her cases, Zara switches
gears and begins investigating Jonathan Nicks, to see if we
can't find some place where both victims cross over. It's a
tedious process, and I can feel my mind going numb as I read
report after report, searching for just the smallest sliver of
evidence that proves these two victims were related in
some way.

In the back of my mind is a clock with no hands, but
ticking down regardless, to the point where we'll find our next
victim. There's no reason to assume the killer won't go after
yet another person, imitating the next book in Stephanie's
series. I hate to say it, but we might need a third victim before
we find the pattern here.

Still, somewhere in all this I can't let go of the Murphy
connection. Even though no one in her world has heard or

seen anything, it *feels* like Murphy is the intended target. Or at least an unwilling spectator.

"Hey," Zara says, poking her head above the monitors.

I halfway get up. "What?"

"Take a look at this."

I stand and circle around to her desk and am immediately assaulted by a dozen web browsers open all at once, filling the screen. "How do you work like this?"

"Easy," she says, "You just think about everything all at once."

"Right," I say.

She highlights one of the browser tabs. "I'm going through Jonathan Nicks' bank records. He's got a series of six deposits, one per month for the last six months, of almost twenty thousand dollars each."

"Where is it all coming from?" I ask.

"So I had a hunch. Remember Green's last case you were so interested in? Eva Nelson. I pulled her bank records and found the exact same amounts debited from her accounts before they were deposited into Nicks' account. Each time it's the same amount, nineteen thousand, seven-hundred and seven dollars. It's debited from Eva's account one day, then deposited into Nicks' account two business days later, like clockwork."

"So he was on her payroll," I say.

"Looks that way." She opens another tab which details who issued the checks. They come from a company called N3, LLC. "I checked with the Secretary of State for New York and found the business has only been in operation since January of this year. And guess who the primary contact is for the company?"

"Eva Nelson," I say, without needing Zara to verify it for me. "Could these be proceeds from her fraud activities?"

"Probably. As far as I can tell, N3 is a front of some kind, a business designed to sell digital products like software, but its real business is taking in all the money from the fraud itself. Nicks could have been unofficially on the payroll."

I scan over the documents she's pulled up. "So Nelson sets up a front company to try and disguise her real source of income, then gets started on defrauding people. Where does Nicks come in?"

Zara shrugs. "He was an accountant. Maybe he helped her manage her books."

"So why kill him?"

Zara looks over her shoulder at me. "There wasn't anything in Agent Green's file about Nicks was there? Or a confidential informant? Green could have been using Nicks to get to Nelson. Eva finds out, and not only kills Green, but kills Nelson for crossing her."

I head back over to my computer to run through Green's files again. "I don't see anything about an informant, but she could have kept that out of the official paperwork. I know I would have, especially after that data breach we suffered. Our CI's identities are the most important secret we keep."

"She must have found out," Zara says. "It's the only thing that makes sense."

This proves that Green and Nicks had another connection that isn't Stephanie Murphy. "We need to find this woman. Have you had any luck tracking her down?"

"Still working on it," she says, opening and closing browser windows faster than I can track. "So far all I have is a box at a UPS store outside of Woodhurst that the business uses as a mailing address. The physical address registered with the Secretary of State is an empty field halfway between here and Richney."

"So she's a local," I say.

"Yeah, I guess." Zara glances over. "Why?"

"She'll be easier to find," I say. "I want to know who else knew about her enterprise, because it's possible they are slated to be the next victim. We need to figure out if she had any partners, employees, other subcontractors, anything. If she's closing up shop because Green got close to her, she might be out there eliminating anyone who ever knew about the business."

"It still begs the question: how do Murphy's books factor in?" Zara asks.

I don't have an answer for that. But this is the most promising lead we've had so far. "See if you can at least find a picture of this woman. In the meantime, I'm going to go speak with Jonathan Nicks' wife. She might know something about her husband's activities that could help us."

"Do you really think she's in any mood to talk?" Zara asks.

I grab my blazer, slipping it on. "If it means getting justice for her husband, then yeah, I do."

I've become so used to Zara accompanying me to interview suspects or witnesses, the car feels strangely empty without her. Back before everything happened with Matt, I used to head out by myself all the time. But it's been nice having her around for some of these more intense cases. As FBI agents, we usually handle our investigations alone, at least until they grow large or complex enough to bring more agents into the fold. But something like this starts out big, and usually doesn't shrink. I'm sure by the time we're done, we'll have roped in half of Detmer's team as well.

When I pull up to the address given from the team, I'm surprised to find Mrs. Nicks isn't in a house at all—she's set herself up in an extended stay hotel. Funny, I figured she would have gone with one of her family members to stay, but maybe no one has the room. Or maybe Mrs. Nicks just needs some time to herself.

I know how she feels.

I head inside, showing my badge to the man at the check-in counter who directs me to room 208. Forgoing the elevator, I climb the short stairs and head down the long, straight hallway until I reach her door. I pause a moment, trying to summon some empathy for this woman so I don't just end up barging in on her and causing her to panic or shut down.

I give the door a little knock, then stand back, my badge clearly on display at my hip.

The door cracks open and I see the bloodshot eye of Mrs. Nicks staring at me. "Yes?"

"Helena Nicks?" I ask. "I'm Agent Slate with the FBI. May I have a moment of your time?"

She closes the door and I hear the chain being removed from the channel before the door opens again, revealing the entire woman. Her face is pale, her eyes puffy and purple from all the crying. A few capillaries have burst in the bags under her eyes, a telltale sign that the crying sessions have been intense. Further inside the room I hear what sounds like an educational game of some kind. Helena notices my attention wandering off her.

"My daughter," she says. "Just trying to keep her busy for the time being. She's eight."

"I'm very sorry," I say.

"Honey," Helena calls out. "Mommy will be right back. Stay here, okay?"

"Kay," the child calls back, distracted by whatever it is she's watching.

"Outside?" Mrs. Nicks suggests. I nod. I'd rather not question her here in the corridor where it is such close quarters, or where someone might be able to overhear through one of the other doors. We head back down the stairs until we're outside the back of the building. Mrs. Nicks produces a fresh pack of cigarettes and a cheap lighter, expertly igniting one before stuffing the rest back in her pocket.

"I haven't smoked in nine years, ever since before Skylar was born. But sometimes you just need a release, you know?"

"I do," I say, thinking back to how I threw myself into work after Matt, working twelve-to-fifteen-hour days; anything so I wouldn't have to go back home. "I know you've already spoken to the police, so I apologize if you've already been over some of this."

She takes a long drag, looking off into the distance. "It's fine."

"How much did you know about your husband's business?"

She raises her eyebrows, giving me a small frown. "Not much, why?"

"We know he worked for Marlowe and Howe. Did he ever do any consulting on the side? Anything outside of the work he did for the firm?"

"Sure, he'd freelance occasionally to drum up some extra cash. We were trying to save for Skylar's college. He told me the more we could put away up front, the easier it would be, even if she got into one of the Ivy Leagues."

So Nicks' consulting wasn't a strange occurrence. Maybe that was how he'd been able to sell it to his wife. Just another freelance gig. "Did he ever mention the name Eva Nelson to you?"

Helena takes another long drag, like she's trying to suck the life out of the cigarette. As if it's the only thing keeping her grounded right now. "I recognize the name. But I never paid much attention to Jon's clients. Even those that would come over to the house. I was usually too busy with Skylar or dinner or...something." She turns to me. "How am I ever supposed to go back in there? I can't stop seeing him like that."

I lean up against the building next to her, staring out at the tree line where she's staring. "I lost my husband about six months ago too. I wish I could tell you it gets easier, but it really doesn't. I ended up selling the place we had together, moved into an apartment with our dog in tow. Staying in that house, just sleeping there…it was too much."

"I'm not sure we can afford to move," Helena says. "Jon handled all the finances. I don't even know how much we have in savings. And now there's a funeral to prepare for, a casket to buy…there's just so much to do."

"I assume that means you haven't looked at your accounts yet," I say.

"You'll have to forgive me, but I'm doing good just standing here," she says, letting the cigarette hang between her fingers. "Much less trying to untangle the knot I'm sure our finances are in." She waits a beat. "I'm sorry about your husband. What happened?"

"The doctors ruled it a heart attack." It's not a lie, but I don't need to go spilling my life history to this woman.

She scoffs, shaking her head. "That's terrible. But I guess if you're standing here, it means I have a chance to get through this too." She finally puts the half-used cigarette out beneath her shoe. "Now that I think about it, Jon was meeting with a woman at the house a lot recently. At first it was only once every few weeks, but lately it had become once a week, if not more often."

"You never got a name?" I ask.

She shakes her head. "He always just said she was a client."

There's still a chance this could be the mysterious Eva Nelson. Even a partial identification is better than nothing; it at least allows us to narrow down our search. "What did she look like?"

"Pretty," she says, crossing her arms. "Not particularly tall, but also kind of a bubblehead. Very animated and seemed overly happy all the time. Blonde hair, like a reddish blonde."

That sounds suspiciously a lot like Erin Burnett. Unfortunately, I don't have a picture of her on me, and if I were to present her picture alone, it could unduly influence Helena's memory. I really need to set up a lineup of similar-looking candidates. "Do you think you could recognize her if I showed you a picture?"

"Probably," she says, reaching into her pocket for her cigarettes again.

I glance up at the extended stay. "Do you plan on being here a while?"

"We sure as hell aren't going home," she replies.

"I don't blame you," I say. "I'll be back later and maybe you can help me identify this woman. In the meantime, I'd take a look at your finances. I have a feeling you're going to want to get ahead of things."

"Do you think she had something to do with Jon's death?" she asks.

"I can't say yet, we need to continue our investigation. Sit tight, and I'll be back," I say, pushing off the wall and heading back to my car. As I'm headed off I see a news van pull into the Extended Stay's parking lot.

"Ah hell," I hear Helena say behind me. "Why can't they just leave me alone?" It doesn't sound like she's in a mood to deal with them.

I turn back to her. "Are they harassing you?"

"You're damn right they are," she replies. "I'd like to know who the hell told them I was even involved in this. The last thing I want to do is deal with the media." She disappears back through the door of the Extended Stay before the reporter can even get out of the van. He spots my badge and motions for his cameraman to follow him as I make my way to the car.

"Agent, are you working directly with the Nicks family regarding the murder of Jonathan Nicks?" he asks, shoving the microphone in my face.

"No comment," I say.

"What about the rumors that this murder is connected to the earlier murder of Melissa Green, that both people were killed in a manner described by local author Ruby Black-thorne's books?"

"No comment," I reiterate, reaching my car.

"Does the FBI have any leads on who this killer is? What do you say to the public who is depending on you for safety? If an FBI agent can be killed in her own home, what chance is there for the rest of us?"

I just give him a quick smile as I get into my car and drive off, leaving him and the cameraman standing there. I wouldn't be surprised to see myself on the eleven o'clock news, refusing to give a statement to the media, but right now we're not prepared to release anything.

Though I do find Mrs. Nicks' attitude toward the media puzzling, considering I thought she was the one who informed them. She still may have and realizes now she's bitten off more than she can chew. But what if she didn't?

Who else would?

Chapter Twenty-One

"I NEED HELP," I SAY, HEADING BACK INTO THE OFFICE WHERE Zara sits, joking with one of Detmer's guys.

"That's why I'm here, isn't it?" she asks, shooting me a wink. The other agent gives us both a smile and a nod before heading back out to the bullpen.

"Aren't you just the social butterfly lately," I say, slumping down into my chair.

"Just passing the time until you got back," she says. "Any luck with Nicks' wife?"

"She thinks his most recent client could have been Nelson, but she never heard the woman's name. She was in the house a few times though. I was going to build a lineup to take back to her."

"A lineup of who? Random people?"

"Of fair-skinned women with strawberry blonde hair," I say.

Zara sits up at the revelation. "Wait, you don't think...not Erin?" she says.

I hold my hands out. "She has a flimsy alibi for both murders."

"So did Adrijus. That doesn't mean she killed anyone. You

said yourself she didn't seem like the type."

"Hence, why I need the help." I lean back in the chair, rocking it back and forth on a stiff spring that creaks with every bounce. "Let's say Erin Burnett created the persona of Eva Nelson just like Nelson created the company as a front for her illegal activities. It's obvious why she'd do it, so any investigation into Nelson would lead back to no one. You said you couldn't find any concrete information on her, right?"

Zara shakes her head. "Nothing in the DMV databases for either New York, New Jersey, or Connecticut. And I can't find anything in the birth records that conform to anyone who isn't seventy-five or older. I'm guessing our mastermind is middle-aged."

"If it's the woman Mrs. Nicks described, then yes," I say. "So Burnett creates this person to shield her activities, and sets up a shell company to run the money, hiring Nicks to what? Keep the books?"

"Or keep everything off the books. As an accountant he was in a good position to hide as much of this ill-gotten gain that he needed for her. Which makes him an accomplice and also her most important asset." Zara says.

"If it is Burnett, what's the motive? Just money? She said Steph Murphy gives her whatever she needs if she's ever short."

Zara sits up. "Right, but how long can something like that go on? Maybe Burnett got tired of mooching off her friend. Or maybe Murphy decided to cut her off. Perhaps not all at once, but slowly pulling back. I doubt she would have admitted that to us, but she did seem a little perturbed at Erin at the Funeral this morning."

"Okay," I say, my mind running through possible scenarios. "Erin knows the money is drying up, or is trying to make a future for herself. She hoped to be an author, but that hasn't panned out. And she can't support a kid on a café barista's salary. So she decides to get into defrauding people. Not for a lot, but enough that, compounded over hundreds and hundreds of individuals, really begins to add up."

Zara jumps in. "And maybe she's not great with money, so she hires an accountant to help, with the promise that he'll get a bonus at the end of every month that he does a good job."

"It fits," I say. "But is there any truth to it?"

She returns to her computer. "I found one other interesting item of note while you were gone. Going back into Agent Green's file, it seems the FBI was tipped off about Eva Nelson from an anonymous source. I went back and pulled the original tip, which is a series of text messages from a now-dead phone number. Probably a burner phone. Still, the FBI didn't discover this on their own. Someone called it in, and Agent Green was assigned the case."

"Who? Someone they defrauded?" I ask.

She holds her hands up. "That would make sense, wouldn't it?"

"But why do it anonymously? Why not leave your name in the event something is recovered? Wouldn't you want your money returned?"

Zara crosses her legs under her, pulling them up on the seat of the chair. "Who knows. Some people just want revenge; they don't care about the money."

I guess she's right, but something still feels off about this somewhere. I decide to push it away from my mind and focus on figuring out the rest of the details. "Assuming Nelson is the killer. She finds out that Agent Green has begun an investigation—though I don't know how she would know that, unless she has a contact inside the Bureau—and she realizes that if Green gets to the D.A. and starts issuing warrants, her deception is going to fall apart quickly." I stand and begin pacing the room, trying to work through all this. "Burnett said she is familiar with all of Steph's books. And maybe she's never killed anyone before. So she decides to take her cues from what she knows. She goes after Agent Green first, staging her body so that it takes us some time to figure out what's going on. Then she goes after Nicks, as he can incriminate her."

"But why kill him if Green is already dead?" Zara asks. "Doesn't that eliminate the immediate threat?"

"You're right," I say. "Unless she suspected Nicks of being the one who called in the tip. You said it was from a burner phone, right? What if she found the phone and realized what Nicks was doing? So she decided to kill him before he could squeal on her."

Zara gets up as well, matching my stride. "Tell me you really believe Erin Burnett is capable of shoving a hunting knife so hard into a man's chest that it breaks two of his ribs."

"It's a stretch," I say. "This whole thing is. Maybe it's not Burnett, but given the physical similarity that Helena described, along with her knowledge of the books and a possible money motive, I don't think we can discount her. And remember, her alibi for the murders is paper-thin. Of course, her kid is going to corroborate her story—what kid wouldn't?"

We stand in silence a moment, my mind reeling with all the possibilities. Part of me wants to just arrest Burnett now and see if we can squeeze it out of her, but we'll need a lot more before we can do that. Proof, for one, that Eva Nelson and Erin Barnett are the same person. If they're not, we're back to square one.

"There's another problem," Zara says. "Eva—or Erin—has to know that by killing Green and Nicks, she's only inviting further scrutiny on her. She looked completely surprised yesterday when we showed up. Wouldn't you think if you killed an FBI agent you'd expect another pair of them to show up not long after?"

"Remember she first met us at the house. She could have seen us through one of the windows and prepared herself before she barged in, making it all look innocent. We don't exactly blend in." I swipe at Zara's platinum hair, knocking a small bit of it away.

"Or she just happens to look like this Nelson woman and it's nothing more than a coincidence."

I nod. "Until we get a positive ID, this is all just conjecture. But you have to admit, it fits."

"It *mostly* fits," she corrects. "Theory still has a couple holes in it."

"No one is perfect." I shoot her a wink.

"Do you want to set up surveillance on Erin?" Zara asks.

"Not until we have a positive ID. Which is why I need the lineup, for Mrs. Nicks." I prepare to head out to the bullpen to speak with Detmer about printing one off. "Oh, there was one other thing. I'm not so sure Mrs. Nicks called the media. They showed up while I was over there and she seemed more than a little perturbed that they were trying to harass her."

"Those vultures are relentless sometimes. Maybe she just didn't know what she was getting herself into."

"I had the same thought." But then again, given her condition, I'm not sure I can imagine her phoning up the local TV station and telling them her husband was murdered when she can barely make it out of her room in one piece. Her fingers were shaking like a willow in the wind when I first arrived. She only calmed down after a cigarette. "Still. What if she didn't?"

She gives me a quizzical look. "Who else would have done it?" I suppose some member of Agent Green's family could have notified the media, though I feel like they would know better, and not want a lot of attention, given the nature of what she did for a living.

"I think this whole thing just has me twisted up in knots. I'll feel a lot better once we have Burnett in custody and can get this all sorted out."

"And if it isn't her?" Zara asks.

I stare at her a minute before leaving. "Then I guess we'll have to wait for another body."

Chapter Twenty-Two

IT ONLY TAKES FIFTEEN MINUTES TO GET A COUPLE OF LINEUP cards created and printed off so I can bring them to Mrs. Nicks. I hope she'll still be in a talkative mood when I get back over there. As I'm heading out to the parking lot, the cards in hand, my phone vibrates. My heart almost leaps from my chest when I see the number belongs to Janice. Could she finally have some news for me about my apartment? Have they finally caught the woman who killed my husband?

"Slate," I say, doing my best to keep a calm veneer over what is nothing but nervous energy.

"What's your progress on the Green case?" she asks. My boss doesn't waste time on chit-chat.

"I'm headed back to a witness now to hopefully provide a positive ID on a potential suspect," I say. "It's the first real lead we've had since the second murder."

"I saw the report come through. You still believe both of these murders to be related?" she asks.

"I do. The medical examiner has discovered the same substance on both, which we believe to be canine hairs. We're still trying to determine a breed. In the meantime, the wife of the second victim thinks she's seen a woman we believe to be the link between both Agent Green and this accountant. A woman who seems to have perpetrated advanced fee fraud, catfishing unsuspecting victims into sending smaller payments in promise for a larger one later." I slip inside the Bureau car and toss the cards on the passenger seat, shutting out the outside world.

"Good," she says. "I don't need to tell you how important it is you wrap this case up quickly. The Bureau already has egg on its face, allowing one of its own to be taken and murdered so brutally. The Deputy Director has his eyes on this one, Slate, so make sure you get it done as fast as you can."

"I'm working the evidence," I say. I can't control the speed of a given case; it goes as fast as it goes. I'm not about to cut corners just to ensure we get a suspect in custody quicker. I've made that mistake in the past and it's come back to bite me. Part of me can't believe Janice is actually asking me to speed things along. From her tone, I get the sense that she knows what she's asking and doesn't care. She's under a lot of pressure on this as well. "I'll bring in some of the local agents to help. Maybe that will speed things up."

"Good," she says. "Keep me updated." It sounds like she's about to hang up without giving me an update.

"What's the status on my apartment?" I can't help but blurt it out. It's been almost five days with no word. I can't just sit here waiting any longer.

"There's been no movement," she replies. "We have our teams in place and the surveillance is still keeping an eye out, but whoever put those cameras there, they haven't come back for them, despite Agent Foley's assurances they were nearly full."

I let out a sigh. It was too much to hope there'd been some development on that front.

"Listen, Slate, we're not about to let *another* agent get

blindsided here. One killed in her apartment is one too many. In the event no one shows up, we'll move you until we know it's safe. I can only keep these agents on this so long, because of the sting set up in a couple of days. If no one shows up by then, I'll have to pull them."

"Yes, ma'am." I should have anticipated that. Janice hangs up without another word and I shove my phone back in my pocket. I'm more than a little deflated; I had really thought there would be a development on that front. I have to remember the assassin is very smart. She could have spotted our surveillance and decided not to take the risk. But that also might mean she knows I'm no longer in town. Whatever is going on, I don't like the idea of her out there in the shadows, watching and waiting. I'd much rather confront her head-on.

Feeling more than a little sorry for myself, I pull my phone back out and dial my in-laws. I don't know why I think they'll actually pick up, but part of me just wants to be verbally close to Timber, even if I can't see him. The past six months have been brutal, and I just need a small bit of connection to get me through.

"Hello?" I freeze upon hearing my sister-in-law's voice. I didn't think she would answer. "Emily?"

"H-hello Dani," I manage to say.

"Is everything all right?"

Dammit, why am I so stupid? Why did I even call? It isn't like she can put Timber on the phone and he can bark at me. "Yeah, fine. I'm sorry, I didn't mean to disturb you."

"It's just…you don't usually call when you're out of town."

Now I need to figure a way out of this mess I've gotten myself into. "I know. I just…how is Timber? Is everything okay?"

"Of course, we'd call you if something was wrong." *Would you, though?* I don't think they would ever let anything happen to him, but I'm not sure Chris would let his wife call and tell me if Timber accidentally swallowed something or if he got sick. They already see themselves as his primary caretaker, they've made that much clear to me.

"Right," I say. "I guess I was just missing him."

"Emily." Before she can even get out the words I know what she's going to say. How it would be better if they kept Timber full-time. I've heard it all before. I've even considered it sometimes late at night after I've had a few. But I can't let him go. I can't stay in that apartment all by myself, with nothing but my thoughts and empty hallways to keep me company.

"Don't," I say, warning in my voice.

"It's what's best for him." Her voice is soft...kind. I know she's not trying to start a fight, that she really believes he would be better off staying with them. But I can't help my muscles tensing as she speaks, my entire body gearing up for a battle. "Max and Waldo love rolling around in the yard with him, and the three of them get along well. You should have seen it earlier, all three were napping together huddled up with each other."

Tears sting my eyes. I don't know if they're for Timber, for my dead husband or maybe they're nothing more than pity tears I'm crying for myself.

"What is she doing calling here?" I catch the familiar voice of my brother-in-law in the background, and I wipe the tears from my eyes, as if he's in the car and will see them.

"She's checking on Timber," Dani says. The phone rustles and all of a sudden her quiet is replaced by Chris's heavy breaths.

"What are you doing?" he demands.

"Just checking on my dog," I say, immediately defensive. Of my in-laws, my brother is definitely the more combative of the two.

"Think we're not taking care of him, is that it?" he asks.

"No, it's just—"

"If you don't think we're up for the job, you are more than welcome to leave him with someone else," he says. "That is, if you even *have* anyone else."

"What the hell is wrong with you?" I hear Dani say on the other end. I recall what Zara said back when we were dropping Timber off.

"You know what, Chris? Fuck you," I say, still wiping at the tears. "I know you blame me for Matt's death and that's fine. You want to blame me, go right ahead. If it makes you feel better to put that on me because you can't deal with his loss, then I'll bear that load for you. But there is nothing you can say that will make me feel worse over what happened to him than I already do. It may not have been my job to monitor him twenty-four-seven, but it was my job to protect him, just as it was his to protect me. And I failed in that. Is that what you want me to say? I *failed*. Maybe if I'd been there, I could have done something. But I wasn't. And now we all have to live with the consequences."

There's nothing but silence on the other end. I don't know if he's still listening or not, but I continue anyway.

"If I could take it back and give my life for his, I would do it in a heartbeat. I would do it a hundred times over. Because Matt was the better of the two of us. I know how I come off— I know I'm abrasive and not always outgoing and not the most social of people. And he balanced all that out, he was the one who was always there to help out whenever you needed, he was there to comfort you or Dani when you had bad days. I've never been good at that kind of thing; I don't know why. So I get it. I get why you're pissed that it was him and not me. But let me be very clear: you can't make me hate myself any more than I already do. And no matter what happens, I am not going to let his death be in vain."

The tears have stopped for the moment, but I feel

emotionally spent, like I've pulled the scab off an old wound and it's raw again. I don't know where all that came from. Maybe I've just had enough of my brother-in-law's abuse. Maybe I'm not going to let anyone else tell me about how guilty I should feel for something I couldn't control.

"Emily," he finally says, confirming to me he heard it all. "I never said I thought it should have been you instead of him."

"You implied it often enough," I say.

"It's just...he was my little brother," he says. "It was always my job to look after him. When he found you, it actually made me feel a lot better. Who better to watch his back? And then to learn that he'd died of a heart attack of all things —something so completely random and...and..."

"It didn't make sense," I say.

"No. I know I've been a dick. I've just got all this anger and nothing to do with it."

"So do I." I rest my head on the steering wheel, feeling like I've run a half marathon. My eyes slide over to the clock on the dash. "I need to go. I have a witness to interview."

"Timber will be fine until you get back," he says. "Maybe...we should put aside some time to talk when you do."

I lift my head, surprised. "Yeah. That sounds good."

"When are you due back in town?"

My mind goes to my earlier conversation with Janice. "Not until this case is finished. Could be days, could be weeks."

"Well, just let us know." He waits a beat before hanging up. I lay the phone in the passenger seat, surprised, for once. I haven't felt anything like that from him in six months. I had initially expected Chris and Dani to be there to support me after Matt died, and I could do the same, only to find them cold and out of reach. Dani has softened some in the past few months, but it seems like Chris has only grown angrier. Which is why this turnabout is so surprising. Maybe I just finally needed to say my piece. I'd been holding it in to spare his feelings. Still, I don't want to get my hopes up. I'm not very good at connecting with people, so who is to say it doesn't all fall apart when I get back home?

I start the car, and pull out of the lot, wiping my eyes one last time. Time to find myself a killer.

Chapter Twenty-Three

By the time I get back to the Extended Stay, the sun is on the verge of setting, bathing Woodhurst in a series of dark shadows, highlighted by pinks and purples all across the sky. Heavy storms are always good for pretty skies the following days, especially around sunset.

I give the guy at the counter a wave, and he throws a half-hearted wave back at me. I'm still reeling from my discussions with both Janice and Chris, but I do feel like some of the weight has been lifted off my back. For the first time in seven months I'm not dreading returning to their house to pick up my dog. But at the same time, I'm concerned that the assassin hasn't returned to pick up those cameras. Has she followed me here to Woodhurst? Is she out there right now, still watching?

I shake my head as I climb the stairs to the second level, heading down the hallway. I need to focus on the case at hand, and to get a positive ID on Erin. Once we've got that, we can set up surveillance on her, and hopefully catch her planning her next kill. Zara will probably want to arrest her right away and see if we can't get a confession, but if she really is behind all of this, there's no way she'll break. Her demeanor both times we've spoken has shown no signs of guilt. She plays the part well, and I have no doubt she'd be able to keep it up once in custody. A professional of that quality we'll need to catch in the act, but before she can strike. It's the only way to guarantee she can't hurt anyone else and ensure this case is closed to the Bureau's satisfaction.

When I reach room 208 I raise my hand to knock, but the door is already partially ajar. Not much, as the spring on the other side keeps it pushed closed, but there's a piece of glass blocking the door from fully closing. A piece of broken glass that looks like it came from one of the glasses they provide for use in the room.

I draw my weapon and keep it at my side, leaning up against the door, trying to see inside the dark room beyond. There is no sound other than the air conditioner clicking on.

My heart hammers in my chest. What could have happened? "Mrs. Nicks?" I call out. "It's Agent Slate. Answer if you're in there." No response. I drop the lineups and draw my phone from my pocket, hitting the first quick dial I have saved.

"Yo," Zara says. "She identify her yet?"

"I need backup over here, right now," I say. "Possible B and E, I'm not getting any response from inside."

"On it," Zara says. By the way her breath sounds, she's jumped out of her chair and is in the process of gathering backup. "Don't go in there until we arrive."

"I can't wait," I say. "Someone could be hurt."

"Em," Zara says, warning in her voice.

"Just hurry, I'm keeping the connection open," I say and slip my phone back in my pocket without terminating the call. If there is someone dangerous in there, they know I'm here and they'll suspect I'm heading inside. But I can't wait out there for the ten minutes it will take Zara and the others to get here from the Bureau office.

Raising my weapon, I lean harder on the door, giving it the smallest push. "Whoever is in there, identify yourself," I say. "I will not hesitate to fire." Still nothing. No movement, no sound. I don't like it. What could have happened in the few hours I've been gone?

I slowly push the door open with my shoulder, keeping my gun extended in front of me as the multi-room suite is revealed to me. The curtains have been pulled and the entire suite is bathed in darkness. I focus on the sounds, listening for anything that could indicate danger. Once I'm satisfied no one is going to charge me from the darkness, I check around the corner of the door, finding no one hiding behind it. I reach over and flip on the light in the primary living room and kitchenette, to find them both empty. There's no sign of Mrs. Nicks or her daughter. But some of the plates and glasses in the kitchenette have been disturbed. A few of them are smashed on the tile floor. I don't see anything else out of place, which tells me the struggle was quick.

"Hello?" I call out, but there's no answer. The suite is divided up into three rooms. The main living area with the kitchenette upgrade—I'm guessing when she booked the room, Mrs. Nicks wasn't sure how long they'd be here—and two bedrooms off the main room, both sharing a bathroom.

I move slow, taking my time as I inspect the scene, looking for anything that might indicate what happened. There looks to be some dark marks on the carpet that lead to one of the bedrooms, but the carpet is naturally dark, and those could be nothing more than water. I head over to the main window and pull back the shade, though it does little good as most of the light from outside is gone already. I recall I still have Zara on the other line. "No indication of anyone in the main living area," I say for her benefit. "Heading into the bedrooms."

It's very possible someone could be waiting in there, ready to pounce. I tense myself as I approach the door, doing my best to check the blind corners. The bedroom closest to me is pitch black, no light anywhere inside. Keeping my gun extended and my breathing as regular as I can, I enter the room, sweeping back and forth for any hostiles. It takes me a moment to find the light switch, which illuminates a lamp on a desk right next to the bed.

But when I see the bed itself I nearly cry out. "One victim," I say. "Helena Nicks, deceased," I say, trying not to let the body of Mrs. Nicks distract me from the fact someone could still be in here. She's splayed out on the bed, a rope around her neck, which has turned purple. Her eyes are wide, staring up in horror and her hands are splayed out by her sides. Except she's missing the tips of all ten fingers. They've been cut off, the wounds raw and ragged. It's as if someone took a pair of pruning shears and snipped them like dead twigs. Large, crimson stains have pooled beneath both hands. If the strangulation didn't kill her, the blood loss certainly did.

Shit, shit, shit, I think. Where's the kid? "Skylar?" I call out, not wanting to go into the other bedroom. "Is there anyone else here?" I make my way to the attached bathroom, flipping on the light to reveal nothing but a standard hotel facility, complete with two sinks, a tub, toilet and shower. No sign of the girl. Pushing forward, I head into the second bedroom through the other door, which is also pitch black. My hand shakes as I reach for the light, but I manage to flip it on without losing my nerve, and keeping my weapon extended out in front of me.

The bed is empty, no sign of anyone else. I make a quick sweep, then holster my weapon. A few of Skylar's toys litter the floor, along with a backpack and some clothes. Whoever killed Mrs. Nicks must have taken the child, though I already recognize the atypical death as yet another from a Ruby Blackthorne book. Her third, *Deadly Stacks*. Just like Zara thought they would. It's distinct enough that I recognize the staging. I can only assume this is also the work of Eva Nelson.

"Zara," I say, pulling my phone back out.

"Here, what's going on?" she asks.

"Site is clear, no sign of the perpetrator. Looks like they killed Mrs. Nicks and took the child with them. She's staged just like you predicted, like in the end of book three."

"Are you okay?" she asks. "We're four minutes away."

"Yeah, I'm—" A thump interrupts me and I drop the phone back into my pocket and withdraw my weapon again. The noise came from the second bedroom. I enter again, moving slowly and not making a noise. I try to check under the bed, but it's one of those kinds that goes all the way to the floor. I head over to the closet, sliding open the door slowly, but it's empty inside. Nothing but a few extra pillows and a blanket. Furrowing my brow, I do another sweep of the room. I know I heard something. Just as I'm about to leave I hear it again. A *thump* from somewhere in the middle of the room. It sounds like it's coming from under the bed, but that's impossible...unless...

Holstering my weapon, I lift up on the mattress and box springs to reveal the hollow bottom of the bed itself. A small girl is curled up in the space, her eyes watering as they turn to me. "Skylar?" I ask.

She doesn't say anything, doesn't nod or move at all. But I can't hold this mattress up forever. "Can you come out, honey?" I ask. "This is really heavy." I can't even imagine what she's feeling. How did she get up under here? Not by herself, there's no way she could have lifted the bed and springs. Maybe her mother put her here, when she heard a disturbance? Hell of a hiding place though.

"Skylar, please," I say, losing my grip. "I need you to help me out here." I can't hold it any longer. But instead of letting it back down, I push instead, forcing it up and toppling over to the other side of the room. The loud noise seems to shake Skylar into action and she sits up, staring at me.

I bend down, so I'm at the same level with her glassy eyes. I'm terrible with kids, always have been. But she's a victim, and a potential witness. I need to be gentle. "Are you okay?" I ask. "Are you hurt anywhere?"

She shakes her head, her dark curls reminding me a bit of myself at her age.

"Here, let me help you out." I reach out for her and she recoils. "Okay," I say, trying to keep her calm. "It's okay. You can stay in there if you want to. Can you tell me what happened? How did you get in here?"

She shakes her head again. I can't even imagine what she must have heard. Even if she didn't see anything, the trauma was still real. I'm making sure to keep myself positioned between her and the passthrough to the next room, so she can't see anything. But it's almost as if she senses it, because she continues to back away, trying to push herself into the smallest corner she can.

The sound of the door opening draws both of our attention to it and Skylar squeals out in terror. "Em!" Zara calls out.

"In here," I say. She, Detmer and three other agents appear in the doorway. I make a motion of my head behind me, to the other bedroom. "I just found her. Her mother must have put her in here before the attack."

The place becomes a buzz of activity. A female agent comes over and speaks to Skylar in a softer voice than I could, cooing and reassuring her everything will be all right while I take Zara and Detmer back into the other bedroom to show them Helena.

"This tracks with the other two," Detmer says.

"You need to call Crawford," I say. "We need to find—" I take a closer look at the body, at her tank top, specifically. A few small, gray hairs are plainly visible. "—Find out if those are a match to the others. I'm sure they will be."

"Holy hell," Detmer says, putting his hands on his hips. "What a mess. I don't get it. What's the motive?"

"Nelson must know we're on her tail," Zara says. "She might have known Mrs. Nicks could identify her."

"How is she doing this?" he asks. "You were just here a few hours ago. You're telling me she just happened to attack in between your visits? Isn't that a little convenient?"

I shake my head. "She's shown that she's aware of our movements. How, I'm not sure." It makes me think back to the woman I'm chasing. The one who always seems to stay a step ahead of me. "She must have access to the team somewhere."

Detmer gives me a stern look. "That's not possible. My agents are above reproach. Are you suggesting we have a leak?"

"Either that, or she's clairvoyant," I say.

"Listen, Em, I know you said if we get a positive ID on Erin you want to set a trap for her," Zara says. "But I don't think we have that luxury. We need to get her off the streets. Draft a warrant for her arrest."

"We still don't know it's her," I say. "And until we're sure, we can't go around picking people up just because they happen to match the description of a suspect." The three of us begin surveying the hotel room, looking for any other details that might give us a clue to finding Eva Nelson. About twenty minutes later, Crawford and his assistants show up.

"Hello all," the man says. All three of them are clad in white clean suits. "I'll need everyone to vacate as you're contaminating my crime scene."

"The body has hairs on it, like the others," I tell him.

He nods. "We'll do a quick comparison. Should be easy to tell if they're from the same source." He snaps his fingers before he gets to work. "That reminds me. I was about to call you and tell you when I got the emergency call from Agent Detmer. We finally got the DNA back on the canine hairs. They belong to a purebred poodle."

The hairs on the back of my neck rise. "Are you sure?"

"A hundred percent. There's no question about it," he says.

"Em," Zara says. "It's enough."

"Enough for what?" Detmer asks.

"Enough to go to the District Attorney," I say. "We need a search warrant for Erin Burnett's home."

Chapter Twenty-Four

WE LEAVE THE SCENE TO CRAWFORD AND THE OTHERS, AND coordinate with local police to help keep any crowds back. The media has shown up again by the time we're getting ready to leave, but fortunately Agent Nilsson has already taken Skylar and is in the process of contacting her closest relatives.

Zara and I slip out the back, and head back to the Bureau. It's going to take some time to get a search warrant for Erin Burnett's place so we can match the hairs to her dog, so I coordinate with Williamson to keep an eye on Erin for the time being. I want to make sure we don't lose sight of her until we have a warrant for her arrest and get her into custody.

"I still can't believe it," I say as we're driving back. "She must be really good."

"Could be someone else's poodle," Zara suggests. "She did say hers was white."

"Yeah, but if you google white poodles, you'll find that a lot of them look suspiciously non-white. What she might think of as white is actually a shade of gray, the perfect shade to match the hairs we found."

"But aren't poodles notorious for not shedding very

much?" Zara asks. "I remember something about that as a kid."

"Common misconception," I say, having only recently learned the truth myself. "They still shed, but because of the tightness of the hairs, most of those stay on the poodle, and don't fall to the ground. Also, they don't produce dander like a lot of dogs, which is what makes them more hypoallergenic."

"So, Erin is just dropping dog hairs on all her victims?" Zara asks.

"What happens every time Timber comes over to stay with you?" I ask, pressing harder on the accelerator.

"I'm cleaning hair off my clothes for a week or more," she says.

"Right. Dog hair can be insidious, getting into everything. Burnett might not even realize she's tracking the dog hair to the crime scenes. She's careful not to leave any of her own DNA, but she might not even be thinking about the dog's. It's sure to be on whatever she's wearing to commit these murders." It all fits, but it's not as clean as I'd like it to be. There is still a lot of circumstantial evidence that happens to fit Burnett at the moment. That's why I want the warrant, so we can prove without the shadow of a doubt the hairs are from her dog. Once we have that, we'll have her cold.

Once we get back to the Bureau we begin working on the paperwork to submit to the D.A. By the time we're finished, it's nearly ten. I doubt we'll get the go-ahead tonight, but as long as Williamson has eyes on Burnett, I'm satisfied to wait until morning. Not to mention we'll need Erin out of her apartment if we're going to be searching it and taking samples from her dog.

By the time Zara and I return to the hotel, I'm beat. The emotional exhaustion of the day has seeped deep into my pores to the point where I feel like the walking dead. Adrenaline kept me going most of the evening, but when my head hits the pillow, I'm out for a solid eight hours.

My dreams are punctuated by a mix of happy reunions with my in-laws and a dark shadow chasing me through the night, always staying on me without letting up. I know deep in my subconscious it's her, waiting for me to come back home. No matter where I go, I can't get away from her. She feels like a monolith, always out there, waiting for me. She killed my husband, and now she's just lying in wait for the perfect moment to kill me too.

I wake up in a cold sweat, my heart beating. I slip out of bed and into the bathroom without disturbing Zara and splash some water on my face. I rarely have nightmares; most of the time my dreams are incomprehensible if I remember them at all. I just know I'll feel a lot better once I'm back home and we can finally catch this woman in the act. That is, if she hasn't set a trap of her own.

I take a quick shower and get ready, anxious to get started with the day. Erin Burnett isn't my first choice, but if that's where the evidence leads us, I'm not going to refute it. At least Janice will be happy.

"Hey," Zara says after she's gotten ready but before we head out for breakfast. "Check your phone. It just came through."

I grab my phone and find the approval of the warrant to take a sample of DNA from Burnett's dog. "Yes, finally," I say. "What's her schedule like today?"

"She said she works Fridays, right?"

"Right. If her shift is the same, she'll be over at the café by eleven." Zara pulls on her blazer, double-checking her holster isn't visible. I find myself beaming a little. I remember when she didn't even want to bother with a gun.

I shoot off a quick text to Williamson to inform me when she leaves her place for the day. In the meantime, we head back over to the Bureau to gather a task force. Since we're limited in scope by the warrant, I want to get as many eyes as we can in there, for the short amount of time we have. We won't be able to seize anything else, but we can at least look. If Burnett has accidentally left bloody clothes out somewhere, we'll be able to take that upon suspicion of harm, though that's a pipe dream. This woman has been as clean and professional as they come, she wouldn't be that careless. But if this DNA test goes like I think it will, we'll be able to come back with a much more comprehensive warrant, *after* we've arrested her.

Two hours later the call from Williamson comes in and I gather the troops.

"You good?" Zara asks as we make our way out to the car.

"Yeah, why wouldn't I be?" I ask.

She shrugs. "I dunno. You seem a little off."

I haven't told her about the call with Chris yet. Seeing as how vociferously she fought for me last time, I don't want to send her into a frenzy. "I think I'm just concerned about this thing at my apartment. Why hasn't she shown up yet? You said the cameras were nearly full."

"They were," she says. "Unless she doesn't care about missing days. Or she got sidetracked. Who knows what else she's out there doing? She could have dozens of people like you she keeps her eyes on."

I guess that's true. I shouldn't consider myself her only target. But that just means more people could be in danger. And if she can make every death look like a heart attack, she basically has free rein to kill anyone at-will, and no one be the wiser. When all Stillwater Medical's tests on Gerald Wright came up negative, I had to assume her method for killing is something as secretive as she is. Which is convenient for her, because it's something I can't prove.

Still. I know she's responsible. Why else would she be watching my apartment?

"Better get your head in the game," Zara says. "We're almost here." We pull up to Burnett's apartment with Detmer's team pulling up right behind us. There's no sign of

Williamson or Burnett's car, which hopefully means she'll be gone for a while.

"I just spoke with Crawford," Detmer says as everyone gathers their evidence cases. "He said he sent you an email. The hairs are a match to the ones he pulled from the other bodies. I guess now all we need to do is verify that this is the dog they came from."

Burnett's place is a far cry from Stephanie Murphy's palatial mansion. It's a small two-story condo in a row of homes, sitting right on the end. It looks as though there is garage access in the back and walk-up access in front. I check for any security cameras or doorbell cameras, but don't see any. Though Zara points to a camera high up on one of the buildings a few hundred feet away. Makes sense, the community provides the security, so the homeowners don't have to. It looks like Erin Burnett has never suspected anyone would break into her home. But given what we're looking at, she also probably didn't want cameras tracking when she was going in and out of her home late at night. We could subpoena that data and use it against her if we needed to.

One of Detmer's men manages to pick the lock and the door swings open easily. Once we're inside, I look for a security system but find none. Again, that's not much of a surprise, though I had figured we'd encounter at least some resistance. Inside the doorway is a staircase and a long hallway where a medium-sized dog lays on a rug. Its head perks up when it sees us and it approaches, its tail wagging.

I get down on one knee and hold out my hand. "Hey there girl," I coo. She gives my hand a little lick and lets me scratch behind her ears. "You're very friendly."

"That's a poodle all right," Zara says. "And look, she's got some gray to her. Like you said, not pure white."

There's no doubt in my mind now that the hairs will be a match. "Get some samples, from her body. Let's make sure to maintain a chain of evidence on this, got it?"

"You say that like I've never collected evidence before," she replies, pulling out a small bag. One of the other agents assists her with collecting the hairs while I continue to distract the dog.

"I have to admit," Detmer says. "I didn't expect it to be a woman. Each murder has had a brutality about it that—"

"What?" Zara asks. "Women can't be as brutal as men?"

"No, it's just that you normally don't see this. The statistics don't bear it out."

"I think we can definitely say this is not a normal serial," I say, giving the poodle one last pat on her head after Zara is finished. "I want to check the rest of the apartment, see if she's been foolish enough to leave anything else out."

We do a walk through, only finding the normal things: a few dishes, kids toys scattered on the floor, a couple of clothes. Not particularly messy or tidy. When we pass by her laptop I have an urge to open it up and to let Zara start digging, but anything we found would be inadmissible. We need to do this one right, especially if the Deputy Director is paying attention. I'm not about to cut any corners on Burnett.

I do notice that for someone who works as a barista, Erin Burnett isn't doing too bad. The townhome is updated and spacious. And it probably wasn't cheap. Maybe she got a settlement in her divorce, or perhaps Murphy helped her out. Or maybe her foray into advance fee fraud wasn't her first time. She could have run other scams in the past with more success. It was just bad luck that someone called in a tip to the FBI and got Agent Green involved. Had they not, Erin would probably still be defrauding people today, and all three victims would still be alive.

"Anything?" I ask Zara as she descends the stairs. She shakes her head. "Time to go, then." Burnett's dog is right beside me, tongue out and wagging her tail. I give her another scratch behind the ears. "We'll find you a good home once all this is over, I promise."

The team makes sure to leave everything just as we found it, and the lockpick manages to secure the home again once we're all outside. "You'll need to speak with the property management company," I tell Detmer, pointing to the camera. "Explain to them what's going on."

He nods. "I'll take care of it. You get those hairs back to Crawford. If they're a match, I'm going to tell Williamson to pick Burnett up immediately."

"We'll be his backup on that." I nod to Zara. "How long do you think it will take to match the hairs?"

"A full DNA match will take a few days," Detmer says. "But they should be able to tell if they're from the same dog without DNA. Crawford knows his stuff. He won't let you down."

"Good. Then I guess it's time to go join a stakeout."

Chapter Twenty-Five

"HOW ARE YOU FEELING?" ZARA ASKS AS WE SIT IN THE CAR about twenty yards away from the Long Gone Cat Café. On the other side of the street sits Williamson, keeping an eye on the place from that side. As soon as the call comes in, we'll move on Erin. We've already been here over an hour, watching the lunch rush die down. All the while, Erin has appeared and disappeared in the windows of the café as she's cleaned tables and helped seat people. It seems the café is a little short on help today. But she's shown no indication that she knows we're here.

To answer Zara's question, something feels off.

"I can't get over how she managed to get in and kill Mrs. Nicks during the hour and a half I was gone. Not to mention when I left, there was a news van there. They might have not had access to the building, but I would think a murderer wouldn't want to go in and strangle someone with the media right outside." I glare at the now-empty window. "Then again, maybe she's just that confident in her abilities."

"The thing I can't figure out is why stage the bodies at all? All it does is draw attention to Stephanie," Zara says.

"That's one of the questions I hope to ask her," I say.

"Maybe it's her way of getting back at Stephanie, for being the success she never was. Maybe she feels like she's had to resort to this, while Stephanie gets to live her comfortable life in her big house where she doesn't have to go in and make coffee all day long."

"That's a lot of resentment," Zara says.

She's right, it is. But people can be strange sometimes. They can seem completely calm and collected on the surface, hiding the storm brewing beneath. Until we get her into an interrogation room and start breaking down some of her barriers, we won't know exactly what she was thinking.

I'm also curious how Mrs. Nicks knew she was coming. Obviously, she hid her own daughter to keep Erin—or "Eva" from finding her—but that means she had some kind of advance warning. There's been nothing from Detmer's team about Helena's phone being used in those precious few seconds. If you knew a killer was coming for you, and you had the number of an FBI agent in your pocket, wouldn't you use it?

"Em," Zara says. "Tell me the truth. Does your gut tell you it's her?"

If I really think about it, it doesn't make a lot of sense. But this is where the evidence has led us, and I can't afford to go off-book for this. There is too much riding on the case. Too many people are expecting a quick resolution, and we have a prime suspect in our crosshairs. If we can just get her to confess, this will all be over, and I can go back home and help with the search for the woman who bugged my home.

"It doesn't matter what my gut tells me," I say. "We're doing our jobs here."

"That doesn't sound very much like the Emily Slate I know," she says.

"That's because the Emily Slate you know doesn't exist anymore," I say, not taking my eyes off the café. "She died with her husband, and this is all that's left. A woman who gets results."

"This the same woman who broke into a man's house because she was sure he was guilty, even though there was zero evidence backing it up?"

I slide my gaze over to her. "We got lucky on that one. I shouldn't have done that."

"If you hadn't, at least four women would still be captive right now," she replies. "Maybe even dead. The whole reason you're so good at your job is because you can see things other people can't. But when you ignore that voice because you're being backed into a corner by a bunch of bureaucrats, things get messy."

"I'm not ignoring anything," I say, even though that's clearly a lie. I'm just trying to do the right thing here and get a killer into custody where they can't hurt anyone else. But if I'm being completely honest, I know there is something more going on. I don't know how or why, but I don't feel like this ends with Erin Burnett. Maybe she can help us out in that regard once we have her in custody.

"If you say so," Zara replies. "I'm just calling them as I see them."

"That's why I like keeping you around," I tell her. "But in all honesty, the Bureau is not going to allow us to spin our wheels on this. If we don't bring someone in soon, they'll take us off the case and reassign it to someone else they feel is more qualified. Then all that work I've done over the past four months just disappears, and I'm back on Janice's shit list."

"So you're willing to arrest someone who might not be guilty to save your career," she quips.

"*No*," I reply. "But I am aware of the time constraint here. Erin is guilty of something. And since when did you become defense counsel for the accused? If I remember it was just yesterday when you agreed with me."

She's quiet for a moment. "I think…in this job we take a

lot of risks. And those have real consequences for the people we accuse. I just want you to tell me you're a hundred percent sure we've got the right person. Because if we don't and there's another murder—"

"My career will be over anyway," I say.

"Yep. It isn't going to look too good to say you've caught the person responsible then turn around and someone else dies like the person in book four."

"How does that one go again?"

"Head crushed under a tractor trailer," she replies. "I imagine it's like running over a cantaloupe."

"That's disgusting," I say, trying to stifle a laugh. "Let's just hope this puts an end to it."

My phone buzzes in my pocket. "Slate."

"Agent Slate, so good to hear your voice again," Crawford says on the other end. "I have good news for you. The hairs are a preliminary match to all three crime scenes."

I turn to Zara, flipping my phone on speaker. "How sure are you?"

"About ninety-five percent," he says. "It would be very irregular for this to come from a different dog, even a sibling. We've been analyzing the structure of the hair, as well as the color and curl. They are all nearly identical. Of course, if you want to be a hundred percent sure, you'll have to wait for the DNA results to come back. But in my professional opinion, there's no way these are from different animals."

"Thanks Crawford," I say. "That's exactly what we needed." I end the call and unlatch my seatbelt. "Ready?"

"As I'll ever be," she says, stepping out of the car. I follow suit and signal to Williamson who perks up. He gives me a nod that he understands as Zara and I approach the café. Williamson pulls out of the spot and heads down the street until he makes a right. He'll cover the back exit just in case Burnett decides to run.

The bell over the door announces our arrival. Most of the

lunch rush has come and gone, and only a few stragglers remain in the café, including one woman working on a laptop, sipping a coffee. We bypass the "seat yourself anywhere" sign and head straight for Erin, who is behind the counter, cleaning. When she sees us her face lights up. "Agents, I didn't expect to see you again so soon! How about a cup of your choice, on the house?"

Zara shoots me a worried look. This is not how someone who is facing two FBI agents after just having killed a woman less than sixteen hours ago should be acting. "I'm afraid not, Erin," I say. "Would you mind stepping around the counter? We need to have a discussion."

"Oh," she says, her face falling. "Well, I understand if you're in a hurry. One second." She gives the back counter one more good wipe then heads down and around the counter back to us with a smile on her face. "How can I help today?"

I can't help but feel there is something seriously wrong with all of this. I have arrested a lot of people, and none of them have ever acted this aloof, as if they don't have a care in the world. But to Erin Burnett, it's like we're a couple of old friends here for a chat. I wince as I pull out my handcuffs. "Erin Burnett, you're under arrest for the murders of Melissa Green, Jonathan Nicks and Helena Nicks," I say, gently taking one arm and pulling it behind her back.

Her face falls, but she doesn't fight me. I thought maybe it would kick in at the very last second, when the clamps closed in. "What?" she says. "This is some kind of practical joke, right?"

I pull her other arm behind her and lock them together with the cuffs while Zara gives Burnett her basic Miranda rights.

"There must be a mistake," she says, even as we begin to lead her out of the café. "Are you sure you have the right person?"

"Evidence was found that puts you at all three scenes," I tell her.

"But I don't even know anyone named Nicks," she protests. "I only know the FBI agent's name because Steph told me she went to the funeral. But I didn't kill anyone."

"What about the name Eva Nelson, does that ring a bell?" Zara asks.

"No, should it? Is she another victim?" Erin asks. People are staring at us now, the woman on the computer has stopped typing and is looking directly at us.

"Erin!" A heavyset man with a stained apron on comes running up from the back of the café. "What's going on?"

"I'm sure it's just a mistake, Marty," she tells him. "Can you get Cynthia to cover the rest of my shift? I'm going to try and straighten this out. You can dock my pay for the hours I'm not here."

"Are you kidding? I'm not docking your hours when you're being arrested," he says, then turns to us. "What is she charged with?"

"Triple homicide," I tell him.

He practically laughs out loud. "This has to be some kind of set up. You know this woman has never had a violent thought in her life? She's the best employee I have."

"Unfortunately, that doesn't mean she isn't capable of murder," I say. "We wouldn't be here if we didn't have evidence to back it up."

"What evidence?" he demands.

"Who are you, her lawyer?" Zara asks.

"No, her boss and friend. And I can tell you right now, there is no way she killed anyone. I've known this woman too long. It's not in her blood."

"We'll see about that," I tell him.

"I need to make a call," Erin says as we take her through the doors out onto the street.

"You can call when you get back to the Bureau," I say.

"My son...I'll have to get Steph to pick him up. Her kids go to the same camp, so I'm sure it won't be a problem, but I just need to let her know. Otherwise, he'll sit there, alone, while all the other kids go home."

"Like I said, we'll let you call as soon as we get over there," I catch sight of Williamson's car peeking out from the alley half a block down. I wave him on, motioning that we've got this.

"Watch your head," Zara says, helping Erin into the back seat. She isn't putting up any kind of fight. A pit has formed deep in my stomach and is only seeming to grow larger.

"I sure hope you're right about this," Zara says as she passes me to get into the other side.

"Me too," I say.

Chapter Twenty-Six

THE BRIGHT LIGHTS OF THE INTERROGATION ROOM WASH OUT Erin Burnett's already pale complexion. She's sitting at the metal table alone, looking around like a bird who has just flown into the eagle's nest. Her eyes flit to the mirror on the wall and back away again, as if she's afraid someone will catch her looking.

I'm on the other side of the two-way mirror, my arms crossed, waiting to see if she'll react before we go in there. So far all I've witnessed is a lot of fidgeting and furtive looks. Nothing out of the ordinary for someone who has been brought in for questioning. She hasn't offered up any additional information since we brought her in, and other than her phone call to Steph Murphy asking her to pick up her son, she hasn't spoken to anyone.

I steel myself for what I'm about to do. We need to get a confession out of her; that's the quickest way to wrap this case up. Otherwise, we'll have to wait on the evidence, which could mean we'd have to release her if we don't have something solid. With a confession we wouldn't need a second warrant for corroborating evidence, but I really want Zara to get into her computer. I'm willing to bet "Eva Nelson" is all over that machine.

I take a deep breath, pushing down the pit that's been in my stomach ever since we picked Erin up. The sooner we can resolve this case, the better. Zara and I can get back to D.C., and I can focus on what's really important.

"Go ahead," I tell the tech sitting in front of me, and she turns on the room's speakers so anyone in the booth can hear what we're saying. I leave the booth and meet Zara in the hallway. Detmer passes us with a nod as he heads into the observation room.

"Ready?" Zara asks. A water bottle dangles from her hand.

I set my gaze, and we head into the room. Erin looks up as soon as we enter, the mask of relief on her face. "I thought you'd forgotten about me," she says, half-joking.

I remain silent as I take the seat in front of her. Zara stands off to the side, though she does set the water bottle on the table, and I slide it over to Erin. "Thirsty?"

She takes the bottle. "A little. It's dry in here." She cracks the seal and takes a sip. "This isn't laced with truth serum or anything like that, is it?"

I raise an eyebrow. "Why? Do you have something to hide?"

She shakes her head. "No. I don't know why I said that." She takes another long sip, keeping worried eyes on me. "Just nervous, I guess," she says after swallowing.

"Erin, are you sure you don't know Eva Nelson?" I ask, diving right in. I find jumping into the questioning helps illicit stronger answers than if I try to ease the subject into it. But then again, everyone is a little different. I suspect if we let Burnett stall, she'll take the opportunity and run.

"That's the woman you mentioned before, right?" She shakes her head. "I don't think I know her."

"Are you one-hundred percent sure?" I ask, looking for

any micro movements that could indicate she's lying. This is her last chance to fess up that will give her any kind of leeway. It will only get worse for her from here on out.

Burnett squeezes her features together. "I really don't think I do. Do you have a picture of her? I remember faces better than I do names."

I shoot Zara a look, wondering if she's buying this. She sends a worried one back. If Erin is the killer, she is one hell of an actor. I decide it might be better to change tactics. "Can you tell us, have you been having any financial issues in the past six months or so? Anything out of the ordinary?"

She kind of cocks her head and gives me a sympathetic smile. "I mean, doesn't everyone? Especially single moms. Supporting a kid through the summer months can be difficult. During the school year it's easy because they're there all day, but in the summer you have to schedule activities and camps for them to stay busy. It all adds up."

"So then you'd say you're under significant financial pressure," I offer.

"I mean, no more than any other year. I don't make a ton from the café, but the tips help. And I think I told you before, Steph helps me out whenever I need it. She's been very generous over the years."

"Do you think Steph resents needing to give you money?" I ask, playing that angle. If Erin suspects Steph's attitude toward her, it could explain why she staged the bodies in the manner she did.

"No, Steph is a great person," she says. "She wouldn't resent me. And I would hope that if she did, she would come talk to me about it. I don't want to seem like a mooch, it's just…I have limited job skills, unless you need me to pump out a manuscript really fast." She gives us a little laugh, trying to break the tension in the room, but it falls flat. "I realize how it must look."

"How is that?" Zara asks.

"Like I'm just mooching off my successful friend. But you have to understand our relationship, it's more like family than friends. She's always been there for me, and I've always been there for her. If our roles were reversed, and I was the successful one, I'd be doing the exact same thing."

"So you don't know any reason why she would be upset or annoyed with you?" I ask.

Erin shakes her head, an earnest frown across her face.

"What about Brad?" I ask.

She hesitates a second too long, and I see something change in her features. She drops her head, so we can't see her eyes. "I don't guess there's any point in denying it."

"Denying what?" I ask.

When she looks up again, her eyes are shimmering. "It was a mistake. I knew it at the time, but it was just…" She lets out a long breath and wipes both of her eyes with the back of her hand. "I was just feeling so lonely."

"How did it start?"

"I've known Brad for years," she says. "Obviously. I was Steph's maid of honor. For the longest time he was like a brother to me. I was around them all the time; I don't have a lot of close family so being with them was like creating one of my own. For the longest time it was never sexual. But I still loved him like he was my own family."

I motion for her to continue.

"A couple of years ago, after Steph's third book came out and…it didn't flop, but it didn't hit expectations either, I could feel a change in him toward me. He joked with me more, and there was the errant fleeting touch every now and again, just enough to start sending shivers up my spine. I came to look forward to going over to see them because I knew he would be there, and I could sense he and Steph were growing distant.

"I never set out to hurt her. In fact, the first time Brad and I were alone after that I asked him what was going on. He said that they had drifted apart, that Steph had become increasingly obsessed with her books, and with making sure this next one was a hit. She couldn't deal with the pressure of the books not performing like her first breakout hits. But at the same time, she was neglecting everything else in her life. I had seen it too because we hadn't been spending as much time together. But you have to realize that Steph is like that sometimes. When things are good, they're good. When she feels like she needs to be working harder for her success, she'll shove everything else to the side." Erin takes another sip of water. "She's a professional, that's what professionals do."

"So how long did the thing between you and Brad go on?" I ask.

She shakes her head, shooting a glance at the mirror. She knows this is being recorded, and I'm sure she's worried about Steph finding out. But at the same time, she doesn't have a lot to bargain with.

"It started when we were in the kitchen while Steph was in her office, working. He'd been complaining about how they hadn't been close in weeks, and he just wanted his wife back. I'd had a couple of glasses of wine and I remember placing my hand gently on his chest, just to see what it would feel like. I could almost feel the strength radiating from him." A sob hitches in her throat. "And maybe I wanted to know what it was like to be her. To have everything." She swipes away another tear. "So when I looked up into his eyes, I didn't try to stop him from kissing me. The first time was right there in the kitchen. And the worst part about it was I could hear her typing in the other room."

"She didn't hear you?" I ask.

"We were quiet. But no, she usually wears noise-cancelling headphones when she's writing. She says it helps her concentrate." Erin takes a few breaths. "After it was over, I just left. I couldn't face either of them after that. When I got home, I promised myself I'd tell Steph the next day, even if it meant we couldn't be friends anymore."

"But you didn't," I prompt.

She shakes her head. "When I showed up at her door the next morning, she welcomed me in with a big hug, telling me that she and Brad had spent a passionate night together, and she'd had the best sleep she'd had in months. She was so happy; I just couldn't shatter that. She told me her writing had improved and that she'd figured out a few key scenes and that she was sure the book would be a hit. After that, I told Brad we couldn't do it anymore. He seemed to agree."

"But it didn't last, did it?" I ask. She shakes her head. "How many more times were you with Mr. Murphy?"

"I don't know, a few times over the years, before I finally put an end to it last month. We argued about it. He said it was what was best for everyone. He was happy, I was happy and Steph was happy, why did I have to go and ruin it? And I told him I couldn't just keep lying to my friend like that. I told him I couldn't keep it from her; that she deserved to know she'd been betrayed by the two people she trusted most." Tears continue to stream down her face, but Erin doesn't stop. This is a lot more than I expected. I figured it had just been a one-time thing, and that it really hadn't had much of an impact on anyone.

"He told me if I ever said anything to Steph, I would be sorry. It broke my heart, because I *loved* him, and here he was threatening me. It made me finally realize I was nothing more than a tool for his enjoyment, something to warm him up for his wife." She raises her eyes to the ceiling. "I don't know how I could have been so stupid."

I lean forward. "Did you tell Steph?"

She shakes her head. "I keep trying, but I guess I'm too much of a coward. Every time I think I'm about to tell her, I just can't get the words out. Can you imagine what that will be like for her? It will destroy her. I don't know if I can ever do it." She sniffs loudly, the wet sound of mucus deep in her nose. "I'm sorry, do you have a tissue?"

"Yeah," Zara says, heading for the door. "Hang on a second." While she's gone, I keep my eyes glued on Erin Burnett. She alternates by lifting her head back to drain the snot and looking down at the ground in shame. Zara returns with a box of tissues, and hands her one.

"Erin," I say softly. "Can you tell us where you were yesterday from seven until eight-thirty?"

"At home," she replies without looking up. "With my son."

Damn. Three for three. She effectively has no alibi for any of the murders, and yet I cannot believe the woman sitting in front of me is capable of killing three people in cold blood. I don't see a woman who is so concerned for her friend's well-being who can just switch off her empathy like a light and head out into the night to stab someone through the eye socket. Or cut all their fingers off. It doesn't track.

"Let's take a small break," I say, standing. "Do you need anything else?" She shakes her head, but doesn't look up. "We'll give you a few minutes, okay?" Zara and I head back out into the hallway, where we meet Detmer.

"There is something wrong about all of this," I say.

"What do you mean?" Detmer asks. "She admitted to sleeping with the husband. You don't think she could go out and kill a couple of people if it solved her money problems? Especially if she knew that by telling her friend could very well mean she's cut off financially?"

"I just don't believe it," I say. "I don't think she's capable of it."

"Yeah, well I do," Detmer says, his voice harsh. "We've got evidence tying her to each of the crimes, and she's already admitted to being an impeccable liar. She just needs some time to stew."

"Is that your professional opinion, Agent?" I ask, my own voice hard.

"It is," he says, hitting right back. "And if you don't think you can perform this investigation, I suggest you remove yourself from the case. I'll be happy to take over. Maybe what she needs in there is a man to flirt with. She obviously likes doing it."

It takes everything I have not to slug him. But I get right up in his face. "I'm going to let that one go because I know that's your pain over losing Melissa talking. But you suggest to me that a woman's worth is defined by who she has slept with again, and I'll make sure you need a permanent appointment with your dentist." I storm past him, my nerves frayed.

"What's her problem?" I hear him ask Zara, who doesn't respond.

"Em, come on, let's get some air," Zara says, taking my arm and leading me to a pair of doors that open on a second-floor patio. There are a few metal chairs and a table out here, all of them showing wear from the elements.

"Never thought that guy was such an asshole," I say, gripping the railing so tight I feel like I could rip it right out of the joints.

"You weren't wrong," she says. "We finally got a suspect, and he wants her to be the one responsible for losing the woman he loved. He's being a dick because he doesn't want anything to disrupt that worldview."

"I just don't see it, do you?" I ask, shaking my head.

Zara leans over the railing beside me. "She's not showing any of the hallmarks. Doesn't mean she didn't do it."

I know she's just playing devil's advocate. This is why it's good to have more than one agent on cases like this, to help us keep our minds open and from getting too bogged down with one view or the other, like Agent Detmer in there. Zara helps balance me out and I do the same for her.

I turn around and lean my head back against the railing, looking up at the night sky. A cool breeze has blown in from the ocean, the last remnants of the storm having blown back out to sea. My gut tells me we're on the wrong track. That we need to examine the evidence again; there's something we're missing. "Let's give her some time," I say. "If she doesn't give us anything by the time tomorrow morning rolls around I want to get another warrant for her computer."

"You really think we'll find anything on there?" Zara asks.

I shake my head. "That's just the thing. I don't think there *is* anything on there. This isn't a woman who makes a living off defrauding people."

"You think that Helena Nicks saw someone else," Zara says.

I do. But I'm not willing to admit it yet. I just can't get over these damn dog hairs. Why are they the only evidence on the scenes? And how did Mrs. Nicks know her attacker was coming? With enough warning to hide her daughter?

I let out a frustrated breath. "Let's get her somewhere she can sleep for the night. And put in a request for the electronic warrant. We'll see what she says tomorrow."

"And if it's the same?" Zara asks.

I don't know what to tell her. But I do know that something stinks about all of this. We just need to find the source.

Chapter Twenty-Seven

"DON'T YOU GET IT? SHE'S *PLAYING* YOU," DETMER SAYS AS Zara and I head out of the building. We've remanded Erin Burnett to a temporary room with a bed where she's being watched, and a guard is posted on her door. We also made sure there was nothing in the room she could use to hurt herself in the event I'm wrong and she's looking for a quick way out.

"I don't like your tone," I call back to Detmer as he follows us out into the parking lot.

"And I don't like the fact that you have this case buttoned up and you're willing to rip it back open again! We got her, close the damn file!"

I spin on him. "Not until I'm sure. We're going to wait for the electronic warrant to come in and do another search of her apartment. I'm not willing to condemn a woman to life in prison because of some errant canine hairs."

He shakes his head. "You're wasting resources. This is why people don't trust the government. Because we can't get anything done."

"Hey," Zara says. "Cool it. Why don't you go home and

take a Xanax or something. You're letting your personal feel-ings interfere with this case."

Detmer just shakes his head and returns back to the build-ing. I'm sure he'll find his cot in there somewhere and spend yet another night sleeping in the back rooms. I don't even know if he's been home yet since we arrived. It seems like the man is more of a workaholic than I am. But I'm still in charge of this case, and I'm not about to let him persuade me we have a guilty person in custody when that's far from certain.

"Guy needs a cold shower," Zara says as we slip into the car.

"His emotions are just high," I say. "He's allowed this to become personal, which is why they brought us up here to begin with. Can you imagine if he was the one in there inter-rogating Burnett? He'd have her confessing to killing Kennedy before it was all over."

"Nightcap?" Zara asks as I pull out of the parking lot, headed for our hotel.

"Not for me. I want to get a good night's sleep so I can take a look at this with a clear head in the morning. If Detmer hasn't calmed down by then, I may have to chain him to his desk until the case is closed."

"I'm sure *that* will go over well with the rest of the office."

She's right. The last thing I want to do is create a rift between us and the people we need to help us with the case. If Erin isn't the killer, it means we still have a perpetrator out there, and I'm going to need everyone's help to make sure we get them before they can kill anyone else.

By the time we reach the hotel it's almost ten and I trudge up the stairs to our room, stifling a series of yawns. Zara is right behind me, though I thought she might stick by the bar for a quick drink.

As I'm removing my shoulder holster, my phone buzzes twice, indicating a new email. I'm resigned to leave it until the morning, but I know I'll obsess over it for ten minutes if I don't just read it and get it over with. Maybe it's the approval for the electronic warrant, though that would be fast.

The subject line of the email reads *URGENT*, and as best I can tell, the sender is a long string of numbers and letters I don't recognize. More than likely spam. Still…working for the FBI I have a strong spam filter on my mailbox, so things don't often squeak through. Not to mention there are always a few CI's in the field who sometimes try to contact me using clandestine means. It's best if I read it just to make sure.

I open the email and my eyes scan the text, though I feel my heartrate rise in time with each progressive word, not quite believing what I'm seeing. I have to read it again to make sure, then a third time.

"Em? What's wrong? You're as pale as a sheet." I'm having trouble breathing. "Here," Zara says, and her hands gently guide me down to the settee in front of one of the beds. My legs go out as soon as my butt hits it. She takes the phone from my limp hand, but I barely feel it.

"Agent Emily Slate," she reads. "I am contacting you not out of desire but instead necessity. You have been deceived and betrayed. Your husband was not the man you thought he was. I have attached records showing his job at Covington College was a cover, and that neither he, nor his boss actually worked there. Furthermore, he lied to you about his true profession. You can see from the given documents that he never received a degree from Georgetown University, nor did he have a license to practice psychology in either Washington D.C., Virginia or Maryland."

Zara looks over at me, but I feel like there is a weight on my chest and I can't get a full breath.

"I am sending you this information because your actions have given me no choice. Not only do you insist on continuing your investigation into your husband's death, you have now involved multiple parties in your conspiracy.

"If it isn't clear by now, I have the power to end you. Your life was spared because I believed you were not a risk. End your investigation and move on. Do not make me re-evaluate my position." She pauses. "No signature, obviously."

I hear her tapping on my phone, looking at the attached documents while I do my best to catch my breath. I'm not normally intimidated by cryptic emails with no signature or idea where they came from, but this is different. Whoever sent this knows a lot more about Matt than they should. Maybe they know a lot more about Matt than I ever did.

"You don't buy this, do you?" Zara asks.

I look up. "What?"

"This. It's obviously bullshit."

"Did you read those documents?" I ask. "No license. No indication he ever even attended Georgetown, much less graduated."

"Documents can be forged," she says, handing my phone back to me. "Someone is screwing with you."

"Who?" I ask. "Who has the resources to break the FBI firewall *and* knew about my husband's record?"

"Didn't you meet with Matt's boss a few weeks after he died?" she asks.

I nod. "When I was on leave. I wanted to thank him for coming to the funeral. We had lunch at some café in the city, I can't remember which one."

"Look, this is easy enough to clear up," she says, pulling out her own phone. "And because I know you're not going to be able to sleep until it's resolved, we're going to take care of it right now." She dials a number and puts the phone to her ear. "University directory, please." She covers the receiver with her hand. "What's his boss's name?"

"Brian Garrett," I say.

"Garrett, Brian," she says into the phone. There's a small beep indicating there's no match. "Garrett, B." The beep again. "Operator." She taps her foot in time to the music on the other end. "Hi, yes, I'm trying to find Professor Brian Garrett."

I can hear the young-sounding voice on the other end. Probably a student keeping an eye on the phones for the evening. "Sorry, ma'am, we don't have anyone by that name on staff."

"What about from a few months ago? Would have been back in January."

"Nope. I don't see any record of a Garrett in our directory, past or present."

"What about Matthew Hunter?" she asks. It's been a while since I've heard anyone use Matt's name other than me. It sends a wave of sadness through me.

"I have a Miranda Hunter, but no Matthew," she says.

"Can you give me Miranda Hunter's information?" Zara asks.

"I'm sorry, Professor Hunter has been retired for almost fifteen years. I'm not even sure she's still alive," the student says.

I shake my head. "All right, thank you," Zara says, hanging up. "This is just a mistake, Em. Don't worry, we'll get it figured out."

I lean forward, covering my mouth with my hands and resting my elbows on my knees. "I just don't know what to do with all of this." Matt and I kept very different professional lives. My work schedule was always all over the place, while he was always out the door at the same time and home at the same time. But our professional paths never crossed. Even when I was close to Georgetown it wasn't like I could take time off from a case to meet him for lunch. He was always just so nonchalant about things; I never had any reason to question it. But could it all have been a ruse?

Zara bends down. "Look, we'll perform a trace on the email, figure out where it came from. And I'll get the EC lab back home to look at the documents they sent over, confirm they're fake. Someone is screwing with you; I don't know why, but we're not going to let them get away with it. And the last thing we're going to do is quit looking into Matt's death."

"What if it's true?" I ask. "What if his job was a lie? He never let me visit him at work—not that I ever had time anyway. And I only met his boss a few times: at our wedding and his funeral. And he came to that Christmas party that one year, remember? What if…somehow, it all was fake?"

She shakes her head. "You knew Matt. He wouldn't have kept this from you. Plus, the FBI does a thorough background check on all spouses of agents. You think they really would have missed something this big?"

I can't deny that. There's no way the FBI would have accepted my application if Matt hadn't been who he said he was. So then why try to convince me otherwise? What is so important about his death that someone doesn't want me looking into it? "Do you think this is from *her*?" I ask.

"The woman?" Zara furrows her brow. "Possibly. Looking to throw you off the tracks by supplying you with a bunch of false information. She knows you're determined, maybe she's trying to do whatever she can to convince you to drop it."

"I guess you're right," I say, relenting. I can't believe the man I fell in love with and married could have deceived me for that long; it's more than ludicrous when I really think about it. Why was I so affected? I try brushing it off and getting ready for bed, but the thoughts linger in my brain, as if they're calling out to be examined and re-examined. I start thinking back to every interaction I had with Matt, every happy memory. Could it all have been a ruse? To what end?

Then I have to remind myself what I'm doing isn't healthy, and that I can't let a random email throw me so far off my beliefs about my husband.

But as I lay my head down on the pillow, I can't help think

that the email wouldn't have struck me so hard if somewhere deep down I didn't know there was a kernel of truth to it.

What else have I been wrong about?

Chapter Twenty-Eight

THE FOLLOWING MORNING I'M UP AND READY BEFORE THE SUN has even broken the horizon. Sleep came in short bouts, punctuated by long periods where I just stared into the dark, thinking about my past and everything it envelops. There are moments when I feel like I can just let it all go, and then when my mind is trying to relax, it all comes screaming back at me at once, forcing me to re-examine everything I've ever known.

"You look like hell," Zara says, sitting up and rubbing her eyes.

Needless to say, I feel like it.

"First thing," she says, throwing the covers off. "Send that email to HQ. Get them to back trace it."

"And when they hit a wall?" I ask.

"Just get it out there first," she says. "We'll worry about that bridge when we cross it." I fumble with my phone, sending the email and attachments to our electronic communications investigative wing. They should be able to get at least some basic information off the email, maybe even the geocoordinates of where it was sent from. That would be a start.

"You need to eat something," Zara says. "Otherwise you're going to collapse."

I manage a meager breakfast at the hotel's free breakfast bar. It all tastes the same going down. I don't know how I'm supposed to interrogate Erin Burnett again this morning. My mind feels like someone has run it through the agitator on the washing machine. The worst part about all this is if it is true, and Matt was really deceiving me all those years, what does that say about me as an investigator? I'm supposed to be able to tell when a person is lying at any given moment, and I couldn't tell my husband was lying straight to my face for four years? How can I trust that any judgement call I've ever made was accurate? I feel like everything is closing in on me and there is no relief in sight.

"Okay, okay," Zara says as she's finishing her own breakfast. Groups of tourists or families surround us, their conversations centered on what they're going to do for the day or who they're going to see. Part of my brain tells me that is normal, but another, stranger part tries to analyze the conversations, listen for anything deceptive. Is everyone lying all the time? Or was I just too stupid to see it?

Zara takes me by the arm and leads me to the small alcove where the bookshelf sits, along with Ruby Blackthorne's books. It's empty this morning as everyone is preoccupied with breakfast.

"What is going on?" Zara whispers. "You look like you're either about to kill everyone in here or break into a thousand pieces."

"I don't know what I'm doing," I say. "I don't even know what's happening right now."

"Listen to me," she says. "You need to focus on what you can control. And in this moment, you can control your own emotions. You can't control that email, or its contents. But you can control how you react to it. Are you going to let one email upend your entire life? You are a respected special agent with the FBI. You wouldn't be in that position if you didn't know what you were doing. If you didn't have the skill to pull it off. Do you understand?"

She's right. I need to pull myself together. I still have a job to do. There's no need to freak out over an email that may or may not be genuine, not until I'm sure. If I wasn't capable, I wouldn't still be here. And as much as Janice likes to ride my ass, I know she does it because she knows I can take it; because I'll use that pressure to focus and do the job correctly.

I can't forget there is a case I need to solve. I close my eyes, take a deep breath, and push the email and everything with it into the back of my mind somewhere. I'm not about to let an innocent woman take the rap for something she didn't do. And right now, I'm the only one who can stop it.

I open my eyes. "I need you to promise me something."

"Anything," she replies.

"As soon as you hear something from intelligence, you'll let me know. No matter if it's good or bad. I can handle it."

She takes a long look into my eyes. "Okay."

"Okay," I repeat. "Then let's go get this warrant. We're still on the clock."

When we get back to the Bureau, I'm surprised to find that Erin is not in the room where we left her with her guard. I look around for Detmer, but don't see him either. Maybe he finally took a break and went home for once.

"Hey Williamson," I call out, seeing the large man lumbering down the hall. "Where's our suspect? She's not in the holding room."

He tilts his head at me. "Detmer said you ordered her back into the interrogation room. Said you gave him permission to debrief her."

Shit. I take off running for the interrogation room, Zara close on my heels. "Get in the observation side!" I tell her as I reach the door to the room itself. The same guard that was outside her door last night is posted outside the interrogation room. He blocks my way as I try to go for the handle.

"Get out of my way, Henry," I say, warning in my voice.

"Sorry, Agent Slate. Agent Detmer ordered that he not be disturbed while he's interrogating the suspect."

"Move. Or be moved," I growl.

His eyes go wide and for a second, I think he's going to call me on it, which will be fine with me. I'm in need of some practice. I've been neglecting my training lately; this would be a good warm up. Finally, he steps aside and I swing the door open.

Detmer is perched like a vulture, standing over a sobbing Erin Burnett, as he berates her over and over about the details of Agent Green's death. He doesn't even look up when I come in, he's practically spitting on her he's so exuberant in his words.

I storm in the room, grab him by the collar and yank him back so hard he flies off his feet and hits the ground. He rounds on me, so wound up that he actually tries kicking at my shins, which I manage to sidestep.

"What the hell do you think you're doing?" Detmer yells, getting back up.

"Saving your job," I say, grabbing his arm and yanking him toward the door.

"I'm in the middle of an interrogation here!"

"Your interrogation is over," I say. "Unless you want all our work going down the drain because you're badgering the suspect." I can still hear Erin's sobs as she tries to recover from the mental assault.

"Get your hands off me," he says, pushing away and breaking my grip. "This woman killed Melissa and I'm going to get a confession if I have to beat it out of her."

I turn to the window, looking straight at where the camera is. "Did you get that? All of it?" I can't see any kind of response, but I know Zara is in there making sure none of this can be swept under the rug.

"Agent Detmer, I'm going to say this once and only once. Leave this room right now, and go home. You're on leave until I can speak to your superior."

"You can't do that," he says, raging.

Steel forms in my gut. "I'm the lead on this investigation and you've purposely interrogated my suspect without my approval or knowledge. You'll be amazed at what I can do."

He grumbles and shoots one look back at Erin before finally leaving. I return to her as she does her best to wipe away the tears. "Are you alright?"

She nods. "Just tired. He's had me in here for hours."

"I didn't sanction that," I say. "Sit tight. I'll be right back." Back out in the hallway, I direct Henry to get Erin some water and something to eat. I head over to the observation room. Inside, Zara and the tech are going back over the recordings. "What the hell was that?"

The tech shakes his head. "He said he had clearance; I just run the machines."

"Looks like he's been in there for at least two hours with her," Zara says. "It starts out civil enough, but only devolves as Erin refuses to give him any answers."

"Great," I say. "Doesn't he realize he's just put this whole thing in jeopardy? All her lawyer would have to do is claim we put her under undue duress trying to coax a confession out of her. I'm surprised she hasn't called for one yet."

"She was too scared," the tech says. "He's barely given her a chance to answer, and when she does, it's always the wrong one. If she did it, her mental fortitude is beyond anything I've ever witnessed."

"What do you think?" I ask Zara.

"I think he's just looking for a scapegoat, and Erin happens to be a convenient target," she says. That's my assessment too.

There's still that little voice in the back of my head questioning whether I have any right to be here at all, but I ignore it, instead focusing on the matter at hand. We've got a suspect who doesn't fit the mold, and isn't showing any of the signs of a serial killer. And yet we have three bodies which lead us directly to her. We need to go back over everything, re-examine it all from the ground up.

I point to the tech. "Make sure all of that is on a backup. I don't want to come back and find the footage has 'mysteriously' disappeared. Understand?"

He nods. "Yes, ma'am."

Zara and I head back out to the bullpen. I spot Williamson in a small huddle with a few of the other agents. "Did that warrant come through yet?"

He turns to me. "Suspending Detmer? You sure think a lot of yourself, don't you?"

"He gave me no choice," I fire back. "His actions may have compromised this investigation. And I don't see any of you rushing to uphold the rules and regulations that we live by. This is the entire reason we're here, because all of you are letting your emotions get in the way of your jobs. Now. Did that warrant come through or not?"

Williamson sighs, then grabs a folder from his desk. The front is marked from the D.A.'s office. "Came through this morning."

I take it, opening the folder and giving it a once-over. It's enough. "I want a crime scene team to meet us at Burnett's apartment."

"Crime scene, why?" he asks.

"I believe someone is trying to frame that woman in there," I say. "And they may have broken into her home to do it. We're going over the whole thing, and bagging anything that might be evidence. Besides, if she did do it, it won't hurt to have more than just circumstantial evidence."

"I'll call it in," he says.

"Good. Thank you." I motion to the door and Zara
follows me out.

"That didn't sound like a woman doubting herself," she
says once we're back outside.

"Couldn't afford to look weak in front of them," I reply.
"All these old boys respect is strength, and you can't show
them an ounce of hesitation, otherwise they'll think you're
incompetent." When we reach the car, I look over the roof to
her. "I can't afford to have any self-doubt in front of them. But
it's raging. I already made one mistake by arresting Burnett in
the first place. I can't afford to make another."

"You won't," Zara says. "Because you're a badass."

I flash her a fake smile. Inside I don't feel like a badass. I
feel like a woman teetering on the edge of doubt.

If I'm wrong about this, I don't know how I'll ever be able
to trust myself to work another case again.

Chapter Twenty-Nine

WHEN WE ARRIVE BACK AT ERIN BURNETT'S APARTMENT, I'M surprised to see the forensics team is already on site and is suiting up.

"You guys sure got here fast," I tell them, getting out of the car.

"We just finished at another site," one of them says. "Williamson called us while we were on our way back. Figured we could squeeze it in."

"I appreciate your promptness." I grab a pair of gloves and boots for my shoes and Zara does the same. I let them take the lead and wait for them to get set up inside the apartment before Zara and I enter.

"Anything special we should be on the lookout for?" one of them asks.

"No, I want it all," I say. "I know it's a wide net, but we need to figure out the truth about what's going on here, instead of just following the breadcrumbs that are laid out for us."

"No dog," Zara says, looking around.

That makes sense. "I guess Steph picked her up when she

took Erin's son. It wasn't like she could have left the dog here to fend for herself."

"I'll start upstairs. Again." Zara heads up while I stay on the main level, my primary interest on Erin's computer. One of the techs is booting it up as I walk into the makeshift office.

"Are you cloning the hard drive?" I ask.

He nods. "We'll take the whole unit anyway. But I always get a copy of everything before we take it all apart. In the event something is damaged in transit." He pulls out a large hard drive and connects it to Erin's computer. "Never know how much data we'll need to copy. This could take a few hours."

"That's not a problem," I tell him. Once he's finished setting up the transfer, he leaves the office to join his colleague as they go through everything else in the apartment. I take a seat at Erin's desk, watching the progress bar inch by. I doubt I'll find anything with a quick search and my limited skills, but I start poking around anyway. Maybe she was stupid enough to leave enough of a clue that it won't be that hard to find the information about Eva Nelson and N3, LLC.

Thirty minutes later I give up, having been through most of the directories I know how to access. The progress bar is barely at twenty percent, though so far it hasn't been the gold mine I'd hoped. I know my skills are limited in this regard, but I had at least hoped to find something. The fact that there's no mention of any of this anywhere on her computer only lends itself to my theory Erin isn't the real perpetrator here. I even went back and checked her browser history, finding nothing of interest.

A few minutes later Zara comes into the office. "How's it going?" she asks.

"I should have let you take a crack at this thing rather than wasting my time," I say, standing.

She shrugs. "I'd be happy to teach you. You have to learn eventually."

I wave her off. "Nah, it's not my field of interest." I crouch down and begin opening drawers on the desk, going through the documents inside. While her desk is clean, the inside of her drawers is not. Everything is haphazardly thrown about, all jumbled up. Papers litter the inside of the cabinets. "Here," I say, pulling out a large stack. "Help me go through these." I split the stack in two and hand one to Zara while I sit on the ground and begin going through my own. It's mostly bills, statements, or catalogs.

"It's junk," Zara says.

I agree and toss my stack to the side. This is what tends to be infuriating about this job. It can be so tedious sometimes. I reach back into the drawer and pull out a couple more stacks of documents, and a few large sealed envelopes. The envelopes are large and heavy, like they have thick stacks of paper in them. I set the documents aside and flip over the top envelope. It's marked with Erin's address, from Steph.

"What's that?" Zara asks.

I turn it back over to find the envelope is sealed, like it's never been opened. "I'm not sure," I say. "Get your phone out. I want to document opening this."

She nods and starts recording as I fish a letter opener from the desk and slide it along the top of the envelope, making sure the camera can see what I'm doing. I reach inside and remove a large stack of papers, bound with one of those big metal clips. The front page of the stack is emblazoned with the words *Flame's Ember by Ruby Blackthorne.*

"It think it's Steph's first book," I say.

"Why is it in a sealed envelope?" Zara asks.

I shake my head. "No idea." I flip the first couple of pages, finding a date listed on page two. "Looks like it might be a first draft. It's dated two years before the book came out." I sit back and think for a moment. I can understand why Steph would send Erin her first draft, but why didn't Erin ever open it?

"It's probably worth something now," Zara says. "Maybe she was saving it as a souvenir to sell."

I start flipping through the pages. Everything is printed on eight and a half by eleven paper, double-spaced, like it came right from a word processor. Like Steph printed it out herself. "I suppose that's a possibility." But something doesn't feel right. I would think if she was keeping it for its value, Steph would have at least signed it for her. I keep flipping through the pages, scanning the words. But when I get close to the end, something catches my eye and I have to go back.

"Wait a second," I say as my eyes scan the page. That pit in my stomach is back. I stand and place the manuscript on the desk. "Is there a copy of the published version anywhere?"

"I think I saw one in the other room." Zara disappears for a moment then returns with the hardback version of the book. I open the front cover to find a signature in this one.

"To my best friend," I read. "Here's to the dream for both of us. Love, Steph."

"What's going on?" Zara asks.

I flip open the printed volume of *Flame's Ember*, fanning the pages until I get to the climax. "Look at this," I say, pointing to the passages that describe the murder in the book. The murder that someone took as their inspiration to kill Agent Green.

Zara scans the words. "Yeah, so?"

"Now look at this one," I say, pointing to the typewritten manuscript. I show Zara roughly the same passages as they appear in the book. But there is one big difference.

"Wait a second," Zara says. "The original manuscript describes the victim as an FBI agent. That's not in the printed version."

I nod. "Steph must have made the victim an FBI agent in the original manuscript, then changed it before it reached the final draft. Changes like that happen all the time, as books go through edits, I'm sure. But it tells us something important."

"The killer has seen the original manuscript," Zara says. "Either that, or they were just extremely unlucky."

"I'm betting on the former," I say.

"So what does this mean?" Zara asks. "Did Erin really do it?"

I glance at the other envelopes. There are two more, both addressed to Erin from Steph. I'm willing to bet they both contain similar manuscripts, either additional versions of this book, or first drafts of other books. "I don't think so. I'm not sure Erin even knew that detail," I say. "The envelope was sealed."

"Steph could have told her," Zara suggests.

I nod. "Yes, she could have. Erin might not have known about the FBI detail. But Stephanie definitely did." I flip the empty envelope over. It has a postmark from over two years ago. "The question is why she would mail it to Erin in the first place."

"I've got it," Zara says, looking up from her phone. "This site says that if you're an amateur author, one of the easiest ways to solidify the copyright to your work is to mail yourself a sealed copy of your manuscript, in the event you'd ever need to prove the original date of creation."

"But instead of mailing it to herself," I say. "Steph mailed it to her best friend for safekeeping." We lock our gazes. "We need to get eyes on Stephanie Murphy, right now."

Chapter Thirty

"I DON'T GET IT," ZARA CALLS OUT AS THE WIND WHIPS HER hair around her. "Why would Murphy want to frame her best friend? What's the motive?"

I push harder on the accelerator as we drive out to the Murphy house on Marnmouth Island. "I'm not sure," I reply. "But we have to consider the possibility that she set all of this up. She definitely knew about the murder victim being an FBI agent, seeing as she wrote it."

"But why go after Green now?" Zara asks. "Wouldn't that just bring more heat down on her? If she was re-creating the murder scenes from her own book—creepy, by the way—then why revert to the original draft?"

"I don't know," I say. "I can't even figure out why she's going to all this trouble in the first place. But if she has, she's clearly got an axe to grind."

I can't believe I didn't see this before. What better way to throw suspicion off yourself, than to make yourself your own target? Or at least make it look like you're the target. If Steph has been behind all of this all along, it would explain how the killer had such detailed knowledge about the murders and how they were able to match them up to what happened in the books so precisely.

But why go to all of this trouble? As best I can tell, Steph has been little more than annoyed by Erin's presence in her life. It isn't as if she loathes her, so why all the theatrics? Why all the pretense just to make us think that Erin was the killer? The only way we're going to find out is if we confront her. I wish I could call for some backup, but given Williamson's coldness toward me after what happened to Detmer, I don't know that I could fully trust them. And I'm not about to go into a dangerous situation with people I can't trust. For now, it will have to be the two of us. At least until I can substantiate my theory.

We give the guard a wave as we pull up and he opens the gate for us, allowing us to pass through without a word. Steph kept talking about needing extra security—and yet, if she is behind all of this, she was never in any danger. Maybe that's why despite her talk, nothing has really changed.

The road winds down past the giant houses on the island, until we come to the Murphy home. None of the cars are outside on display like normal. I drive past the house, not slowing. My plan is to keep an eye on Murphy, and see how she acts now that Erin is out of the way. If this really has been about framing Erin, she's done with the killing. No more people could die while Erin was in custody, otherwise like Adrijus, Erin would be exculpated. Tactically, though, this is dangerous. I don't know what Stephanie Murphy is capable of. But my guess is she has an accomplice, given the brutality of some of the murders. I just don't believe she has the kind of strength needed to pull something like this off.

"Over there," Zara says, and I pull off to the side of the road beside some dense bushes.

"See anything as we drove past?" I ask.

She shakes her head. "Doesn't look like anyone is home."

"Going through the house without a warrant is off the

table," I say. "With so many eyes on this, we can't pull a
Douglas Krauss and hope we get lucky once we're inside."

"Then how do we go about proving she had anything to
do with this?" Zara asks. "She has alibis for at least two of the
murders. We never asked about the third, but she's obviously
smart. She wouldn't leave herself open like that."

"First we need to find her," I say. "See how she's acting
now. She said she normally writes in the mornings, but maybe
now that Erin is in custody her schedule has changed." I pull
out of the bushes and do a U-turn, heading back past the
house. Her security cameras might pick us up on the way past,
but hopefully she won't recognize the car. When we get back
to the guard station, I bring the car to a full stop. "Good
morning, Gus."

The man inside looks up with a smile. "Mornin'," he says.
"Didn't realize I introduced myself."

"You didn't," I say. "Stephanie Murphy was kind enough
to tell us how much she appreciated your efforts."

He nods. "There's been a gate guard at this post for the
past ninety years, ever since horses were more common than
cars in these parts. Residents take pride in the heritage and
history here."

"I bet they do," I say. "Did you see Mrs. Murphy leave this
morning?"

"Sure," he says. "That woman is like a machine, runs one
of the tightest schedules I've ever seen."

"Is that so?" I ask. "You don't know where she would be,
do you? We're just trying to sort out this small matter and I
can't do it without her help."

"Normally she heads down to the Long Gone Cat on
Saturdays for brunch. Friend of hers works down there. Do
you know it?"

I nod. "Sure do. Thanks, Gus."

"Be safe out there, and don't be a stranger," he says, giving us a little wave. He opens the gate again and we drive back off, headed for Richney.

"Do you really think she's there?" Zara asks. "Given everything that's happened?"

I have my doubts as well, but save putting out an APB for her vehicle, I don't know where else to start. We also need to find Brad Murphy. If anyone was assisting Steph with this, it was him. Now that I think about it, this could have all been his idea, if he wasn't so aloof. He said he'd never read any of Steph's books, but that could have been a lie. Maybe we'll get lucky and find them there together.

"Whoa there Furiosa, ease off the pedals," Zara says. I look down and realize that I'm pushing seventy in a forty-five.

"Sorry," I say, dropping the speed. "I'm just anxious about this. This whole thing has me questioning everything. Not seeing the threat from Steph in the beginning, working too hard to go after Erin. And don't even get me started on that email."

"I understand," she says. "But getting us killed on the way there isn't going to make any of that easier."

She's right. I've been taking this too personally and it's clouded my mind, making me call everything I know into question. Maybe if I hadn't found those cameras in my house I wouldn't have been so distracted when we got here. And maybe I would have seen right through Steph in the beginning. But none of that matters now. What matters now is that we find her and figure out how to connect her to the murders. There is likely an innocent woman sitting at the Bureau right now.

I shake my head. None of this makes sense. Steph is a successful, smart, capable woman who is living the dream, writing books and living life to the fullest. Why would she go after a woman she says is the best friend she has in the world? As it has been for this entire case, something isn't adding up.

When we finally get to Richney, I begin canvasing the small town slowly, looking for Steph's car in any of the parking lots. Finally, I spot it behind one of the buildings in an out-of-the-way spot, tucked into a small corner. I have to remember, Murphy is something of a local celebrity. People probably know who she is and what she looks like, even if she does use a pen name. Which makes a place like the Long Gone Cat perfect for her to visit, because it's so small and out of the way itself.

"It looks like there's a little alleyway," I say, pointing to her vehicle. "Leads out to the storefronts. She probably uses that to get in and out without being spotted by many people."

"So what's the plan?" Zara asks. "Just stroll up and ask her if she murdered three people?"

I shoot her a side glance. "I just want to get eyes on her first. See if she's acting out of the ordinary. Then I want to pull her cell phone records. They might be able to tell us if she's been anywhere unusual in the past few days."

"Unusual?"

"Like scoping out Agent Green's apartment, or the Nicks' house. Or even if she was following me to where Mrs. Nicks and her daughter were staying. It won't be an exact ping, but it might tell us something."

"And how are we supposed to requisition those with everyone in the local office actively wishing you were dead?" She gives me a wide grin.

"Very funny. Why don't you call one of your friends down in intelligence? You know, all those connections you're always talking about."

Zara pulls out her phone. "Always saving your ass, Slate, I swear," but she says it with a smile. While she's getting one of her contacts to pull Murphy's phone records, I find a place to park. The Long Gone Cat is too small for us to enter unnoticed, but I'd still like to get eyes on Murphy. We can probably set ourselves up across the street, if she's not situated too far back into the café, seeing as it has large windows out front.

"They're working on them," Zara says, hanging up. "Happy?"

"Very. Ready for some good old-fashioned spying?"

She wiggles her eyebrows at me. "I thought you'd never ask."

Chapter Thirty-One

THE STREET THAT RUNS THROUGH THE MIDDLE OF RICHNEY IS barely two lanes wide. Bike paths have been integrated on both sides, which cuts down on the amount of room vehicles have to drive, and there are plenty of crosswalks and wide sidewalks that run the length of the downtown area. It's not an area built for commercial traffic. Not even one of those large pickups with the double wheels could make it through here.

But it's good for us, because as I stand across the street next to a wall while I pretend to look at my phone, I have an almost perfect view of the inside of the café. Zara is about thirty feet away, on the other side of the street, but seeing as the street curves to the right, she has a different, but still visible angle into the café. Both of us have a clear view of Stephanie Murphy, who is sitting alone, drinking a cup of coffee, seeming not to have a care in the world. She keeps taking long inhales through her nose, then exhaling and giving herself a satisfied smile as she does. She has no laptop, no phone out, nothing but her and the cup in front of her. It's like everything else has just melted away from her world.

Not the type of behavior I would have suspected from

someone whose best friend was in custody. From the way Erin described it, Steph should have been the first person down at the station, arguing for Erin's release. Instead, she's here, enjoying her Saturday morning while shoppers, joggers and dog-walkers stroll on by past her.

She's just drinking coffee, Zara texts me. Though the word coffee is replaced by an emoji.

Without a care in the world, I reply. *She's too relaxed.*

U sure ur seeing what u think ur seeing?

On the surface, I have some doubts. But when I look deep inside, this *feels* right. I don't believe Erin could have masterminded this; she just doesn't have the wherewithal. Steph, on the other hand, has the resources, the time and the mindset to set something like this up. I just need to figure out why.

Got a 2nd person, Zara texts.

I look up and see a bald man in a button-down enter the café. He wanders around the back for a moment before finally coming to sit down on the other side of Murphy. She barely glances up as he does—apparently she was expecting him.

Got an ID?

Couldn't get a picture from here, she replies. *No clue.*

Steph makes a motion with one hand, and one of the servers brings a second cup of coffee for the other man. He's a far cry from her husband. This man holds himself like someone who is not to be messed with. He's rigid, and showing little to no emotion on his face, even as Steph begins talking. From where I'm standing, it looks like he has a tattoo that begins just below the base of his skull, but it disappears below his collar. His hands, likewise, are covered in tattoos. There's a spiderweb on the left one, which is the one most visible to me from this angle.

Looks like a bouncer, I text. I could see someone like this standing outside a nightclub, intimidating all the entrants. Even with the long sleeve shirt, I can see bulging muscles trying to break through. *It's him.*

What?

They're in on it together. He's the muscle while she's the brains.

A second later my phone rings. "Yeah?"

"Em, are you sure?" Zara asks. "We don't even know who this guy is."

"Why would she be meeting with someone like this on a Saturday morning, in a place where few people will see them?" I ask. "This is not a man who runs in the same circles that she does."

"That's a lot of assumptions," she replies.

"You were the one who told me to go with my gut," I say. This is what feels right to me, despite the circumstances. But I'm not reckless enough to destroy the entire investigation because I'm getting too far ahead of myself. If the evidence doesn't bear this out, then I will accept that. For now, I need to follow this train of thought. It might just lead me right where we need to go. "It's just a theory right now. We need to find out who this man is, and if he has a record. That will go a long way to supporting the theory."

"And in the meantime?" she asks. "Erin is still in custody."

"Then we'll just have to work fast."

Across the street, I see Steph slide something across the table, but it's too flat to tell what or how large it is. Before I can get a good look, the man has stuffed it in his back pocket."

"Looks like they're about done," Zara says.

"Yep. When they leave, you stick to him, I'll stay with her. Reconnaissance only. No engagement." Whatever she gave him could be the exact proof we're looking for.

"Um, excuse me," she says. "Aren't you the one who's a black belt in like ten different things? And you want to stick me on the burly guy who looks like he can break a telephone pole in half?"

I chuckle. "Fine. I'll watch the big guy, you tail Murphy. I'll stay on him as long as I can without a car."

"She's getting up," I say. "Make yourself scarce." I end the call and get ready to head down the street half a block, so Murphy won't see me when she leaves. As soon as I begin walking, however, my phone buzzes in my pocket. Thinking it's Zara, I answer without looking as I need to get out of the way before it's too late.

"Z, look, I said I'd—"

"Agent Slate," a sultry female voice says. A voice I've never heard before. "I see you received my email."

I stop dead in my tracks. "You," I say. "What do you want?"

"I've tried being nice," she replies. "And I've tried to give you fair warning. This is the last chance you'll get. The information I sent you was genuine; stop trying to find me. And tell your boss to give up. I'm never coming back for those cameras now that you know about them." She hangs up before I can get in another word.

"Wha—" I begin and open my call log to try and redial the number, but it's coming up as unavailable. I try calling back anyway, but there's no connection.

"Agent Slate?"

I turn and look up, Stephanie Murphy is looking straight at me, her hand gripping her purse tight. The man she was meeting is right behind her, and upon hearing the words come from her mouth, he grabs her in a headlock and pulls her back, producing a gun from his waistband and pointing it at her head.

Stephanie Murphy screams, while what few people on the sidewalk yell out, turning and running away from the man with the gun.

"What is this?" he hisses. "Some kind of double-cross? That why you brought me to this shit little town? Catch me off guard?"

"Whoa there," I say, holding both of my hands out in front of me, my phone still in one of them. "Just calm—"

"Shut it or her brains become window dressin'," the man says.

Stephanie is clawing at his arm, trying to get him to release her. "Xavier, this wasn't me, I didn't call them!"

The man—Xavier—turns to his right as Zara gets into position behind one of the benches along the road, her weapon drawn and trained on him.

"Drop it!" she yells.

He moves his arm so that Stephanie blocks more of his body and positions his head right behind hers. He's not a large man, but he's *dense*. "That ain't how this is gonna work," he calls back. "I ain't goin' down for this. It was all *her* idea."

"You son of a bitch," Stephanie yells, and tries kicking his shins from behind with no luck. Xavier increases the pressure on her neck, and I can see her face beginning to purple. Much longer and she'll pass out.

"Just tell us what you want," I call out, my hands still up. "You can't hold her like that forever."

"No shit," he calls back. "I want a car, and free travel past the border. I'll drop her off on the Canadian side when I'm sure I'm not bein' followed. I see any cops, I kill both of us."

That's obviously not going to happen. But I need to figure out how much this guy knows. I might be able to stall him, though I'm not sure Murphy would survive long enough. "You said it was all her idea, what did you mean?" I ask.

"You know what I'm talkin' about," he calls back. "She said it would be clean. That there'd be no heat. But obviously she *lied*. It was nothin' but a trap. Well I'm tellin' you, she came to *me*. Wasn't my idea to kill those people. She needed some muscle. Think I'm gonna say no to half a mil? No way, brother. And I sure as hell ain't goin' to no gas chamber or whatever it is they've got these days cause someone else told me to get my hands dirty." He changes position just a little so that he can see me a little better. "I'm just the tool lady. She's the operator."

There it is: proof positive that Stephanie was behind all of this. But now I need to get both of them out of this alive. I'm going to have a much harder time building a case against her if Zara blows this guy's head off, and I can't let him choke out Stephanie. He could inadvertently cause brain damage and I need her to be cognizant enough to admit to the charges. Or take the stand. Whichever she prefers.

"Okay," I say back. "Let me call for that vehicle for you, okay?" I ask, motioning to the phone in my hand. My impression is this guy might be deadly, but he's not very bright. He has to know there's no way he'll get very far even if he does get a car, which isn't happening. I'm not about to put him in a position where he can kill them both by just slamming into a wall if he so desires.

"I want a Ford F-150," he says back. "Blue, with good tires."

"With good tires," I repeat back, "Got it."

I raise the phone to my ear and he presses the gun harder to Stephanie's head. "Don't think about whatever you're thinkin' about," he says. "I want to hear you make the call. Come over here and put it on speaker."

Not as stupid as I'd hoped. Still, he can't really expect he'll get out of this. One of the locals has to have called the town authorities by now. But they could end up adding kindling to an already out-of-control fire. If local cops show up and start shooting, I'm going to lose everyone.

I make my way over to him, still keeping my distance. "There's good," he says, once I'm on the sidewalk on their side. "Put it on speaker. Let me hear the other side."

I put the phone on speaker and dial through to the Woodhurst office. "Williamson," I say when I get the operator. "Tell him it's Slate."

"Slate, huh?" the guy says as we wait. "I like that name."

I want to roll my eyes in disgust. But I can't afford to piss him off. Stephanie stares at me with wild eyes, like she's scared for her life, but also defiant in some way. My first priority is clear: saving her life and the lives of anyone else in this man's range. After that, she's mine.

"Williamson," he says. "Having fun, Slate?"

"Looking at a hostage situation," I say, keeping my voice completely neutral. "Armed suspect has requested a vehicle be delivered to the corner of Hollow and 3rd, a Ford F-150 specifically," I say.

"And tell 'em no more cops," the guy says, lurching forward with Stephanie.

"He says no more law enforcement," I say. "The vehicle needs to be delivered within the next ten minutes."

"Um…right," Williamson says. "We'll get right on that. Ten minutes. Ford F-150. Got it." He hangs up.

As I go to slip my phone back in my pocket, Xavier shakes his head. "Nah. Toss it. You don't need it anymore."

There's nowhere I can throw my phone where it won't shatter as soon as it hits the ground. But if I do that, any data regarding the call I just received from the assassin could be lost. I can't afford that. "If I throw away the phone, they won't be able to contact me if there's a problem," I say. The gun in my shoulder harness hangs heavy. I'm not even sure he knows it's there, given my blazer covers it completely. Though I'm afraid if I go for it, Stephanie will end up with a hole in her head.

Xavier jerks his head in Zara's direction, who still doesn't have a clear shot. "They can call her. Lose it." He digs the gun into Stephanie's head and she squirms from the pain.

I spot a plot with a tree close by and do my best to toss the phone so it lands on the soft dirt, instead of the concrete surrounding it. Unfortunately, I hear the dull thud as the device smacks against the concrete. I wince.

"Don't worry, sweetheart, I'm sure you can afford another one," Xavier says, relinquishing his grip on Stephanie slightly. I need to find a way to de-escalate this situation. There's no telling if Williamson will actually try to follow through with the request or not, but the longer this goes on, the more likely someone dies.

"Is that your payment, in your back pocket?" I ask. I can't see it from my vantage point, but I recall him slipping it back there earlier.

"Yeah. Cashier's check. Too much cash to be carryin' around. Look like a damn gangster or somethin'," he says, a gleam in his eye.

"You know no bank in the country will cash that, not now," I say. "Even if you get out of the country, you won't have anything to live on."

He looks down at Stephanie as he's holding her. "You said this was foolproof! That I could deposit it anywhere."

I shake my head. "She lied to you. Anything over ten thousand dollars is going to require an immediate investigation by the bank in question, who will check with local and federal law enforcement. They'll have to make sure the money is legitimate, and they'll look into your history. Banks have safeguards against this kind of thing due to money laundering. Trust me, I just spent the last three weeks elbow deep in the financial sector. There is no where you could cash that check that wouldn't send up a dozen flares to five different government agencies." I'm embellishing a little here, but the idea is to throw him off, see if he won't make a mistake we can exploit.

"Then we're gonna need to stop by her bank on the way," he says. "She's gonna hafta issue me fifty ten grand checks instead. Yeah, that'd be better anyway. Spread it around, not all my eggs in the same basket."

I catch Stephanie roll her eyes, which is strange, given her situation. She's still attempting to claw at his arm, but isn't as fervent about it anymore.

"How did you meet?" I ask, trying a different tack.

Anything I can do to keep him talking, to keep his focus off the fact the truck isn't here yet.

"Ain't you payin' attention? We been havin' *relations* for the past eight months." He shows his teeth when he sees the look on my face. "That's right. In 'er bed n' everythin'. Right under 'er husband's nose. Idiot had no clue. I even wiped my ass with a couple of 'is shirts." He looks down at Stephanie. "He went to that stupid club of 'is with those on, didn' he?"

"You really hate him, don't you Steph?" I ask, leveling my gaze with her.

"The guy's a massive twat," Xavier replies for her. "Goes off and sleeps with 'er best friend, then pretends like none of it even happened. And then, they find out she's pregnant from it!"

Stephanie's eyes go wide. "You idiot!" she yells, driving her elbow back into Xavier's stomach. It causes him to stagger back, releasing her. I go for my weapon, but Xavier is already raising his.

"One more inch and I fire!" Zara yells.

Xavier looks behind him and Zara has him dead to rights. He considers it for a second, then drops the weapon, putting his hands up.

Stephanie takes off running.

Chapter Thirty-Two

"STOP!" I YELL, CHASING AFTER STEPHANIE. MY WEAPON IS IN my hand, but I'm doing everything I can to keep up with her. I can't shoot her, not even a warning shot. There's too much of a chance I'll miss her or my aim will be off and I'll accidentally turn a warning shot into a fatal one. Firing a gun while trying to pursue a suspect is a bad idea. And Stephanie seems to know it, because she's not slowing down.

Thankfully, I'm in good enough shape to keep up with her. She's hauling ass down the street and makes a quick turn into the alleyway. I'm sure headed back to her vehicle. But she has to be in full panic mode; there's no way she'll be able to get anywhere before she's stopped. She must know it's over, which makes me fear what she might do.

"Murphy!" I yell out. "This only ends one of two ways! You come with me, or someone takes you down!"

"I'll take my chances," she yells back at me, though her eyes widen when she sees how close I am.

I grit my teeth and push harder, doing everything I can to catch up with her. When I finally reach her, she screams as I tackle her from behind, sending us both to the pavement. Given she's in a dress, I imagine her legs are pretty scuffed up.

Still, she's trying to fight me off with everything she's got. She manages to squirm out from under me as I'm trying to get her hands behind her, and delivers a blow with her elbow to my stomach, which knocks the breath from me. I almost drop my weapon as she scrambles out from under me as I catch my breath.

"Stop," I say, forcing the word out with the pain of not being able to breathe. I have the gun leveled at her back before she can take off running again. I suck in air, but my arm is steady.

Steph turns, her eyes wide. They flit down to the weapon, then back to me. Maybe she isn't ready to push me as far as she thought she was. Or maybe there's something about having a gun pointed at your back that makes you reconsider your life decisions.

"Nowhere to go," I say.

"Wrong," she says, turning all the way around to face me. "There's one way out of this." She points up.

"Didn't take you for the religious sort," I say, pushing up on one leg so I'm standing, both of our gazes locked.

"I can't go to jail. I can't live that life," she says.

"Just tell me why." I'm doing the best I can to be empathetic to her, but knowing that she orchestrated the deaths of three people, including an FBI agent, then tried to pin it all on her best friend makes it difficult. "What was the point? Was it Joey?"

Her eyes flash.

"It was. Your husband had an illegitimate child with Erin and you couldn't stand it. You wanted the kid for yourself."

"That woman has always been better at everything than me," Steph growls. "Ever since college. She was always more popular, had more boyfriends, got better grades. She was the favorite in more than one class. And she met her husband there."

I cock my head. "Seems like you were the one who ended

up with everything. A successful career, a family, a nice house and a great future."

"Does it?" she spits. "Let's see, my husband cheated on me, my career is failing, and if my next book doesn't sell, I doubt we'll be able to stay in that house. The one thing, the *only* thing I've ever been better at than her is writing. And most of that was just luck. She always got everything else. I already knew about their affair. But when I found out the kid was his, I just lost it."

"How did you find out?" I ask. "One of those gene tests?"

She nods. "I had my suspicions. So when Joey was over playing with the kids, I swabbed his mouth, pretending like he had something stuck in his tooth. But I already knew. You can see it in his face, it's just like Brad's."

"I assume your husband knows." I keep the weapon leveled on her. She could try to run again at any moment. I'll have to wait for Zara before I can hope to get her into custody safely.

"Please, he's clueless. Just like he thinks I am," she replies. "The man isn't very bright. He's more concerned with his image than with what I'm doing most of the time." She shakes her head. "Maybe if he'd just listened when I tried to talk to him…" She trails off, looking out into the distance. "Doesn't matter now."

"So you were willing to kill in order to frame Erin…to what end? Get her out of your life? Get custody of Joey?"

"I'm his godmother," she says. "Custody would have fallen to me and Brad. And yes, to keep her out of my life for once. Do you realize how annoying it is, having someone come around to your house day after day, planting in *your* garden, using *your* kitchen to fix meals for everyone, living the life *you're* supposed to be living?"

"Why couldn't you live that life?" I ask.

"Because someone in this family had to work and provide. And I don't know if you know much about writing, Agent

Slate, but it takes every bit of your being. It sucks you in and devours your world to the point where you can't think about anything else. You don't have time for friends, family, nothing. All you know is the muse, and trying to keep her satisfied. It's exhausting."

"I'm sorry to hear that," I say, checking my peripherals, but seeing no one. "But it doesn't give you the right to take someone's life. Especially not three people's."

"Necessary evil," she says. "It needed to get enough attention that someone would eventually figure out it was Erin."

"That's why you started with an FBI agent," I say. "And N3, LLC? The advance fee fraud?"

"All set up by Jon," she replies. "He thought we were going to be rich together. I had him take care of making sure all the financials were in Eva's name and that it would all lead back to Erin. I couldn't make it too easy; someone might suspect something was off. But if I could make it look like Erin tried to cover her tracks, the story became a lot more believable."

"Classic writer," I say. "You weave a tangled web."

"I had no choice." She holds her hands out. "It was the only way to give her a motive."

"And Xavier, where does he fit in?" I ask.

She actually chuckles, shaking her head. "That moron. I needed my own alibi. And he's a professional. He had the strength to do what I needed done. And I have to admit, it felt good giving Brad a taste of his own medicine, even if he didn't know about it."

"Seems to me Xavier has put a kink in your plans," I say. "He seems ready and willing to testify."

She gives me a small shrug. "It doesn't really matter. I'm not telling you all this because I want you to use it against me in the near future. I'm telling you because I'm not walking out of here alive, and at least one person should hear it, because it took *a lot* of planning."

Classic narcissist, I think. *Can't help but reveal how hard and complicated all this was to pull off.* I want to look behind me to see if Zara is on her way, but I can't afford to take my eyes off Steph. She seems determined to die by my hand, and I can't let that happen. But at the same time, I can't just let her keep pushing me.

"You're the one who called in the tip on Eva," I say, and Steph grins. "How did he get in each of the places? There was no sign of a break in."

"In another life, Xavier worked as a locksmith. He still has all his tools, which partially justifies his high price. He doesn't come cheap because he can get into places few others can."

"Tell me about the bodies? Why stage them?"

"To add to Erin's culpability," she says. "It was the only way. I gave Xavier specific instructions, and he had me on facetime to make sure everything was done correctly before he left. Of course I was home, safe in my bed, just like my security system said I was. But what better way to make myself look like the true victim than by someone copying the scenes from my books? Someone who knows my books as well as I know them myself."

"Apparently she didn't know as much as you thought," I say. This causes the first flash of interest I've seen from her. "We found your sealed manuscripts, still in her apartment. She'd never opened them."

Realization dawns on Steph when she figures out what was in them. "I'd completely forgotten. The FBI agent in book one. Of course. No wonder you came after me." She shakes her head. "I can't believe Erin kept those all these years."

"She's been your biggest fan and supporter," I say. "It's going to devastate her to find out what you tried to do."

"Why couldn't she have just thrown those away?" Steph says, her eyes beginning to well up. I don't think she's upset her friend believed in her that much, but rather that it was the lynchpin that brought everything down around her. "God dammit! If she'd just taken the fall for this, everything would have been better. It would have fixed all of it!"

I shake my head. "It wouldn't have. It would have just made everything worse. You would have had to live with the guilt of what you'd done to her, just like you have to live with the guilt of three deaths on your conscience. You might not have done the deed yourself, but they still fall on you."

She wipes her eyes. "It's just not worth it," she says. "The world is not worth all this bullshit." Funny, coming from someone who looks like they have it all. But the truth is, Stephanie Murphy is isolated, angry, and depressed. It's a vicious cocktail that's led to disastrous consequences.

"I've learned that not everyone is what we want them to be," I say. "But if we're not honest with each other, the chasms only deepen. You should have discussed this with Erin years ago. Before things got this bad."

"Too late now," she spits. "Now I'm going to turn around and walk this way. You can either shoot me or let me go. Either way, I'm not going to exchange one prison for another. I will be free."

"Steph, don't make me take you down," I say, warning in my voice. I steady my hand again. It's gone lax listening to her sob story.

"No other choice," she replies and turns her back on me. She's no more than ten feet away. I caught her once, and I'm sure I can do it again. But I can't let her get my gun. I toss it a few feet away, where it clatters across the parking lot. "Thank you, Agent—"

I slam my body into hers again, as hard as I can, taking the both of us down a second time. The hit is hard enough to knock the wind out of her and I grab both her hands before she can even begin to squirm again. I have them cuffed in under five seconds, even as Steph screams and tries everything short of dislocating her shoulder to wrench them apart.

Now that she's subdued and flopping on the ground like a fish, I sit back, taking a breath.

"There you are." I look up to see Zara, red in the face from running, as she approaches from the far end of the alley that connects to the parking lot. "I finally got the big one into custody. He's singing like a songbird."

"*NO,*" Steph yells.

"Took you long enough," I tell Zara. I stand and retrieve my weapon. "I was this close to shooting her."

"Do it! Shoot me! *Please.*" There's such an urgency in those words I think the first thing I'm going to have to recommend is that we put Murphy on suicide watch. Given her volatility, I don't think it's premature.

"Williamson finally showed up," Zara says. "I'll get a couple more agents down here to help you out."

"Thanks," I reply.

"Did you get what you needed?" she asks.

I look down at the woman who masterminded this whole thing. I can't wait to see her behind bars. "Yeah. I think I did."

Chapter Thirty-Three

"GIVE ME SOME GOOD NEWS," I SAY, HOLDING MY NEW PHONE up to my ear. It's an identical model to the one I had before, with all the proper protections and restrictions for a phone that has access to information that's not freely available to the public. I had no choice but to get a new one seeing as mine won't even turn on anymore after I threw it on the ground.

"Good news is in short supply today, Slate," Janice says. "No one has shown up to claim the cameras, and I have to pull the agents on surveillance for the sting operation."

"She said she wouldn't be back to retrieve them," I say. "Somehow, I believe her."

Janice sighs. I can just see that mirthless look on her face right now. "I'm assigning you a junior agent when you get back. To keep an eye on you."

"No way," I say. "I'm not walking around with a babysitter on my back. I won't be able to get anything done."

"It's not a request," she says. "I will not have my agents' lives threatened. Plus, he's a recent grad. He'd benefit from some on-the-job training with you."

I crease my brow. "Who?"

"Special Agent Coll," she says. "I believe you're familiar with him."

For a brief moment my heart is in my throat. "*Liam* Coll?" I ask.

"Yes, Slate. How many Agent Coll's do you think work for the FBI? That was a rhetorical question, don't answer it."

I swallow again, not ready to deal with the flood of emotions that come along with that name. I haven't seen Coll since we both left Stillwater, and with everything going on I hadn't expected to see him again for a long time. But I can't say I'm disappointed. "Fine." I say. "But he's got to give me my space. I can't work with someone hovering over me all the time."

"Given that you have now received both an electronic and a verbal threat from this person, I can't ignore the danger to your personal safety. Hopefully it will only be temporary until we track down this mystery person. I understand Agent Foley is bringing your phone back for analysis."

"She has what's left of it bagged up."

"If this person is as good as you say she is, I doubt we'll get anything from it. But everyone screws up eventually. Maybe we'll get lucky."

Somehow, that doesn't make me feel any better. "Any luck with the email trace?"

"Dead end," she says. "But as far as we can tell, she was right, the documents weren't faked. We're still trying to track down your husband's boss. I have to say, Slate, I don't like where this is leading."

"That makes two of us," I say. Even the insinuation Matt wasn't really who he said he was is enough to turn me straight into fight mode. Despite her warning, I *need* to find this woman, no matter the cost. Now that I know she's on my trail, I have to assume she's never very far away.

"When will you be back?" she asks.

"Tonight. We have some last-minute housekeeping, and then are slated for the eight p.m. out of LaGuardia."

"Safe travels, see you when you return," she says. Before I can say anything else, she hangs up.

Typical Janice. She never has been one for long goodbyes.

"It was one hell of a job," Williamson says. He's taken over Detmer's desk until he returns from leave, and is provisionally in charge of the small team here in Woodhurst as his boss, SAC Warburton, has been called away for some kind of emergency. "I guess I owe you an apology."

"Apology?" I ask. It's been three days since we arrested Xavier McCabe and Stephanie Murphy. Both are awaiting trial without bail. "For what?"

"For thinking you weren't up to it when I first met you at Agent Green's apartment," he says. "Turns out, you were just what we needed."

I exchange a grin with Zara. "We were just doing what we do best."

He gives me a knowing nod and leans forward, folding his hands together on Detmer's desk. "It's a tragic thing, but had you not been here, I think an innocent person might have gone down for this."

"That was the idea," Zara says. After the arrest, I filled Zara in on everything Steph told me while I was working on my official report. More than likely I'll have to come back up to New York if there ends up being a trial and my testimony is needed. Though with as much information Xavier has given up already, I can't see how any defense attorney won't advise Steph to take a plea deal.

"Heard from the D.A.?" I ask.

Williamson nods. "Just this morning. There's enough evidence to charge them both with three counts of felony murder. She's not getting out of it just because she didn't hold the weapons."

"Good," I say. "Though I imagine it's going to be quite the shock to her husband to have to try and manage everything on his own now."

"I also got word that her latest book has been cancelled," Williamson says. "Apparently her publisher didn't like the idea of representing a serial murderer."

Zara scoffs. "Nowadays I'd be surprised if she didn't get another deal immediately. Some tell-all that will probably sell a million copies or more. A writer who gets someone to act out the murders she writes about? Someone is jumping on that." She turns to me. "You probably just made her more famous than ever."

"Infamous is more like it," I say. "Doesn't matter. It isn't like she'll ever see the light of day to enjoy that money. And maybe it can make a better life for her family."

"Here's hoping," Williamson says. He holds out his hand, which we take in turn, giving it a hearty shake. "Thank you again."

We give him a nod and head out.

"Oh, and Agent Slate?" I turn back to the man behind the desk. "I spoke with Agent Detmer this morning. He wanted me to tell you were right. And he should have listened. He's going to be taking a leave of absence for a while."

I purse my lips, giving him a small nod. "Sometimes love makes us do crazy things. Tell him good luck."

———

The taxi pulls up to the apartment complex and I open my door to get out, but stop when Zara remains put. "Aren't you coming?"

She shakes her head. "Not really my thing. I'll wait in the car for you."

"Really?" I let out a frustrated grunt. "You're going to make me do this alone...*again?*"

She gives me a small shrug. "What can I say? I'm not good with praise."

"Neither am I," I hiss. I catch the cab driver's eyes flit up to the rearview window. "Fine. I'll be back in a minute." I slam the door and head over to the last apartment on the block, knocking on the door.

Somewhere inside a dog barks before Erin opens it and almost collapses into me before I even have a chance to say hello. "Thank you," she whispers. "You saved my life."

I return the hug for only a second before I begin to pull back. She gets the hint and lets go. Her strawberry blonde hair seems more vibrant today, like all of her. "How are you doing?"

She glances behind her and I see a small boy playing with some Duplo blocks further into the apartment. Strange to think four days ago a team of FBI agents was combing through this place looking for evidence. "We're doing great," she says. "Not perfect, but better. I was just glad you managed to clear all of this up."

"Have you heard from them?" I ask.

She shakes her head. "Brad has tried to call a few times, but I've just ignored it."

"Good," I say. "It's better that way, for now. Keep your distance, at least until everything has been resolved. And honestly, probably after that as well. It isn't the same environment you're used to."

"Seems like it never was what I thought, was it?" she asks. "I can't believe I was so naïve. I should have just confronted the issue from the beginning. And I realize that this is partly my fault as well. If Brad and I had never gotten together—"

"It could have been a million other things," I say. "Steph was spiraling, whether she knew it or not. She has some deep-rooted issues that have nothing to do with you. So try not to put too much blame on yourself."

"You give me too much credit," Erin replies. "But thank you. I just want to start over, raise my son in a new, healthy environment. Leave all of that in the past." Her words make me think back to what the assassin told me over the phone. A conversation that now only exists in my memory.

"Sometimes that is best," I reply. "I wish you the best of luck."

"Thank you, Agent Slate," she says, and reaches in for another hug. "Could Agent Foley not make it?"

I smile. "Zara isn't really good with goodbyes."

She gives me an extra squeeze. "Tell her this is from me. For all her help."

I pull back again. "I'll be sure to do that."

"And safe travels back home."

"Thank you," I say, giving her a small wave as she closes the door. It's not the trip home I'm worried about. It's what I'll find when I get there.

Chapter Thirty-Four

WALKING UP TO THE FRONT ENTRANCE, I GIVE THE HEAVY wooden door a solid knock before stepping back. It seems like I'm doing this every time I come home from a big case. Land, drop Zara off at home, then drive out to my in-laws' house to pick up my dog. Their home sits on a large lot with plenty of land, which is a far cry from my tiny two-bedroom apartment in the middle of the city.

At the sound of someone at the door, I hear at least two dogs howl. That would be Max and Waldo, their two rescues. Timber isn't much of a barker, not anymore. He kind of just likes to investigate quietly, see what's going on.

A moment later, my raven-haired sister-in-law answers the door with a smile. "Emily," she says. "Come in."

This is new. Usually I stay out on the porch while they hand Timber over. Something must be wrong. "What's happened?" I ask, more panic in my voice than I'd like. "Is he okay?"

"Timber is fine," she says. "He's right in here, waiting for you."

I cautiously follow her inside. I haven't been in this house since before Matt died, and it's strange being back inside.

Familiar smells of wheatgrass and bourbon fill my nose and I'm transported back to all those nights the four of us sat out on the back patio, talking and joking long into the night. It produces a warm feeling deep within somewhere and I find myself relaxing the further I follow Dani into the house. But I can't allow myself to drop my guard, not knowing where my brother-in-law is.

Before I can get halfway down the hall, I'm assaulted by a medium-sized terrier and a large chocolate lab, both of whose tails are wiggling when they see me. Both of them sniff me up and down, giving my hands small licks and waiting for me to pet them.

"Hi guys," I say in a soft voice. "I've missed you." They both look up at me with those puppy-dog eyes, even as their butts wiggle out of control. I give them both head scratches at the same time before I spot Timber standing at the far end of the hallway, beyond Dani. He's watching me with an intense gaze and the moment I make eye contact he bolts down the hallway, nearly knocking the other dogs out of the way to get to me. Timber slams into my legs, his entire body vibrating with joy. "Hi baby," I coo, nuzzling my head into his. I don't think I realized just how much I missed him this time. Maybe it was knowing that the woman who killed my husband could have gotten to either of us at any time they wanted. That fact in itself is sobering.

"Hi, Em."

I look up and see Chris standing near the kitchen island. Next to him are three glasses, all with a finger of brown liquid in them. I give Timber a couple more pats on his side. "What's all this?"

"A peace offering," he says, and offers the bottle. I'm shocked when I see the label.

"Where'd you even get this? Isn't it like a five-hundred-dollar bottle?"

He tilts his head slightly, telling me that it's probably even more. He's a handsome man, his sharp features and dark complexion from being out in the sun all day complements his wife's fair skin tone. They're a good-looking couple. But this is the first time I've seen my brother-in-law with anything other than rage on his face in the past six months. Ever since the funeral. His wife takes his side and all of a sudden I feel like I'm about to be blindsided.

"I wanted you to know I thought about what you said, and you were right," Chris says. "It wasn't your fault what happened to him. And it was stupid of me to blame you for it."

"Thank you," I say, though I'm still anxious about what might come next.

"I also wanted to say I'm sorry for pushing so hard about Timber," Dani adds. "You need someone in that apartment with you. I shouldn't have tried to butt-in."

I can't believe what I'm hearing. As each consecutive month following Matt's death has worn on, the tension between us has only grown. And now it's like it has all melted away. Maybe Zara was right, and what I needed was to finally confront them both about how they were treating me. "You were just looking out for his best interests," I say.

"Emily," Dani says. "You're still family. And we don't want to lose you. These past six months have just been...hard."

"For everyone," Chris adds.

I find it hard to meet their gazes, so I stare at the glasses instead. This is what I wanted after Matt died: a support system of family so we could lean on each other. But I still feel like a stranger in this house. Is it too late? Can we start over?

I take a deep breath, realizing that there is no way I can open myself back up to them unless I lay everything out. I can't keep secrets from them anymore, even if it's a violation of protocol.

"Em? Are you okay?" Chris asks.

"I need to tell you something about Matt," I say. "Because

if I don't, then all of this will be for nothing, as much as I appreciate it." I motion to them and the drinks at the same time.

"Okay," Chris says, stiffening. "What is it?"

"I don't think he died by accident," I say.

Chris narrows his gaze. "What?" Dani's eyes have gone wide.

"I encountered a woman, on my first case back after my leave. I believe she killed a suspect of mine and the circumstances of his death matched Matt's exactly. I've been looking into her and I believe she has me under surveillance. I found cameras in my apartment before I left for New York."

"Wait," Chris says. "Are you saying that Matt was murdered?"

"That's my working assumption, yes."

His eyes flare. "How long have you known about this?"

"That's the problem. I don't have any proof. This woman, she's a professional. She didn't leave any evidence behind. All I have is a working theory." I decide not to tell them about the phone call I received in New York. That doesn't concern them, because no matter what threats I receive, I'm not giving up.

Chris turns his back to me and places his hands on the counter, staring out into the darkness of the evening.

I turn to Dani. "That's why…I've decided it's better for Timber to live with you for the time being. This person managed to get into my apartment undetected. I can't have him exposed to that kind of danger."

"Em, you can't stay there either," she says.

"I'm still working on that. This woman, this…assassin knows my every move. But she's only after me. I don't want to put him or anyone else in her crosshairs. Which means I need to isolate myself until I catch her." I haven't told any of this to Zara yet, because I know she'll be pissed. But I'm not about to have her risk her life when I'm the one she wants. Same goes for my dog. I finally reached my decision on the plane ride back home.

I catch Chris's back heave as he takes in a deep breath, though I already know what's coming. I was hesitant to tell them any of this before because he already blamed me for Matt's death. But his recent change of mind means he deserves to know the truth: that he was right all along. Matt was killed, and I wasn't there to stop it. I don't care what some cryptic email or phone call tells me. My husband was a good person, and he didn't deserve that.

Chris turns back around, glaring at me. I match his gaze, ready to take the punishment. Instead, he picks one of the glasses up and holds it out to me.

Furrowing my brow, I take it in my palm, unsure what's happening. He takes the second glass and hands it to his wife, while taking the third for himself. "If you're going to find this person," he says. "You're going to need all the help you can get. And I know my brother would kill me if we weren't there for you."

My mouth hangs open like a fish that's been hooked. I can't believe what I'm hearing.

"To new beginnings," he says, holding out the glass.

"To new beginnings," Dani repeats, clinking hers with his.

I smile, my heart full for the first time in a long time. "New beginnings," I say, and happily add my glass to the mix. We all drink at the same time, and it's the smoothest thing I've ever tasted.

"Welcome home, Em," Dani says, and gathers me in for a hug. This time, I don't try to let go.

Epilogue

CHRIS SAT UP IN BED, READING FROM HIS E-READER AS HIS WIFE finished getting ready in the en-suite bathroom. As soon as she was done, she shut off the light, then headed out their bedroom door, only to reappear a few moments later.

"She out?" he asked as she closed and locked the door behind her.

Dani nodded.

Chris lay the e-reader off to the side as his wife climbed under the covers with him. Her long, sheer nightgown leaving little to his imagination. But that would have to wait. "Cuddled up with Timber. She'll wake up with a headache for sure. Still, she held her own against you."

Chris smiled. "Em always could drink almost anyone under the table." He sighed. "I'd hoped it wouldn't have come to this."

"What are we going to do, now that she knows the truth?" Dani asked.

"She doesn't know. She just suspects," he replied. "The bigger problem at the moment is Camille. How could she have been stupid enough to get found out like that? Cameras in her apartment?"

"*Shhh*," Dani said, putting her finger to her lips. "She'll hear."

"Not with half a bottle of the Colonel's finest in her, she won't." He sat, thinking for a moment. Every time he'd pressed Emily over the past six months, she had never said one word about anything other than Matt's death being an accident. He had tried his hardest to get her to admit she knew more. He already knew from Camille's reports that she suspected something wasn't right ever since she came back from that little town in Virginia, but to actually hear her admit it and tell them her theory was something else altogether. She was wading into dangerous territory, and it seemed Camille wasn't doing a very good job of steering her in another direction.

"I need to make a call," Chris said, reaching over for his phone.

"Now? It's two in the morning."

Chris smirked. "Trust me, they don't sleep. But we can't not report this."

"I really like Emily," Dani said. "I didn't want it to come to this."

"Me either," Chris admitted. The woman his brother had married was one of the strongest-willed people he knew. He should have guessed she wouldn't just let his death go. "But if she finds out about the—"

"I know, I know," Dani said, folding her hands in her lap. "You're right. I just…at least we can give Timber a good home once she's dead."

Chris grabbed his phone, calling up his most recent recipient and pressing the 'call back' key. "Yeah," he said. "At least there is that."

The End?

To be continued...

Want to read more about Emily?

A shot rings out, piercing the night...

Following her return from a case that has turned her world upside down, Special Agent Emily Slate finds herself sidelined once more because of circumstances beyond her control. Instead of focusing on the investigation that could lead to the woman who killed her husband, Emily is ordered to keep her distance, and assigned a murder in a small Chesapeake town.

But when Emily arrives with newly-minted Special Agent Coll, they find themselves in the middle of a power struggle between two law enforcement departments, both accusing the other of improper conduct. And in the middle of it, a body that seems to have no answers.

As Emily and Agent Coll examine what on the surface looks to be a random killing, they soon find dark desires are driving their killer. And when a second body is found, Emily realizes nothing about this case is by chance. But when she discovers a new revelation about her husband, Emily will find herself ripped between her duty to her job and her duty to the man she still loves.

The killer is out there, and they haven't missed their target yet.

Find out what happens in *Can't Miss Her*, available now from Amazon. Click HERE to get your copy now!

To get your copy of CAN'T MISS HER, CLICK HERE or
Scan the code below!

FREE book offer!
Where did it all go wrong for Emily?

I hope you enjoyed *Her Final Words*. If you'd like to learn
more about Emily's backstory and what happened in the days

following her husband's unfortunate death, including what almost got her kicked out of the FBI, then you're in luck! *Her Last Shot* introduces Emily and tells the story of the case that almost ended her career. Interested? Scan the code below to get your free copy now!

Not Available Anywhere Else!

You'll also be the first to know when each book in the Emily Slate series is available!

Download for FREE HERE or scan the code below!

The Emily Slate FBI Mystery Series

Free Prequel - Her Last Shot (Emily Slate Bonus Story)

His Perfect Crime - (Emily Slate Series Book One)

The Collection Girls - (Emily Slate Series Book Two)

Smoke and Ashes - (Emily Slate Series Book Three)

Her Final Words - (Emily Slate Series Book Four)

Can't Miss Her - (Emily Slate Series Book Five)

The Lost Daughter - (Emily Slate Series Book Six)

The Secret Seven - (Emily Slate Series Book Seven)

A Liar's Grave - (Emily Slate Series Book Eight)

The Girl in the Wall - (Emily Slate Series Book Nine)

His Final Act - (Emily Slate Series Book Ten)

The Vanishing Eyes - (Emily Slate Series Book Eleven)

Coming Soon!

Edge of the Woods - (Emily Slate Series Book Twelve)

The Missing Bones - (Emily Slate Series Book Thirteen)

A Note from Alex

I hope you enjoyed *Her Final Words*, book 4 in the new Emily Slate FBI Mystery Series. My wish is to give you an immersive story that is also satisfying when you reach the end.

But being a new writer in this business can be hard. Your support makes all the difference. After all, you are the reason I write!

Because I don't have a large budget or a huge following, I ask that you please take the time to leave a review or recommend it to fellow book lover. This will ensure I'll be able to write many more books in the *Emily Slate Series* in the future.

Thank you for being a loyal reader,

Alex